BLUE VALENTINE

THOMAS CUMMINGS

XENOCENTRIC PRESS

BLUE
VALENTINE

If you want to come along, you'd better keep up. We move fast because we're not going to find much in the way of nice, not here, not with me. We keep on moving because people play games and we don't want to get trapped in rules scrambled toward someone else's advantage. I promise you I'll never play games with you; you'll always know where I stand.

The Wheatpenny Tavern's not far now. Just down the road. See that glow making roses in the points of the treetops? That's where we're headed, just around that copse of conifers. When the country music hits you, bleeding out across the parking lot, you'll know what kind of bar we're in for. The twang just scrapes along your sinuses. The low tones get stripped while melodies roll across the parking lot to the blacktop's gravel edge. All those pickups and 4x4s pointing every which way make a maze you could get lost inside. There are no painted lines, so the shitkickers just sail in at any angle, brake, kill the engine, and amble right on into the bar. That's why I didn't drive. You're just asking for chipped paint or a dinged fender in that snarl. The tavern's just a mile's walk from the house, anyway, and I plan on getting myself around on someone else's gas tonight. Don't know whose yet.

Tell you what, if you like wood paneling, neon, Stetsons, baseball caps, and jukebox twang, the Wheatpenny Tavern is every inch of awful as you might hope for, packed shoulder-to-shoulder with rednecks, blue collars, and bar sluts. I up the ante for the last group, and the second I step across the threshold I get the stink-eye from some fellow travelers. The men, on the other hand, tend to give me a wink or raise a mug to send a beery cheer.

There's one who does neither. He sticks out because of his faux-hawk, popped collar, John Lennon glasses, and an unpleasant twist to his face. I don't know if he's aiming that twist my way, but I'll steer clear of him in case he thinks he's got some sort of score to settle with me. I'm not planning on staying here long, anyway. There are better bars further down the road, and good ones in town, ones that don't play this family-God-and-country hallelujah, gimme a beer twang free from a crowd hopped-up on self-entitled grudges and crushed under the heal of fifth-grade educations.

Hey, I'm not a graduate, myself, but I made it to twelfth grade. I got expelled only because someone always wanted a fight with me. Didn't matter I was on the honor role. Didn't matter I went out of my way to never start shit with anyone. The only thing that mattered was that most of the time I finished the shit that got started and that some of the noses I broke belonged to kids whose parents lived on the east end of town.

At the bar there's a slim kid who looks like he's having his first time around booze and boozers. His brown hair is parted methodically to one side as if he thought he was going to church. The jeans jacket he wears probably represents the toughest piece of clothing in his wardrobe. That jacket might have worked on someone else, someone older, someone who doesn't have a sad little mustache struggling for respect over his upper lip. You can tell he's trying to hide his baby face behind that mustache, and I wouldn't be surprised to find out he'd secreted some of his mama's mascara to thicken it up before he left the house.

I sidle up to him. There's no available stool nearby, so I move my hand across his shoulders, real casual, like I'm just trying to scoot in between him and the guy next to him. He turns to look. I rest my hand right next to his on the bar top and give it a quick, friendly scritch with one pinkie nail.

His eyes go wide, then shy.

"Hi," he says, quick, clipped.

"Hi." I smile and lilt my voice. I don't want to scare him off. "Crowded tonight." I lean toward his ear to give him a confidential whisper, just between the two of us. "Staff likes ignoring anyone with cleavage. Can you do me a favor and signal the bartender over here?"

"Sure." He's eager to impress and turns immediately to wave down the barmaid. It's Shell. She'd have served me no problem, but I want to give my knight in shining armor a chance at valor.

"The lady would like a drink," Babyface says.

Shell looks at me, smirks, but doesn't say, *That ain't no lady.* "What'll you have, hon?" she asks me.

"What are you drinking?" I ask Babyface.

He lifts a glass and clinks ice in an orange-hued libation.

"A Mai Tai."

Wipe that smirk off your face.

"Mm-mm," I say. "Sounds great."

"One Mai Tai," Babyface tells Shell. "On me."

"Sure thing," Shell says, moving down the bar to make the drink and rolling her eyes at me along the way. Hey, man, I didn't serve the kid a foo-foo in a cosmopolitan glass.

Babyface doesn't catch the look; he's too busy goggling over me. *Goddamn*, he just can't believe his luck! "My name's Randy," he says. Of course it is. He offers his hand and I give it a demure shake.

"I'm Nicki." I smile and hitch my shoulders. "Thank you for the drink, Randy."

"No problem. Um..." He checks the length of the bar, left and right. "Do you want to sit?"

"Sure." I lean into him. "Just scoot over a little." I wind my arm around his waist. He grins and lets a giggle slip out his nose, and then slides over so we can each settle a single ass cheek on the fake leather.

It's not long before I decide he's not nearly as lucky as he'd like to think. I have to give him props for moseying his narrow ass out to the Wheatpenny all by his ownself, but the kid's really got to up his game. He's boring as fuck. I nod and flare my eyes in rapture as he talks about his job at the Ford dealership and figure I'll give him another five minutes before I try to convince him to take me into town where I can wriggle loose of him.

We're both rescued from that miserable fate when a voice outside our sad little soirée tickles my ear.

"Hey, Sparks."

I turn—and find my favorite person in the whole world!

"Holy shit! Quinn!"

I bound off the bar stool to wrap a hug all over him just as Patsy Cline comes over the juke, timed just like the first kick of a theme song in a movie. I don't remember the name, but thank god for small miracles. I turn back to Randy. He's looking hurt and desperate. His eyes flit back and forth from me to Quinn.

"I'll be back in a second, sweetie."—No I won't.— "Gotta dance to this one." I lean in to give him a kiss on the cheek. "Thanks for the drink."

"My pleasure." Defeat in his voice. He doesn't seem like a bad guy. He doesn't know it, but I'm doing him a favor.

I grab Quinn by the wrist and lead him onto the dance floor. He grins like a rogue the whole way. We love doing this shit. I have no idea why the two of us dancing together freaks people out so much in a town where every other father is putting it to his daughter and date rape is considered a rite of passage, but it doesn't save us from the icy stares and twisted frowns that shoot our way.

Other couples are hanging all over each other, hands on asses, faces kissing-close. Quinn and I keep a steady thirteen-year-olds-at-the-dance distance from each other, his hand lightly on my waist, mine on his shoulder.

"What the hell are you doing here, Sparky?" I say. He calls me Sparks sometimes to irritate me. I call him Sparky sometimes for a similar reason.

He gives me a look. I know damn well what he's

doing. Same thing I am.

"I didn't ask what you were *doing* here. I asked what you were doing *here*."

He chuckles. "Lowering my standards, I guess."

"Shit, any lower, you'll be waking up in fields with cattle."

"Hey, I'd just be following in your footsteps."

"Well, I'd say *fuck you* but I'd just be putting on airs."

"What say we keep thinking highly of ourselves and roll over to McNamara's after the song?"

"*McNamara's*. Ain't we just all fancy tonight?"

We sway to Patsy on through the second chorus, then a flannel jacket, Steelers cap, and salt-and-pepper beard wants to know, "Now, what would your daddy say if he saw the two of you right now?"

It's Rudy Foreman. He's drunk off his ass. He's swaying, but not to the music. There's an alpha dog look on his face.

Quinn says, "He'd probably say the same thing to me he's said for the past twenty-five years: fuck-all."

I say, "He'd tell me to make him a sandwich and get him a beer, then fix the goddamn dishwasher while I'm at it."

A mean, thoughtful smile slides up the side of Rudy's face. He's trying to fuck with us, to start shit with Quinn, or to start shit with me to start shit with Quinn, but he's got enough sense to know already that we're not biting.

"Mind if I cut in?" he says. It's barely a question. "Just trying to respectable-up the place a little."

Quinn's tensing. Got to head him off at the pass. I say to Rudy, "I'll give you a dance next, if you want. Just wait till Patsy's done."

"Not really one for waiting," he says. "'Sides, dancing's not what I had in mind." He goes Neanderthal, hooking an arm around my waist and lifting me off my feet. I'd holler if he hadn't stunned my diaphragm doing that. Quinn takes an angry step toward us as Rudy carts me away toward the bar. I wave him back, trying to keep the shock of Rudy's pincer move from betraying Quinn's wavering composure. Quinn watches us go, mouth slashed at an unhappy angle. Quinn's a scrapper, but Rudy's a half-wit pit bull on his best days. Besides, I don't want Quinn getting into a fight. I'll just have someone else kick Rudy's ass.

Rudy says to me over his shoulder, "Just trying to save you from yourself, Peaches."

Peaches? If I didn't already dislike him.

We sail past Randy. He watches us go by, looking miserable. I twist to a more comfortable position in Rudy's arm and give Randy a wave and blow him a kiss. He turns and slumps back to his half-full Mai Tai, sitting glumly next to my empty one.

Rudy tows me onward, legs unsteady but determined, past a line of curved backs and hunched shoulders, peppered by the looks of five or six faces, male and female, turning to watch with mean amusement the sight of a woman—a woman of a particular style and class— being hefted caveman-style and carried about like an errant sack of grain, before finally depositing me back onto the ground. Rudy turns to call for Shell and I grab a deep breath, wincing as a xylophone of needles shoots up my ribs. The melody ebbs with a second.

A shock of stale alcohol stench and disinfectant stings my nostrils. We're at the far end of the bar. An empty stool presses against my hip. Immediately to my left, a big guy with a Sam Elliott mustache and a Stetson is just finishing tossing back a shot, copper colored, probably whiskey. There's a pale band of untanned skin on his wedding ring-finger. Could be divorced, could be on the down-low. Either way, my luck's in with him. To Rudy I whisper, "I'd love a Heineken, baby," tracing my fingers along the back of his neck, adding, "Let's drink 'em fast and get out of here." He gives me a jackal-grin and raps his knuckles against the bar to hurry up Shell.

Rudy's attention elsewhere, I hook my arm around 'Stache Elliott's bicep. He looks mid-forties, but there's honest, working man's muscle under his sleeves.

"Hey there, outlaw." I make my voice husky like a sex

phone operator. "Rescue me from Grizzly Adams over here and I'll walk you to the dance floor. If you want, we can just keep on walking out the door and maybe take a stroll under the stars, just you and me."

He gives me a sidelong look, suspicious, but he wants to get an eyeful anyway. No fool, he; here's a guy who knows he's being played when he's being played.

Fair enough. I shift in my seat to press the swell of one tit against his arm for incentive.

He smiles, cuts his eyes toward Rudy. "Boyfriend's not going to get a little hot about that?"

"Don't know." I lock eyes with him, let my eyebrows bow all coy. "Are you getting a little hot, boyfriend?"

"All right, honey." He winds one arm around my waist, sucks down the final dregs of his Budweiser, and begins to lead me away from Rudy. "Let's go take in the night air."

We're barely three steps from the bar before Rudy's circled over in front of us like a mama bear after her cub.

"Hey there, partner," Rudy says to 'Stache Elliot, sidling up. "Think you got the wrong girl there."

"Buddy, seems to me you came in with the wrong girl."

I back away from them, hands raised. "Hey, guys, I'm not worth it. Plenty of dates around here for everyone."

Rudy grabs my arm, bruise-hard, and yanks me toward him. I yelp and stumble against him. Would have preferred it to be all show, but it gets the desired effect.

"Hey, easy there." 'Stache Elliott bristles, genuine pique in his voice. He steps forward. I feel a little guilty now; the guy's practically a gentleman. I hope he pounds Rudy's ass. I don't plan on sticking around to find out, but I hope he does.

"Fuck off, fucker," Rudy shoots back. "Here, go fetch your hat, cowboy." He reaches out and flips 'Stache Elliott's Stetson off his head by the rim. I told you Rudy was a half-wit pit bull.

'Stache Elliott takes Rudy by the lapels with both fists and wheels him toward the bar. Rudy almost takes me with him before his arms start to pinwheel for balance. A crowd immediately presses in, and I fade back into it to the sound of a beer mug shattering. I hope it was over Rudy's skull.

Quinn's at the entrance, arms crossed and looking surly until he catches sight of me breaking out of the throng.

"That was quick," he says.

I take his arm and we're out the door.

"Years of practice," I say. "Besides, men are easy."

"Easy's something you've put a few years of practice into yourself."

"Ooh, look who's talking."

He looks around and pats himself like he's just discovered his body for the first time. "Might be me."

"I'm easy and you're a stud. How fair is that?"

"I didn't write the rules. I just read 'em with a stupid look on my face."

He puts his arm around my shoulders. "Come on. Let's go to McNamara's and treat ourselves to some prime cut."

I let him lead me to his Mustang.

McNamara's is the preferred watering hole for folks from the east end of town. East end is where you find sports cars and minivans, working streetlights and gated houses, manicured lawns and manicured people who rake in eighty grand a year at a minimum. McNamara's is too good an establishment for the likes of Quinn and me, but each of us is sure to find some warm body tonight in the mood for some slumming. They don't make a habit of it, but East Towners are more than willing to take out the trash every once in a while.

We're howling Tex Ritter's "Rye Whiskey," complete with yodels and hiccups, as Quinn wheels the 'Stang into a spot unbelievably close to the entrance. There are lines painted on this parking lot; they're fresh, bright yellow, and just screaming class. I feel so swanky right now, I tip back the last swig of Jim Beam from Quinn's flask.

"Don't tell me you just killed it," he says.

"I'm high class like that, baby."

We're shouting *West Enders!* as we walk inside McNamara's. Quinn's black tee is tucked into his faded Wranglers. His scuffed steel-toed work boots leave a trail of dust over the red carpet. My own jeans are rolled up nearly to the tops of my boots. It's not to show the boots off; it's for practical reasons when I go out. I catch my reflection in a wall mirror and find that my burgundy blouse is buttoned low enough to flash the lacy cups of my black bra. I hadn't quite meant it to be that way, but I'm not going to fix it.

The attire for the clientele at McNamara's is strictly the nines. For guys, it's either button-ups or polos and khakis, or a Sunday-goin'-to-meetin' western ensemble, with a flashy bolo tie and shiny boots that have never touched an open field. For the girls, it's Capri's or skirts that drop below the knee, thank you very much, and just enough cleavage and shoulder exposure to flirt with slutty without risking tumbling over into tramp. No worries now, ladies—my presence will rescue any daffodil unlucky enough to have misjudged the cut of her wardrobe.

The DJ, out beyond the dance floor, is spinning fistfuls of earworm hip hop. Christ—out of the frying pan, into the fire. Hopefully, he'll mix the playlist up some. Quinn and I are getting a jungle of looks from the people we pass. It's all the same. First, the men bulldog and browbeat Quinn, while the women take in the sight of his tight, small muscles under the fabric of his shirt and then catch the quick, blue sparks of his eyes and start sliding off their seats.

Not all of them, of course. Some of them have had it hammered into their heads that they are way too good for the likes of Quinn. But most have looks on their faces that tell of dreams of getting a down-and-dirty animal-fucking later on tonight. I've never seen Quinn fuck, so I wouldn't know what they're in store for. He did tell me once what he did to Annabel Planter and how she sent him flowers and CDs and money for the next two weeks. Shit, any guy did the same thing to me I'd send him his dick in a ham tin. You want to talk about easy and liking it? Only on the east end.

Once Quinn passes by, the men and women switch roles. The girls give me wrinkled noses and stink-eyes. They scoot themselves back up proper onto their seats and whisper *slut* to each other as if they weren't making a secret wish to be treated like one a second ago. That shit's just funny to me.

The men aren't any better. They go from fight to fuck in less time than it takes the women to switch gears. Of course, by the angle of their eyes, my presence stops dead just above the valley of my tits. Guess what? Not one of them has an ass hair's chance of getting fucked by me tonight.

There is one guy, though. He's staring right at me. Oh, that'll catch my interest. I take his face in. Score! He's good-looking; dark haired and clean shaven, too. He's got a bit of a western thing going, but no bolo and no hat. His eyes are crisp as dark whiskey. Could I have found true love?

He nods at me without breaking eye contact. "Evening."

"Evening." I reach out and trace my hand along his chest. "What's a girl gotta do to get a drink around here?"

"What're you needing?"

"Heineken, maybe?"

"One for your boyfriend, too?"

I grin at him. "I don't know, you like Heineken?"

The guy's steady as a wolf. "I'll find you," he says before the crowd washes us apart. I turn, my eyes still ringing with his eyes, and follow Quinn on to wherever it is he's leading us. Turns out to be an elevated two-seater at the corner of the bar.

"Think I might have scored us some drinks," I tell him.

"From who?"

"My boyfriend."

"Boyfriend already? We just got here."

"Hey, there's a lot to be said for a guy who can look you in the eye the first time instead of the tits."

"Well, *hello sailor*."

I bat him on the shoulder. "He's not queer."

"Don't mean shit to me either way, but if he's got a swish in his step, he'd better keep it in check around here." He turns to nod at someone in the crowd. A pretty blond waitress with a tray full of empty glasses sidles up to him.

"Hey, baby," she says as he loops an arm around her waist. "What brings you to the shiny side of the tracks?"

"The staff," Quinn answers. See, that's the funny thing about McNamara's, or just about any place east-end. Even though the business might be owned by a guy with a Maserati in his driveway and frequented by customers boasting no less than an Aerostar and a Saab, the uniforms are all worn by people who sleep in trailer parks out past Cowen Road.

This waitress here is no different. I know her. Her name is Marshall. Jesus, what kind of a name is that to stick on a girl? Probably no worse than Nicki Valentine, no middle initial, and thanks for the porn handle, Mom and Dad. *Nicki*, I should add, is what you'll find on my birth certificate. Not *Nicole*. Not something cool like *Nikita*, as in *La Femme*. Not even the standard double-K spelling. *Nicki* is what they saddled me with, as if I couldn't be anything else but.

Marshall's always been nice to me, and if that's only because she's always had a crush on Quinn, well then, I can bear it. She has wide brown eyes and an infectious smile. I've tried to practice that smile in a mirror, but I can't quite find it. A smile like that you probably need to mean.

"Hey there, Nicki." Listen to that sweet tone. I can almost believe she's using it because she's happy to see me, not because she's trying to score points with Quinn.

"Hey, Marshall."

"We got a special on shooters tonight," she addresses

the both of us. "I'm on a run right now. Want me to grab two for you?"

"Sure," Quinn says. "Actually, better make that three. We're expecting Nicki's boyfriend to show up pretty soon."

"*Boyfriend*?" Marshall goggles her eyes at me in admiration and places her hand on my elbow. "Anyone I know?"

"I don't even know him."

Marshall creases her brows, then laughs. "You two are bad." She waggles a finger at me. "I'll be back with those shooters." She disappears barward.

"You're a fucking asshole," I tell Quinn.

"What?"

I look away into the crowd for my boyfriend.

Marshall shows up with the shooters before I find him. When Quinn tries to pay, she waves his money away. "There's a table back in the corner that's crocked," she explains. "I'll just put it on their tab." She winks.

"Thanks, babyheart." Quinn leans forward and gives her a quick kiss on the cheek. I swear, Quinn is the only guy I've ever seen who can get away with that. And calling a chick "babyheart?" Marshall giggles and vanishes with her tray again into the crowd. Quinn leans over the table and reaches out to poke my elbow.

"Check that guy out." He points to the dance floor. "What? Did his mom tap a pack of D cell batteries up his ass before he left the house?"

I laugh, and Quinn moves on to a couple dirty dancing like two retards on a surfboard. I throw my head back and guffaw, so Quinn launches into a running commentary on a third of the people in our view and has me doubled over by the time my boyfriend finally shows up with the Heinekens. Three of them, no less. Check this guy out.

"Hi there," he says.

I recover myself. My boyfriend watches me. He smiles at the way I laugh.

"Hi back," I say.

12

He slides a bottle to me, to Quinn, and keeps one for himself. "Sorry it took so long. Bar's packed." He looks at the shooters on the table. "Looks like you've got connections."

"They're just trying to move us out of here faster," Quinn says. I kick his ankle. My boyfriend chuckles good-naturedly. He reaches out, offers me a handshake.

"Todd, by the way."

"Nicki."

"Nicki, pleasure to meet you." He turns to Quinn, proffers a hand. "Todd."

"Quinn."

"Quinn, pleased to meet you."

Todd's smile is easy. His eyes are confident. He holds Quinn in his gaze with no challenge and no hesitation. Quinn can be a cock-block when he wants to, just to be a fucker about it, but this guy might be more challenge than his time and effort are worth.

Quinn says, "Thanks for the beer."

"No problem. Enjoy."

Quinn raises the third shooter to Todd. "Special tonight, I guess. Don't know what's in them."

"Well, thank you." Todd takes the offer.

"Enjoy." We all tap our plastic cups at the center of the table and toss the drinks back. The taste is like burnt cherry.

An obnoxious rap song starts to thump over the speakers. I don't understand how women listen to this shit. (Annabel Planter probably thinks it's the Peake's Hill of romance.) Todd's wincing within the first few beats. The two of us start talking about music. He doesn't have awful taste.

And then, somehow, the subject of music segues into real estate, which, apparently, is his pursuant career path. Fair enough for him. For me, his voice starts to drone.

Still perfectly worth the effort to look at, though.

Never does ask how me and Quinn know each other.

Pretty soon we've each gone through another bottle

of Heineken on Todd's buck and a shot of Patrón on Quinn's. Last sip, Todd tells me, "I'm sorry, but I do have some friends I'm ignoring. Let me go see if I can get a booth we can all sit at."

"Sounds like fun," I say.

I look sideways at Quinn. He is nowhere thrilled. Todd leaves the table and Quinn gives me a look. "When the fuck did you become a girl?"

"You've never seen me work my magic."

"I've seen you work your magic. I've just never seen you fucking believe it."

"What're you getting nasty for?

"*He didn't look at my tits,*" he mocks me in a warbling falsetto. "*Meeting his friends will be* fun."

"Jesus."

"What?"

"Fuck off."

"It's your new dream to marry an east-towner and become a trophy wife and a soccer mom?"

"You're an asshole sometimes."

"You got *me* beat."

"Why don't you trot off and get a blowjob from your trailer park waitress, cheer yourself up some?"

He looks off toward the dance floor.

"What the hell did *I* do?" I poke him in the shoulder.

He keeps his eyes fixed elsewhere.

"It was your idea to come here," I tell him.

"Yeah."

"Yeah, what?"

"I thought we were going to hang out tonight."

"I thought we were going to get laid tonight."

"I bet."

The hell? I have no idea how we went from fun to fuck-you in sixty seconds. Tracking the conversation backward and forward in my head, I still can't figure out its course. The effect of the Patrón swimming up on me isn't helping me parse it, and I'm wondering if I lost a detail. Does he really not like Todd. Why? This isn't the first time we've trolled McNamara's. This isn't even the first east-towner I've picked up. It certainly isn't like he's never picked up any himself. Is he jealous that the start of the night gave me prime cut and him Grade A trailer park? That doesn't make sense. We've never competed with each other before.

His silence is pissing me off and making me feel guilty at the same time. I want to reach out and touch his elbow. I want to walk around the table and put my arm around him, but I hate the idea of being shaken off. Instead, I tap my short nails against the tabletop. I want to know what kind of shit he's trying to pull, and I almost demand that he tells me, when Todd shows up again.

"I found us a booth over in the corner. A little quieter, so we can hear ourselves."

"Great," I say. I look across the table. "Quinn, you coming?"

Quinn turns and smiles like he hasn't given me the silent treatment for the past eternity. He waves his hand. "I might scout you out later. I think I'll just hang here for now. Have fun." If you hadn't been around when he was dicking me off five minutes ago, you wouldn't have heard the sneer in *fun*.

Quinn turns back toward the dance floor. "All right." I motion to Todd. "Let's go." Todd turns toward his little corner. I lean toward Quinn and say, "Jesus fucking christ, Quinn." Then I move out and find Todd's arm and hook it in mine. I stare at the back of Quinn's head as I let Todd move us away until the crowd moves in to block him from sight.

"Something wrong?" Todd asks.

"I don't know," I tell him. "Quinn went all pouty on me all of a sudden."

"I'm not getting in the middle of anything, am I?"

"No. No. What's there for you to get in the middle of?" He looks at me.

"Quinn's my brother," I tell him.

The booth in the corner is horseshoe-shaped. There are two men sitting at the center, deep in conversation. One of them, on the left, is a skinny, sharp-nosed blond, dressed in a black polo. The one on the right is in a deep green button-up; he's square-shouldered and has a Van Dyke that's a shade darker than his auburn hair. He's not bad looking. He moves with confident body language that the blond tries to mimic. We stop in front of the table and the two men look up. There's a half-empty pitcher in front of them, a fully-empty pitcher next to it, and slightly beery looks in Blondie and Van Dyke's eyes; eyes that flitter back and forth between my face and my tits.

"Hi," they say in stereo.

"Hi," I answer in mono.

"Guys," Todd begins, "this is Nicki. Nicki, this," he gestures toward Van Dyke, "is Parker. And this"—Blondie—"is Donald."

Each reaches out a hand and we all shake with a *hi* and a *pleasedameetcha*.

"Go ahead and sit." He guides me to Parker's side. Donald looks crestfallen. "I'll go rustle us up some more shots. Patrón still good for you?"

"Love me some Patrón," I tell him and flash him a wide grin to show how much.

"Good," he says and leaves me with these two. I peek around for Quinn, but I can't see our table through the crowd, and he's nowhere else to be seen.

Whatever conversation Parker and Donald were having before me and Todd arrived was either private or less interesting than I am, because neither restarts it. My own tongue is a flat tire, and I'm not in the mood to play anymore. Goddamn Quinn.

Parker starts asking me questions, and I give him answers I forget the next second. I notice he has a tattoo peeking out under his cuff. I comment on it to give myself something to talk about. He gladly rolls up his sleeve and shows me a tumble of brightly colored koi, kappa, and Celtic patterns swimming down his arm.

"Been working on this for two years," he tells me, holding his arm over the table and rotating it so I can take in every stretch of the design. "Goes up over my shoulder and a third of the way down my back. Maybe I'll show you the rest of it later."

"Love to see it."

"You have any tattoos?"

"Naw."

"Thinking about getting any?"

"Thinking about it. Don't know what I want."

"Stuck with it for life."

"Sure are."

"Like names."

"So, Parker's your first name?"

"It is."

"What's your last name?"

He shakes his head and chuckles.

"No. Is it bad?"

"Fabian."

"Fabian?"

"Uh-huh."

"Your name is Parker Fabian?"

"Sure 'nough."

"For real?"

"I told you."

"Do your parents hate you?"

He laughs. "What's your last name?"

"Please."

"Come on."

"Valentine."

He whirls on me with goggle-eyes. "Your name is Nikki Valentine?" I can hear the two K's in his voice.

"Nicki. N-I-C-K-I. Valentine."

"Christallmighty."

"Yup. Parker Fabian and Nicki Valentine."

"Together at last."

"Who'da thunk it?"

And we carry on like that until Todd comes back with a round and a beer mug for him and me. He sits on the opposite side of the table next to Donald. I thought he would sit by me. I even started to shift myself toward Parker when he arrived. But now he's settled himself and passes shots of Patrón around the table.

17

I lift my glass to the middle of the table where it is clinked alongside the glasses of the others, then shoot its contents, its flavor lost in the sharp-smooth, knife-blade-dipped-in-dental-anesthetic sensation of it sliding down my throat. Donald finishes his with a *whooo-baby!* Todd starts telling a funny story about a trip to Portland.

He's a good storyteller, and we're all laughing before he even gets to the punch line. I keep laughing even as I feel Parker Fabian's hand creeping over my knee, cupping my inner thigh, and riding his palm upward. He's not trying to hide it, either. Todd is looking directly at me, directly at Parker, and not missing a beat. To test Todd, I scoot a little closer to Parker and wrap my arm around him, like an affectionate girlfriend. Parker takes this as the go-ahead to quicken his hand, but I can't tell if the tiny tick of a smile that takes the corner of Todd's mouth is because Parker and I have increased our amorous fumblings, or because a part of the story amuses him. If he's got some dream of pimping me out tonight, he better also get the idea of handing me over the lion's share of the profits.

The flat of Parker's hand collides with my crotch. The pressure he applies is electric, making me hiss short, sharp breaths as Todd launches into another story and as I keep watching his pretty eyes, his handsome face, listen to his smooth, soft voice, tracing my fingers along Parker Fabian's bicep, his hard muscles hidden under a thin sleeve, and continue to luxuriate in the pressure his hand rubs into me. Quinn's barely a thought at the back of my mind. Quinn? Quinn who?

Parker's hand slows and yields. "What's wrong?" he asks; I've started giggling.

"This song's got the same beat as the last," I tell him.

"They all have the same beat."

"I like the rhythm."

Parker's hand comes alive again and finds the rhythm. I hope they all have the same beat.

Another round of shots arrives, and after the glasses are clinked again, the Patrón goes down smooth but hits my gut like the glowing end of a cigarette, so I grab a nearby bottle, don't know if it's mine or not, and gulp down two swallows of Heineken, tasting bitter now, and sharp, like there are whiskers spinning inside it, but it douses the sizzle.

Parker leans into me as I set the bottle down. I turn to look. He's close, his face is all I see, and his nose begins to loose a ghostly version of itself to one side, making me blink to bring it together again, and he says, "Do you like to get high?" I do like to get high, but his hand is a sickly pressure now, so I grab his wrist and move his arm free. His face drops.

"Bathroom," I tell him.

I scoot to the edge of the booth. My legs are surprised to rediscover gravity. I have to lean one hip against the table's edge and steady myself with my hand flat on the tabletop before I move off toward the bathroom. The Patrón, beer, and whiskey trick my equilibrium and transform my momentum into a deft sway; my feet live in the movement, taking cues from the pogo stick beat of the dance music, finding new and inventive paths through twisting bodies and lunging shoulders. A guy in a green Ducks cap dances at me; I dance away from him with a wink.

I'm still scootin' and shufflin' as I shoulder through the swinging door to the ladies' room. The two girls inside, primping hip to hip in front of the long mirror above the sink, cut their rapid-fire speech as I enter. Their reflected gazes find me as the door arcs shut, track me as I cross the floor behind them. The white chick's hair is a plume of yellow curls held aloft over her head with a blue silk scarf; the black chick's falls straight as rulers over her shoulders. I give their reflections a nod, receive a reflected nod in return, and head to the stall.

Once settled on the cold seat, pants around my knees, I bask in the sensation of the basketball pressure in my bladder waterfalling out of me. It's bliss, despite the tandem snickering outside the stall. My hackles rise only when the voices of the mirror-girls sink into conspiratorial whispers peppered by bursts of tittering squawks. It's a preamble for what's coming, because these two know me, even if I don't recognize either one of them. They look about my age, though, so if they know me how I think they know me, I can guess what's coming.

A silence descends, backed by the muffled thump of dance music outside the restroom. They may just decide to let it go, to keep their own joke private, but, no, they begin to clap in cadence, a peppy, cheerleader rhythm.

Don't do it.

They up the rhythm.

Don't do it.

They do:

"*Go, Nicki! Go, Nicki! Go—go—go, Nicki!*"

My jaw locks and my eyes burn. Somewhere rattling around my head is a knifepoint threat about knocking the both of them flat on their asses and then forcibly de-cunting one after the other with my boots, but my tongue can't find the shape of the words, which probably means whatever it is I'm going to say sounds better inside my head than out loud. Instead, I kick the stall door with the heel of one boot. A shriek of cackles erupts from the other side, cut off sharply as the restroom door snicks shut after them.

I shouldn't let that kind of shit get to me, but I wasn't expecting it; I was having a good time, so it does get to me. I sit in the stall until my eyes stop burning, my sinuses clear, and my cheeks cool. I'd tell you I'm not waiting for the two of them to clear a good distance from the restroom door before I leave, but you'd know better.

Back out in the bar, the DJ is announcing last call over the speakers. Is it that late? I see Quinn on the corner of the dance floor with his arm around Marshall's waist. I walk over to him just as he releases her so she can go tend to some customers.

"Found a date tonight?" I ask.

He turns, smiles. "Found a couple. Looks like you found yourself a couple, too."

"Think so."

"Have fun."

"Do you want to come with me?"

He shoots a look to the corner booth. "I think they might be a little too tight for me. Cut off my circulation."

"You could bring your dates."

"Then I might have to share."

I don't know why I want him to come. Maybe I'm still feeling weird about our spat. He seems to be over it, though.

"Go have a good time," he says. "I'll call you tomorrow."

I hug him, he hugs back, and I leave him for the corner booth where Todd and Parker Fabian are already out of their seats.

"Where's Donald?"

"He has to get up early for church," Parker tells me. There's a wry grin on his face. I can't tell if he's serious or not. Probably he is.

Todd moves close to me. "Do you want to head out to a little private after-hours?"

"Where?"

"House out past Briar Range Road."

Swanky. Like Cowen Road divides the haves from the have-nots, Briar Range Road divides the haves from the have-a-lots. Probably two dozen buck-and-a-half chateaus sit on something like two-hundred acres of privately-owned woodland.

"Your house?" I ask. Shit, trophy wife and soccer mom hasn't got such a bad ring to it, after all.

"Friend's."

"You house-sitting or something?"

"Something like that."

"Just us three?"

"Another friend of mine will be coming out with us. He's around here somewhere. I'll drive, you don't have to worry about your car."

"I don't have my car with me."

"Well, then, I'll take you home whenever you want to go." He steps away. "Let me go hunt him down so we can move out."

Todd leaves and I go to Parker and hook my arm around his waist. He hooks his arm around my shoulders. Damn, but he's tall. I tighten my grip on him to steady him because he's swaying. If he tips over, he's taking me with him.

"Z'at yer boyfriend o'there?" His words run together.

"Quinn? What makes you think he's my boyfriend?"

"Guess I juss can't believe you don't got a boyfriend."

"'Cause?"

"'Cause you're beautiful."

I look up at him. "Thanks." I snort. "I can't believe you don't have a girlfriend."

"Yeah?"

"You got great hands."

That bowls us over. We stagger and sway like Weeble Wobbles.

Parker says, "There's Todd." I look toward the door. Todd's flapping one hand, motioning for us. Parker and I tip and sway toward the door, arm-in-arm. We make it outside. The night's taken on an edge. I button up the front of my blouse. My arms run with goose bumps. I lean into Parker for warmth. I like him. He's not as good-looking as Todd, but I think I like him better.

"There he is," Parker says, and redirects us across the parking lot. I look for Quinn's Mustang, but its parking place is already empty. Todd is standing with another guy next to a Toyota Tacoma double-cab. Who the hell would name a truck Tacoma? No one from the Northwest, that's for sure. The new guy with Todd has his back to me. Todd sees us and says, "Nicki, this is Ellis Ray."

Ellis Ray turns to face me. I stop cold.

"Hi, Nicki." Ellis Ray extends his hand. He's smiling, being pleasant, friendly, but I can still see the ghost of that leer he was wearing at the Wheatpenny.

I step forward, away from Parker, and take his hand. "Do we know each other?"

"I remember seeing you around every once in a

while."

"Uh-huh."

Those tight, round John Lennon glasses of his are a getup nobody wears. It's completely possible I could have seen Ellis Ray "around every once in a while" and remembered him for no other reason than those glasses alone. The popped collar of his salmon polo flares out the neck of his black sports jacket. The neat, black soul patch, which I hadn't noticed in the Wheatpenny, underscores the animal curves of his lower lips and fierce chin. He's not good-looking, but he's lookable, if you know what I mean. At first sight, you might wonder if he was worth getting interested in, and that's what he wants you to wonder. Look, I know which worm to hook when I go fishing, and I can tell Ellis does too. But there's something off about his bait. Something that catches your attention but keeps you at bay at the same time. That give-and-pull can have a sickly appeal, the way shifting whims of his manner keep you wondering whether you like him or you don't.

I don't like him. This I know. I do not like Ellis Ray, not for a second.

No one speaks for a beat.

"Well," Todd says. "Let's get moving."

Parker follows Todd around to the driver's side. To me, Ellis says, "You don't mind if I ride shotgun, do you? I get motion-sick in back seats." He turns and opens the front passenger side door.

I don't care where the fuck he rides. He better not think he's riding me later on. I open the back door and climb in.

Don't think our little tableaux here in Todd's Tacoma doesn't feel real familiar to me. I've been here before. Only difference is, nothing is going to happen that I don't want to have happen—experience and the straight razor I'm slipping from my boot to my pocket say so.

On the road, Parker slides toward the middle of the seat. I meet him there. Ellis is poking at the MP3 player on the front console. He finds something he likes, and thank god it's neither hip hop nor country. It's some new rock I hear on the radio from time to time, but I don't know the name of it.

Parker's hand slips onto my thigh. He leans toward me, puts his arm around me. I shift and raise my head and we find each other's mouths. He's hungry. I am too. I turn and lie my back against his shoulder, wrap my arms around the nape of his neck, neither of us wanting to draw our mouths apart. A new song comes through the speakers now. I know this one. Goddammit, I know this one. Its syrupy intro is the sound of slow, fat, balloon-shaped frogs humping. Prince's falsetto glides in over the music, singing the first lines about a girl that shares my name, and how, when he first met her, she was doing something with a magazine that sounds unlikely and uncomfortable.

I pull away from Parker, slide back to my side of the seat.

"Is that supposed to be a fucking joke?" I'm straightening my blouse; Parker's watching me with a look of desperation.

"Sorry." Ellis minces his words. "Poor choice of music."

"Yeah, well, I hate that fucking song."

Todd turns to Ellis, and voice pitched low, but not low enough for me to miss the words, he says, "What the fuck's that about?"

Ellis smiles at Todd. "Sorry."

Parker reaches a hand out to me. "It's okay," he pleads. "It's okay." I flash him a look that tells him he's going to draw back a stump if he isn't careful, so he settles back on his side of the passenger seat, turns, and shoots daggers at the back of Ellis's head.

Todd hits shuffle and Level 42 comes on with "Something About You."

"Sorry, Nicki," he says. "Sorry about that."

"Yeah, well, why don't you just let me out."

"Nicki." Todd glances over his shoulder. "Ellis'll behave himself."

"I'll behave," Ellis says. "Scout's honor."

"Shut it, Ellis," Todd says.

"You can do whatever you want," I say. "Let me the fuck out. Now."

"Where you going, Nicki?" Todd says.

"Let me use a cell. I'll get a ride." I hope Quinn still has his phone on. He'll be pissed, but he'll come get me.

"Just let's go to the house. I got some weed there. Chronic. Good shit. We'll take a couple of tokes and I'll give you an eighth to keep for your own personal use, as a matter of apology. If you want to leave after that, I'll take you home, no arguments."

I don't smoke weed much, but I could turn that eighth of chronic into some quick cash later on. It's not like I couldn't use the money.

"Fuck," I say. "Whatever."

I turn toward the window and watch the night skim by, making my silence loud to let them know that if the three of them are still hoping for some action tonight, the only place they're going to find it is inside their own private daisy chain.

Two more songs shuffle through. I barely hear them. We're well past Briar Range Road, and the tree line on the shoulder opens every hundred feet or so into a private fenced driveway. Todd slows the Tacoma near the third drive on the right. An iron wrought gate stops us. Todd climbs out, walks over, and thumbs a code into a keypad. The gate parts down the middle and swings open for us. After he climbs back into the driver's seat, we roll up to a two-story Victorian and park between a black Jeep and a red Mercury.

I ignore Ellis as we step out onto the wide drive, the gravel crunching and popping under the heels of my boots. I swear I can hear harder particles shearing and breaking weaker particles under the pressure of my heels, some particles displacing a comfortable divot down inside the dirt, while others skitter off and away, sheared and nicked, but free of the pressure, at least until the pressure of another heel forces them against their neighbors again. I feel as though I have very little to do with all this clatter; I feel more in tune with the echoes the gravel throws into the deadened air in a darkness that's slipped past midnight.

I walk around the back of the truck, where Parker meets me from around the opposite side. I don't look at him but I let him put his arm around my shoulders. "Sorry, Nicki," he whispers. "Don't know what that's all about." Nothing to say. We all walk toward the front door. I'll smoke a bowl, get my eighth, and Todd will take me home. No arguments. I will be a cunt about it.

"Weed's upstairs," Todd announces. He's punching a code into another keypad on the side of the front door. A lock clicks, and Todd swings the door wide. I break away from Parker as we enter—he lets me go without protest—and linger by the door. There's a foyer first thing inside, lightless doorways opening to the left and right, and an immediate staircase that leads to a second floor. Todd takes the stair and the rest of us fall in one after the other. I stick to the rear, behind Parker. Ellis is perfectly fine to remain in back of Todd. I jam my hands into my pockets and curl the fingers of my right hand around the closed straight razor there.

The lot of them is setting me up for something, and I don't like it, not for a second. I don't know what they want. I can't fathom what I possibly could have to offer anyone, and I don't care if I ever find out; but if one of these motherfuckers wants to press me, he's going to find himself sorry and teary-eyed.

At the landing, a furnished open loft breaks into view. Todd's hit a wall switch at the top of the stair, and when I get up there, I check out the lay of the land.

Shelves in each corner, filled with books and DVDs. A fat brown sofa and recliner line the far wall. A choice sound system and widescreen LCD brace the near wall, just at the edge of the balcony railing that looks back down onto the foyer downstairs.

On an oak table in the middle of the room sits a plain wooden box, dark with varnish. Looks like something that might have been made in a high school woodshop to fulfill the most basic requirements of the assignment.

Todd lifts its lid and takes out two vacuum-sealed baggies and a green marble pipe. He hands one of the baggies to me—I pocket it opposite my straight razor—and hands the other to Parker.

"Set this up while I put on some music," he says and turns to the stereo.

Parker breaks open the baggie and starts loading a bowl.

I keep Ellis in view. He's loitering near a recliner in the corner near the curtained window. I go stand on the opposite side of the room, outside the threshold of the dark hallway, exactly opposite the stairs, so I can make a run for it if I need to.

Parker finishes loading the bowl and takes the first hit. Music starts thumping. Todd takes the pipe and hits it. The smell of pot fills the room. Someone once told me that the only way to describe the smell of marijuana is "green." It's true, I think. This is so green it practically paints the air in midday-jungle hues.

Todd brings the pipe to me. I hit it, but easy. If it's as good as Todd says, I don't want it to dumb me down. I hand the pipe back, exhale.

"Like?" Todd wants to know.

"Sure." Todd nods and starts to step across the room to give Ellis a hit. I turn to the bookshelf closest to me and read the spines. A lot of science fiction. I'm not much into SF, but I once knew someone who loved it. Foisted a few titles on me. I find two or three here. They were all right, I guess.

One title catches my eye. It seems utterly out of place in between the other ones on the shelf. It's *Blubber*, by Judy Blume. A hardback. I tap the spine with a fingernail. It's an old copy; the cover's scuffed and beat up.

"Find something you like?" Todd says over my shoulder. Must have snuck up on me while I was reading the titles.

"I used to have this one." I tap the spine again.

"That very one?" he asks.

"Can't be." I turn and look at Todd. He's holding the pipe out to me.

"'Nother hit?" he says.

I look at the pipe but I'm thinking about my old book. Whatever happened to it? I lent it out, right? Lent it out and didn't get it back?

"Whose house is this?" I say.

The hairs on the back of my neck flair. There's movement down the hallway, behind me. Todd breaks away and crosses back to Ellis. I turn to look down the hall. It's dark. Can't see anything.

I turn to the others. "Is there someone else here?"

Todd's handing the pipe to Ellis, pointedly avoiding my eyes. Ellis, on the other hand, is giving me a half-assed smirk. Parker's face is slack and stoned, his lips work on a word that's not coming out, then his eyes cut to me, to Todd, to the hallway.

"Anyone want to give me a fucking answer?"

Todd gives me an answer, all right: without a glance in my direction, he saunters over to the head of the stairs and then parks himself there, resting one hand atop the thick dark oak banister before turning to slide me a placid, unmoving look, a look that tells me he knows he's effectively blocked my only way out.

"That's how it is, huh?" The words are a hiss through teeth that won't unclench.

You see, ladies and gents? This is what happens when you stumble into somebody else's game. Doesn't matter that you're drunk and horny and a little blue and a little hurt, because no one's going to offer you a mulligan once the cards are dealt and the pieces are in place; no use crying about it. The moment you find yourself there, you only have yourself to blame for taking a seat at the table.

The soft lumbering in the dark of the hallway grows nearer, its source not bothering to be subtle, but not bothering to turn on a light, either. I sidestep to the middle of the room, one hand stealing toward the pocket with my razor in it, the other rising as a distraction, index finger out and aimed at Todd, who hasn't budged from his post at the landing.

"Don't think you're not going down those stairs head-first when the time comes, champ."

Ellis honks out a laugh, one single, sudden, loud note, full of surprised delight, lacking anything close to humor, and finalized with a theatrical, deflating sigh. "Oh man, it'd be worth my cut to see *that*."

"*Can it*," Todd hisses. His eyes have cut to Ellis. Muscles in my right leg twitch, ready to send me flying toward Todd, to put my shoulder into his sternum and make good on my promise to him.

The rest of me holds back. I figure if I can take one of them down, the others will spook and back off. But the right one needs to go down.

Todd's distraction won't last long. I saw how his hand tightened on the knob of the banister, how his weight shifted my way in anticipation after I sent my threat after him. Parker's shoulders are slumped, his eyes heavy. His uncertainty about this whole situation playing at the corners of his mouth makes him the easiest pickings, but the least effective example. Ellis hasn't betrayed an ounce of tension since the start. His face stays asshole-calm and unruffled, his frame slouch-shouldered, leaning with one hip against the arm of a couch, one hand hooked by thumb in the pocket of his jeans, the other resting at his side. Ellis isn't the kind to get spooked, is he? No, not a shade. He's going to be the one to fall.

And then a voice drifts from the hallway. The sound of it stops my breath cold, slackens my muscles, and snaps the knifepoint of my offensive off at the tip.

It's a high voice for a man's, soft but projecting, unruffled by the shape of the snare into which it's about to enwind itself.

It says, "Hey, now, everybody, we're all friends here," the diction precise and clipped, forming the words as would a heavy reader, betraying the artless tone of someone who's ghosted outside and between cliques, who's drifted here and there, but never found a way to settle anywhere.

The owner breaks into the light, breaching the absolute darkness of the hallway belly-first. The robe he wears is stretched creaseless over the barrel-shaped bulk. It's gold with a damask-pattern and deep red cuffs and collar. The very tips of the matching belt around his waist strain to stay knotted. Brown leather slippers, visible under the hem swaying an inch or so over the bare, white ankles, whisper out over the carpet. When his face appears, it's a head over my own.

His dishwater hair has thinned in the front. He has jowls now, more baby-like than bulldog, as if his face could ever hold a feral look. His pale hazel eyes are high-set and close together, ever on the verge of squinting. His thin eyebrows are peaked toward the center, nearly forming the top of a triangle over the long dive the bridge of his nose takes that's always seemed to divide his face in half. His cheeks are clear now, but rough with scars of the acne he'd battled even into his twenties.

"Hi, Nicki," says Jonathan Garver. "Boy, you sure haven't changed." He's smiling as if surprised by a chance meeting, as though the two of us have simply run into each other for the first time in years and are about to share a delighted hug of reunion. He glances to Ellis, then to Parker, and I swear there's an expression on his face like he's a proud father.

"Why are you here?" My voice is as weak as my hands, no longer tight and ready for action, but nerveless and slack.

His attention returns to me. "Don't be scared, I hate seeing you like that." He raises his arms, like he might make a lunge for me, might actually make a play for that hug he thinks we owe each other, but his palms are upturned, the way a ringmaster presents the big top to circus-goers. "I *live* here. This is my *place*."

"Jonathan—"

A sharp, high scent stings my sinuses. Cologne. It wafts out into the loft, spreading in the motion of Jonathan's upraised arms, smothering the fat smell of weed and booze and the chemical whiff of furniture polish and carpet cleaner, the last present only in the moment it's scrubbed clear.

"I'm sorry I brought you here like this. It wasn't fair, but I didn't think you'd come to see me if I asked." He tucks his hand back into the pockets of his robe and shrugs. "Couldn't find you, anyway. I figured you were still around but I ..."

His voice trails off, his eyes fixing on mine, unmoving, undistracted, as if finally, really, seeing me for the first time since he's entered the loft.

"We need to talk about something. Okay? Nothing bad. You know ... I'm *looking out* for you."

I snort, a sound less astonished and joyless than the laugh Ellis gave just a minute ago. At the sound of it, Jonathan's eyes go soft and wounded around the edges, like he has any right to feel wounded by anything at all that I do.

He raises one hand from a pocket, holds it out to me, palm up.

"Nicki, please." His voice pitches toward a reedy whine; he catches himself, squares his shoulders and pastes on a smile whose sincerity might be genuine, but whose confidence struggles to stay put. "Just a quick chat, all right? That's all. Then you can leave, if you want to. Or we, you know, we can catch up, the two of us? We can have some fun? We'll do some hits, have a few drinks, we'll have some fun. It'll be nice. Maybe you can dance for us. Do you still like to dance, Nicki?"

There's a whisper to my right. Across the room. A sound like rain but too regular, too rapid and dry, soft, airy, a sound I love but can't identify, my head's so scrambled.

It's Ellis. He's found a thick, over-sized paperback book lying on its side on top of the end table and has started flipping its pages. There's a distracted inelegance about what he's doing; he's using the knuckles of one hand to press down the glossy cover while the thumb raises a corner to let the leaves thrump one on top of the other. He's doing it solely to make the sound of an impatient dealer flipping a deck of cards. It's a careless, thoughtless action.

"Be careful with that, please," Jonathan tells him, thumbnail dinting the side of the opposite index finger in agitation.

The sound of the flipping pages stops. Ellis glances at Jonathan, then glances around the room. He raps the cover of the book twice with his knuckles and places both hands in his pockets.

"Thank you," Jonathan says. He returns his attention to me. He opens his mouth to speak, but another voice cuts him off.

"Uh, hey, look."

All eyes turn to Parker, the guy we've all forgotten about. "Yeah, hey." His voice is plummy, his face dopey, and he seems to be leaning at an angle just short of tipping over. "This may not be any of my business, and I kinda feel like I'm party-crashin', but is everything kosher here? You okay, Nicki?"

If I'd have been able to muster a response, Todd makes sure to step all over it before I can get a word out, answering for me in reassuring tones that seem to do little to convince Parker that the situation is proper and hygienic. I barely hear him; his voice is as senseless as a rush of water, a lapping shoreline, a babbling brook, and all I want to do is stand perfectly still and silent and wait for this to pass, as all things must, but I know I have to screw my head back on, to start kicking and paddling, because I won't have much time before the currents pull me all the way under.

"I have to go to the bathroom."

The room falls silent. I stare into the dark mahogany shadow between the sofa cushions and the back rest.

"Can't it wait?" Jonathan asks. "We won't take long. I've got something for you—"

I fix Jonathan with a no-bullshit look.

"Okay." He steps away from the mouth of the hallway and reaches around the corner to flip a wall switch. The hallway brightens, bleaching the white plaster walls. I move forward into it.

"First door on the left." He gestures with one hand.

Ellis offers Jonathan a resigned warning—"*I wouldn't ...*" —but I'm already stepping into the bathroom and swinging the door shut behind me, flipping the light switch by feel in the darkness only after I've twisted the lock in the knob.

The straight razor's in my hand. I don't remember fishing it from my pocket. I flip it open, securing the tang under my thumb. It can't do me any good. I can't cut my way out of here. All Jonathan needs to do is call the cops, and who are they going to believe? Some fucking white trash slut putting on airs by traveling past Cowen Road, or the owner of the two-story Victorian who made the call? I flip the blade closed, but it feels good in the center of my fist because I can direct the shaking of my hands into its steady steel and ivory.

The bathroom is long and narrow. A tight, tiny window is set mid-height opposite the door. Along my righthand side hangs a broad mirror over a long counter and sink. The toilet sits at its end. On my left, the bathtub lays shuttered behind a burgundy shower curtain.

I pocket the razor, walk to the window. The pane is frosted, like you'd need privacy on the second floor. It's not any bigger the closer I get to it. And if I did manage to wriggle out, which is quickly seeming more and more likely to be my only option, what then?

There's really no time for thinking, so I slide the pane open and knock out the screen, watch it flip end-over-end down into darkness, and pause to listen for the hushed rustle the grass will make when it hits. Takes longer than I'd like it to.

I lean out. My shoulders clear the sides of the frame with at least an inch of space on either side. That's good, but the frame is only as tall as it is wide. If the bathroom were on the first floor, I'd be out and gone like a tiger through a flaming hoop. But the drop on the other side, doused in darkness, driveway lights peaking around the corner helping only to sink vision deeper, must be twice my height; and if there are, say, thorny rose bushes below, or tomato vines on skewering posts, how far do I have to jump to avoid them?

There's a knock at the door. Jonathan's voice bleeds through.

"Hey, Nicki?"

I step up onto the toilet lid. It shimmies, slick as ice on the lip of the bowl. The plastic hinges securing it pop, warning me that they aim to give way if I test them. Christ, how do I fucking do this?

"Just a sec!" I call over my shoulder, leveling my right foot onto the sill, slowly sliding it through, then outside, where it hangs atop open air. I shift my weight to the sill until I'm finally straddling it.

I'm not heavy, and I'm not weak, but gravity is treacherous tonight thanks to the booze and the weed. My balance is an angry bee in a jar, and I can't be sure whether or not I'm swaying, or which direction if I am, until I catch myself. I fold myself until I'm jackknifed into the frame, riding the sill like the world's thinnest mechanical bull. The metal track the window slides on has sharp edges and cuts into one ass cheek. I shift my shoulders left, toward the inside of the bathroom, brace my right elbow against the pane, hoping it won't shatter, bend my left knee, and hook my foot over the edge of the sill. If I can get that leg all the way over and outside, I'm nearly home free.

There's another light rapping at the door. Jonathan's voice floats through again, asking if everything is all right; he must have heard the heel of my boot scraping the plaster wall. Instead of answering, I shift onto my belly, the metal track pressing into my liver now, then turn myself widdershins—that's what it's called, right, making a circle counterclockwise is turning widdershins?—until I can finally anchor my elbow over the edge of the sill and free my left leg to dangle in the open air alongside my right.

"Nicki, please come out." The door knob rattles. I start

to wriggle backward, my blouse riding up, the track digging into my skin, my ribs, cold and sharp-edged. If I hook my elbow over the sill, hang like that, I can maybe set myself up for a controlled fall.

I do, yanking my blouse free because whether or not I make the drop, I refuse to finish this night out naked from the waist up but for a thin, black, lace bra; that'd just be *Porky's*-style shenanigans, and even I'm too good for that.

The door knob starts to click quietly. They're working on the lock from the outside. Enough of this crap—I push myself off into the night.

They say your life flashes before your eyes when you die. I don't have enough time to even remember my name before the ground, yielding but still sudden, hammers my feet, my legs, shoulders and head, and ain't a bit sorry about it. A shot of white light, and I feel like I'm stuck to the wall of the Revolution at the fairgrounds. Hair is in my eyes. A blunt, bruising pain is latched to my left side.

I roll onto my stomach, get my arms and one leg under me, and push up.

"Nicki!" Jonathan's voice, above and behind. "You okay, buddy?" I have no answer for him, don't even bother to look up over my shoulder at him; I just launch myself forward toward the road.

The next voice that reaches me is Ellis'—"She's bailing."—the clarity of the words ebbing in the fast distance I'm putting between the house and myself, but the amused I-told-you-so tone is clear. Having the time of his life, ain't he just?

I should pace myself, but my legs won't tolerate anything else than a haul-ass down the blacktop. These boots are the wrong things to run a marathon in. A quick check over my shoulder tells me the Tacoma's headlight beams are on. They wash the asphalt of Jonathan's driveway. They're coming after me.

I make it to the access road, then dodge to the opposite shoulder and down a shallow embankment right into edge of the woods. I can't see shit. I throw one arm up over my eyes to protect against skewering branches. The sound of the Tacoma's engine rumbles in my ears.

I drop into the uneven underbrush and lie flat on my back. Stiff leaves and pointy branches scratch my skin. Whatever bush I'm lying on better not be poisonous. If it is, I'll come back tomorrow and find it and burn it to ash.

For this, I shaved my legs.

The lowest boughs of the pines crawl with light. They're using flashlights to search for me. My name echoes on the road. It's Todd's voice. Ellis' soon accompanies it, crooning.

"Come back, Nicki, *come* back!"

The Tacoma's tires slow and crackle over gravel. Its engine rumbles closer, the vehicle not more than a dozen yards away. Cold light paints the forest in dazzling emerald. The tang of exhaust fumes douses my hiding place.

The sound of the engine moves on up the road, no slower, maybe a bit faster. Todd keeps calling. I don't hear Ellis anymore. They can't think I've gotten far. They'll be back, and I'll have moved. I hope I'll move. The chronic is making me want to just lie here and blink.

I'm right. Before the sound of the engine fades entirely out of earshot, the Tacoma circles back again. It's moving at a faster pace now. I don't hear my name being called. Maybe they've given up. Maybe they'll just let it be.

I lay still, waiting for it to pass. It does. The crackling of the tires moves back toward Jonathan's house. The rumble of the engine ebbs with it, not quite vanishing into silence, but instead coming to a steady idle. It's soon accompanied by the chatter and yawp of voices, the words dampened by distance and foliage. One voice carries the halting, flat, honking pattern of the inebriated. Parker. He sounds as delighted by the whole situation as I feel.

Conversation stutters to a halt. The silence that

follows is short, punctuated by the tinny clap of three of the Tacoma's doors. Its engine shifts into gear with a hurried whine, and the truck's tires pop the gravel again. The leaves above my head seem to sway in flowing illumination and shadows as the Tacoma passes by, and then the sound of the engine finally dwindles completely into dead air. I'm left alone, at last, my heartbeat a rubber mallet in my chest.

Okay, no fucking around now. I give myself a good shake to knock some of the stupid out of my head, fold my straight razor, pocket it, stand. Twigs rake my cheeks, tug at my hair and keep a few strands for themselves. The lights from Jonathan's driveway break into view beyond the low-hanging boughs. I wasn't as deep inside as I thought.

Breaking out to the shoulder of the road, I look left, look right. No headlights. No tail lights. The night's empty now but for me.

Almost empty: down, beyond the fence, across the lawn, at the foot of the front steps, in a bubble of porch light, stands Jonathan. Hands in the pockets of his robe, he's looking out toward the road. I can't tell if he sees me, but the porch lamps can't possibly shine bright enough to light the edge of the trees.

I stand motionless. So does he. What am I in his eyes, what does he see? I'm not the same person I was, he's got to know that. I'm half-inspired to walk up to him and demonstrate just how much I've changed, how much stronger and more well-placed my fists can be ten years on. But if I move forward, each step across that brief swath of the nighttime between us just might collapse the decade, and I'll arrive before him full of anger and tears and nothing else.

He turns and enters the house, the front door swinging closed behind him with a sharp clap.

Time for me to make my exit as well.

I won't be able to move through the woods. If I'm going to make any time at all, I have no choice but to take the road. I won't run. I'll walk. I'll have to pace myself.

I've got a long, dumbass hike ahead of me, the only sorry motherfucker in the world without a fucking cellphone, and these boots weren't made for walking.

I move out, shooting steady glances over my shoulder every dozen steps. Ten minutes up the road, an iron ache skewers my calves and a dumb red coal smolders in my thighs. I begin a rant in their honor. It's short and simple, and it goes like this:

Fuck you
Fuck you
Fuck you
Fuck you
Fuck you

Right leg *Fuck*; left leg *you*. Maybe I can knock on a door, say my boyfriend dumped me and left me on the side of the road, and can I can use the phone inside to get a ride home; but wouldn't you know it, the next drive I pass has a sign on a post by the mailbox that reads:

BOBBY JAMES SOUNDER
for MAYOR PRO-TEM

Isn't this just my night? I find enough energy to kick the goddamn thing down and stomp it into shreds.

I don't know how long it takes to make it the best part of the way up Briar Range Road, but street lights have broken into view up ahead. Once I get to them, I'll be in a business district. There's got to be a pay phone along the street somewhere.

There's a chill in the air that's making my nose run. The snot's all thin and watery. I wipe it from my upper lip with the backs of my wrists, then wipe my wrists on my jeans. Am I a thing of beauty, or what?

A final look backward shows the road dark and empty. Safe as can be. I cross Briar Range to the corner of Brook Road. The first building that rises to meet me is the Bank of America. I want to drop and rest, but I need to keep moving.

The street's dead and quiet. The good folk are resting

up for salvation tomorrow, I guess.

Four blocks down, I spot a half cabinet mounted onto the façade of a business. I dig into my pockets and find a miracle of change, walk up to it, plug the nickels and dimes into the coin slot, dial Quinn's cell. His voicemail tells me to leave a message. I say I'm walking home, hang up, and start hoofin' it, whistling Golden Earring's "Radar Love" as a little prayer or enchantment. Actually, I think it's the White Lion cover that's going through my head. That'll never work. My stupid brain.

When I was little, my dad kept an overstuffed, unorganized bookshelf in the downstairs family room. That was back when he still bothered to read anything other than the morning paper or Mom's pop culture magazines, but even then, his taste was neither wide nor deep. Still, alongside the World War II books, war novels, and card game guides, I found a few things to keep me interested. My favorite was an oversized doorstop called *Our Weird World*. It ran the gamut of paranormal phenomena, and was broken up into sections with titles like "Unearthly Encounters," "Ghostly Visitations," "Monsters in Our Midst," and "Phenomena of the Mind." This last had a chapter about twin sisters who never willingly left each other's sides, never spoke, and finally died on the same day, at the same time, in two separate hospital wards. Supposedly, when alive, they both acted in tandem, always seeming to know the other's thoughts, and instantly shared things learned while apart. They would even draw the same pictures while sequestered in different rooms. These girls were a wonder to me.

I set about trying to hone my own mind-reading skills, first on my brothers, both of whom I quickly concluded were too dense to be effective subjects, and then on the screaming kids on the school bus, on waitresses balancing heavy trays of plates in restaurants, and on cashiers running the register at the supermarket. I'd search my mind for a stray thought or a point of view outside my own eyes but I could never find an image or an idea that seemed too strained from anything that could be my own.

A while after I discovered Quinn Halliday was my brother—half-brother, if you want to be strict about it—I made him read the piece about the twins. He wasn't as impressed as I was with it, said if two people spent enough time together, they'd probably start growing similar, probably learn how to communicate with each other without words, and even start thinking the same thoughts. That's the way cults worked, too, he figured, or any group of people, in fact.

I was angry with him for a couple of days for blowing apart all my efforts at mind-reading, but only because I realized he had put to words the more everyday explanations I had already started to suspect. Still, I have to admire those two girls for getting one up on the rest of the world; they invented their own house rules and committed to them in the midst of the biggest game of all. That's probably what I really wanted to find in their story, anyway.

I'm still whistling "Radar Love" by the time I pass by the Wheatpenny—darkened, silenced, emptied—even though I've gotten sick of the tune by now. Anyway, I think I've finally managed to lock down Golden Earring's version in my head.

Another three or four minutes to reach the split-rail fence that borders my folks' property; a physical boundary that runs in stretches of fifteen or twenty feet between collapsed boards and broken posts. An especially large gap opens at the southwest corner by the road; that's where I enter the back forty.

The "back forty" is what the family has always called the property enclosed by the fence, although most of it lies on the sides of the house rather than behind it. And I'm not sure just how big one acre is, but the property can't amount to anywhere near forty of them. Still, once

I'm through the southwest gap, it takes about a minute-and-a-half to hump it to the house.

Porch lights glow just across the drive, silhouetting the shambled frames of the horse stalls. My parents owned horses before I was born. My brothers, Lewis and Terry, both of whom have middle names, by the way, remember horses. Myself, I've always remembered the stalls fucked up and tumbled down and empty.

The lights aren't on for me, by the way. My folks couldn't care less where I am or when I'm coming back. Anyway, it's the bungalow we're headed for, which sits just south of the house. It was built for my grandpa before he died, but by the time the bungalow was completed, Grandpa's dementia was so bad he couldn't live alone, not even in a fifteen-by-fifteen shack, forty feet from his daughter and son-in-law. Since it was just standing there, Dad converted it into a pool room. Now I'm renting it out. Have been since I got kicked out of my apartment eight months ago this January. Old couple next door got upset with my hijinks, I guess.

The straw that broke the camel's back, I think, was the night I chased some fucker out the door with my razor and on down the back alley. I'd brought him home from the bar and the poor fella had a stubborn case of the whiskey dick no amount of enthusiastic and dedicated finessing could beguile. The more it flopped left or lolled right, the more upset he got about it, started swearing up a blue storm, started calling me names, and saying things I couldn't pretend were just dirty talk. I tried to explain to him that the night didn't have to be a total loss, since, clearly, his tongue was still working even if his cock wasn't, which, pretty quickly, he took as a slight against his manhood. He batted me away by the forehead with the back of his wrist, sending me reeling, more from the shear act than the boney butterfly impact, and then started getting really mean. I suggested he leave, which he answered with a raised fist, which I countered with a box to the mouth. That surprised him, but not as much as my open razor against his throat. I told him I'd take his fucking head off and flush it down the toilet if he wasn't quick-stepping out the door in the next two seconds. Gave him a full thirty and even tucked his pecker back into his pants for him as a show of good will. He showed his appreciation by wheeling around just before stepping out the door and jabbing a finger out, once at me, then again at the apparent me standing at my side, and said that this wasn't the end of it, sweet cheeks.

I begged to differ, whooping and racing forward, razor cutting the air between us. He found his legs then, turned, and ran across the balcony and down the concrete steps. I gave chase, howling after him, down into the back alleyway, loping like William Hurt fresh out of the sensory deprivation tank and newly transformed into an Australopithecus.

It wasn't the way I'd wished the night would end, but I can't deny its moments of pleasure and exhilaration, and all of it without even having to cook him breakfast in the morning.

The elderly neighbors downstairs were not nearly as amused, though; a day later I came home from work to find a notice from the landlord taped to my front door. Thirty days to vacate.

My stomach still hurts when I think of those next three weeks. I was on the verge of having to throw three-fourths of my monthly take-home into an equivalent unit near the main drag, or rein in my rent payment in favor of a constricted rat-trap over in meth town. Live in poverty, or poverty of life. Couldn't tell you which was which.

I did have a third option, though; it didn't ease up my stomach cramps any.

I dragged myself to my folks' house a few days before I was legally homeless, getting there before noon, when I could be sure my dad would be both awake and at still a good number of bottles shy of insobriety. We gathered in the downstairs TV room, Dad slouching with one elbow on the arm of the sofa under the panoramic painting of four horse-borne cowboys racing forward over a fiery orange and magenta hardpack winter landscape at evening, my mom seated square-shouldered and unyielding in her mossy-green wing chair placed in front of the glare of the picture window. I sat on the far side of the coffee table, across an expanse of carpet, in a brown recliner whose seat sagged around my ass like a deflated tire. We haggled over the details—my cards face up, my mom holding all the aces, my dad sinking deeper into the sofa with each swig of Molson—until an agreement was reached: I would rent the bungalow for an exorbitant fee; I'd pay a percentage of the utilities and groceries (which I have to ask permission to use); and, I would help with odds-and-ends around the house whenever they came up. To give her credit, my mom's not just being cruel, she's being practical. My parents are broke. Mom works two jobs, and Dad hands over the monthly disability check he's been receiving for the past five years. Good thing he fucked up his back when he did; it let him dedicate himself full-time to drinking.

As it turns out, I'm renting only half of the bungalow. Just because I sleep here doesn't mean my dad's going to stop using it as his pool room. On one side lies my mattress and box spring, my dresser drawer topped with a short stack of library books, my nightstand with a lamp and an AM/FM radio alarm clock, and against the far wall beyond the foot of the mattress, my Magnavox TV/DVD player combo, circa 1993. There's also an alcove set into the back wall that opens to a bathroom with just enough space for a stand-up shower stall, sink, and a narrow linen cabinet, so I guess I'm getting a full three-fifths of the place.

The pool table takes up the opposite half of the living space. Roger Hanlon and Pat Saunders join Dad once or twice a week to get fuckered-up, holler a lot, clack their balls back and forth across the green felt, and sometimes even finish a game. I can sleep through pretty much anything when I set my mind to it. Earplugs help. This is what I'm paying six-hundred a month for. Home again, home again, jiggity-jig.

My legs are iron rods. I crawl under my covers, don't even take my boots off, my head sinking into the pillow so deeply I can barely imagine having kept it aloft all night. In spite of the way the whirlpooling dregs of booze, pot, and soured adrenaline make the bed seem like a one-ended teeter-totter, I can get down some serious thinking on just what the fuck I walked into tonight. What I'm gonna do about it. What's your game, Jonathan? What the fuck do you want with me?

He says nothing bad. He says he has something for me. He has my best interests at heart, my hand in his, smiling, pleased with himself. His hair isn't as thin as it was earlier tonight, and his paunch and his jowls are gone; tall, skinny Jonathan Carver. He's replaced his gold bathrobe with a yellow t-shirt and jeans.

My hackles rise. We're not alone up here. Over my shoulder stands Ted Wells, at the head of the stair. His arms are crossed, his black bangs swept left over his forehead. He has his head cocked at an ill-behaved angle. He's locked me in his gaze, making a point of seeing me.

I give Jonathan's hand a squeeze, but my palm is empty. I can't figure out how I ended up back here. It's the last place I want to be. I look down at myself and see I'm in a bathing suit. A two-piece. I'm dripping wet, getting puddles all over the carpet. I must have been swimming in the river with Quinn. The current must have caught me and washed me here.

Someone's coming down the hallway, the same hallway from which Jonathan made his entrance earlier. Even before he breaks into the light, I know who it is. It's the only person it could be to complete our special foursome.

It's Bobby James Sounder. I hope he doesn't know I stomped his signs to pieces.

He comes out, stands, and looks at me. Like Jonathan Garver and Ted Wells, he looks younger than he can

44

possibly be. In fact, he is; he's still thirty. He's so good-looking, with his blond hair and blue eyes, his square jaw and that Kirk Douglas dimple. He was the first guy to make that warmth flutter in the middle of my chest when he smiled at me. He used to have a special smile for me. I loved that smile, but the last time I saw him, he gave me another smile. It's the one he's wearing now. I follow his gaze back down to my dripping wet self. I'm making a mess of the carpet and I just know Bobby James is going to make me clean it up. I'll do it. Just get me a towel. I'll clean it all up, I promise.

I hope you don't make me tell you twice, dear heart, *Bobby James says.* Nothing special about it, sweetie, *Bobby James says.* It's the same no matter what.

I'm always told twice, I try to explain, but Jonathan, somewhere back down the hallway, interrupts me. He's repeating the same thing over and over: It's okay. It'll be nice. It's okay. It'll be nice.

It's not okay. It's not going to be nice. You know how I know? That's not water. Not on the carpet. Not on my thighs. My leg looks like a barber's pole. Red and white streaks running down.

I drag myself up onto my elbows. My jeans are heavy. They're sticking to my crotch, my thighs, because I pissed myself.

"Fuck! Fuck, fuck, fuck."

I'm off the mattress, peeling away my clothes as I waddle to the shower. My jeans are the last to go, and I leave them in a tangy heap on the tile. I turn the water as hot as I can stand it and let it turn my skin red.

The steam's going to lift the dream up and out of my head. That, and the feel of summer ten years ago, the final weeks right before I entered high school. I don't care what kind of shit Jonathan is trying to pull with me right now. All of that is done and gone and over with.

Even if it's never felt that way.

So now, if you don't mind, can you find something

else to do for a bit? I'm going to sit here and feel sorry for myself for a while.

"That boy called looking for you this morning," my dad tells me around noon. We're in the kitchen. He's on his fourth or fifth Molson of the day and halfway through a pastrami sandwich I fixed him. He sticks with beer because he wants to be an active drunk all day long and avoid the pass-out-by-two-in-the-afternoon that hard alcohol demands; his rules and he keeps to them, which is more than you can say for most people. I have the dishwasher pump and motor assembly on the kitchen floor. What I told Rudy Foreman last night at the Wheatpenny was no bullshit. What Quinn told him last night was no bullshit either. "That boy" is how my dad refers to Quinn.

"Why didn't you wake me up?"

"I looked in on you to see if you were in bed. He said not to wake you. Said to call him when you got a chance."

"'Kay, thanks."

I talk a lot of shit about my dad, and for good reason. He's a shiftless, philandering, no-account drunk. But after about two whiskey sours, I can start to tolerate him. I shoot my second one.

Actually, I can't really criticize him for his philandering. It's what gave me Quinn, after all. I need Quinn, even if no one else does.

"Still a little jittery there," he says; it's a verbal note about how the glass rattled after I set it on the counter. "Sure you couldn't use a third one?"

"Sure. I don't want to fix this washer, anyway."

"Hot damn! We'll use the dirty dishes for target practice!"

I give him a wry look. "Tempting as it is to waste a full Saturday with you and Mr. Molson's finest barley—"

"You'll be foraging for your own barley, I'm afraid, chicky."

"—*but*, Mom is coming home in a couple hours."

"Oh yeah." The grumble in his voice is an expression of sympathy.

"And if I can avoid my daily ration of shit from her by fixing this damn thing ..." I flip a corner. It thunks against the linoleum. The sound hangs in the air.

"Everything okay?" he asks.

"Just grouchy. Tied one on a little too tight last night, is all," I tell him. Half-truth.

"You knew the job was dangerous when you took it."

I snort. "That I did." I stand. "This motor's fucked. Think I'm probably going to have to pick up some parts at Coast to Coast. Can I use your car? I'm on fumes, and I won't be able to afford bits-and-pieces and gas too."

I'm setting him up to spring for parts, too, but he doesn't take the bait. Instead, he says "Yeah, key's on the peg."

Beer or clean dishes. Which did you think he was going to choose? Wasn't like he put any thought into it or anything. The lizard part of his brain makes the decisions these days.

I call Quinn before I head out.

"Hey, I got to drive to town for parts for the dishwasher. Why don't you meet me at the Cafe and buy me lunch?"

"You okay?" he wants to know. His voice is tight.

"Sure, I'm fine."

"What was that message about last night?"

"Oh. Nothing. All those fuckers wanted to do was listen to techno and play Scrabble so I had to light out on them. The only tiles I got dealt were a bunch of X's, Q's, and L's, anyway."

He doesn't laugh. "What happened last night?"

I hesitate. I'm not going to tell him about Jonathan Garver. I say, "They brought out a game I didn't want to play, is all."

The line stays dead and I'm starting to think the call got dropped.

"Hello?"

"What did they want to play?" Quinn seems avowed

to defend the last vestiges of my maidenhood, wherever the fuck I left it lying around. Probably explains the attitude he copped last night. Probably thought I was so taken with some east-towner that I wasn't going to be able to save myself from pain and degradation. Like I might end up starring in a snuff film or on the Internet getting sodomized by an Afghan.

I say, "One of them wanted to play Fuck With Nicki. By Hasbro. Killed the mood, is all." I'm thinking of Ellis. Lends a tone of conviction. "Didn't let him get away with it, though," I add to make him feel better. Saying it doesn't make me feel any better, though; I still owe Ellis. Ellis at *least*.

No, no, shouldn't even be thinking along those lines.

"Your boyfriend?" he says.

See? I knew it. Quinn's just looking for a reason to play knuckle-boppity with Todd's noggin.

"No, it wasn't Todd."

There's a long pause. Quinn says, "'Kay, meet you at the Cafe in twenty, Sparks."

I'm there in ten. "The Cafe" is The April Cafe, and it's a little hole-in-the-wall that makes the best country fried steak you'll ever taste. Its picture window looks out on a thrift store across the street, with silver art deco mannequins in the storefront that wear clothes so mismatched, I'm half-convinced the line-up is some sort of bizarre personal joke the designer is playing on pedestrians. The Cafe has five booths and five tables. The color-scheme is what-the-hell. On the wall are pictures of eagles and bears and pastoral scenes all crowded together. The tile floor laminate buckles underfoot every two steps, and the tabletops are peeling. I have no idea what the hell is going on in the kitchen, and if I'm going to continue to eat here, it's probably best I don't. Sometimes eating here feels like ordering blowfish— your life's in your hands with every bite you take.

Quinn enters five minutes after I'm seated, finds me at a glance, and joins me in the booth.

I go, "So, you give Marshall Rowson the thrill of her

life?"

"Marshall? No. She had to close. I hooked up with Carol MacDonald."

"*Carol MacDonald*?"

"Carol MacDonald."

"Jesus."

"No, Carol MacDon —"

"I fucking hate Carol MacDonald."

"Good thing you didn't fuck her then, I guess."

"Shit, if your dick was in her, it's like I half fucked her."

"I don't even want to think about what that means."

The waitress comes around. Her name's Betty. She must be on the high-end of fifty, and her hair is redder than nature allows, but she says "goddamn" and "shit" a lot, so she always puts me at ease. Quinn and I both order the chicken fried steak.

We wait for our food and talk about everything and nothing. I do want to tell him what happened last night; I do want to talk to him about it, not just so he can help me figure it out, but to tell him how I felt, how seeing Jonathan Garver made me small and helpless again, but I can't, because if I do, Quinn might say something I don't want to hear. He might start shit with Todd or Parker or Ellis. Or, god forbid, Jonathan. I don't want him to do that.

If I need his help, I'll ask. But right now, if it's over, then let it be over. If something's just started, well, I'll hold Quinn's hand and cross that bridge when I come to it.

Quinn says, "So how far did you have to hike last night before you could call me?"

"Who cares?"

"I do. So I won't feel so bad about taking time out to make Carol MacDonald feel like the little bitch-whore she wants to be when I should have been rescuing my sister."

Is it bad that that seems like one of the sweetest things anybody's ever said to me?

"It wasn't that far," I tell him. "I barely remember anyway."

"Really?"

"No. Not really. It's cool, though. Seriously, my bad decision. I'll tell you about it later." I want to tell him now, and the need won't stop buzzing my head. Makes me slip a little and say, "Gave me the chance to kick the shit out of one of Bobby James' election signs I saw stuck in a yard, at least."

"Good for you," Quinn says. He eyes me, searching for what I'm keeping from him. "Hopefully he felt a boot up his ass when you did it."

"Probably not. If I could voodoo him, the fucker'd be a paraplegic eunuch by now."

Quinn cocks an eyebrow. I went too far, but I'm saved by Betty and the arrival of delicious junk food. The bliss of too much starch and cholesterol should smother all our troubles, but I can tell the stuff I told Quinn is still churning in his head.

To shake it, I ask, "So what's the difference between a bitch-whore and a slut?"

He snorts. "A bitch-whore can afford to get off by telling herself she thinks she deserves what she's getting."

"A slut can't?"

"A slut's giving as much as getting."

"Hallafuckinlooya."

When we're finished, I slouch back in the booth and prop my feet up on Quinn's seat. My legs aren't as sore as I'd have expected after last night's hike, but it makes them feel better when he rubs my shins. He talks about his job at the print shop and how Gregory Hines—no relation, white guy—is pressing him to take a management position. I think he'd be great at it, but Quinn frowns and shakes his head.

Quinn pays the bill, I leave the tip. We meet outside and stand in comfortable silence together, facing each other, not wanting to part. My hands are in my pockets. I step forward and put my forehead on his shoulder. He rubs the back of my head.

"What's up?"

50

I moan. "I just want things to be like they were."

"Mmm."

He knows what I mean. When we were kids, we were each other's best friend. We're still each other's best friend. In fact, we're nearly each other's only friend, but life is getting in the way. Shit's getting in the way. I can't even put a name to half of it.

He kisses the top of my head. I love him. He's the only person in the world I've ever loved.

Shit. Mom's home. Standing by her Camry, not bothering to shut the door. She just frowns as I coast in and bring Dad's Olds to a stop up alongside her. Jesus, what the fuck now? I climb out.

"Something wrong with your car?" She slams the Camry's door. I guess she'd been waiting to use it to punctuate her displeasure. I'm so impressed.

I hold the Coast to Coast bags up for her to see. "For the dishwasher. I'm on fumes, Mom. I couldn't afford gas and parts."

"So, you're going to take your dad's car to work on Monday?"

"I'll get to work on Monday." I start for the house.

"I hope so."

"Fuck off."

"What did you say?" She's in hot pursuit now.

"I said, do you want me to fix your fucking dishwasher or not?"

"How'd you like me to kick your ass to the street?"

"Yeah. Fine." Lower. "Without my six-hundred, who's going to be out on the fucking street?"

She grabs my arm and spins me around. Her grip hurts as much as it always did, but I don't give her the satisfaction of letting her know it anymore. She's traded her bangs for a short, permed bob that doesn't suit her in the least, but she still glares bullet holes when she's furious. Right now, I think she's just pissed off that she doesn't have anything to spit at me. She can always call me tramp; it's her fallback line.

This time, though, she just looks down at the bags. "Well, why don't you go and make yourself useful, then." She drops my arm and steps back. She adds, "Could you maybe get it finished before you go out and be the neighborhood bicycle again tonight?"

Ah, there it is. She whirls and marches inside.

Here's the thing: I had the temerity to be born on the same day as Quinn. To her, I'm a walking, talking reminder of my dad's infidelity with Marisa Halliday. I was born two hours before Quinn, so, I think, in her mind, I represent that day twenty-four years ago that my dad fucked her, then walked straight out the door and down Ludlow Road to throw a fuck into Quinn's future mom. I don't know if that's how it happened, but it's her truth now.

I found out Quinn was my brother by way of Alice Winterbaum's vicious, little mouth. I do not know how the fuck news travels in this town. Alice was really no one to me, and I can't image how she found out. I can only guess that either my mom or dad or Miss Halliday said something to someone and the gossip made its rounds. I do know that there was the issue of child support, and that it went all the way to the courts, so my dad's paternity wasn't exactly a secret. My mom had to take a job for the first time in her life to cover his child support. She'd told me that once, a few years ago, when she took a second job after my dad's disability; said it like it was my fault, like I'd banged Quinn's mom and knocked her up.

It was at Robert Chambers Elementary, so me and Quinn must have been around nine or ten. There'd always been three separate classes for each grade, and students would always get remixed each new school year, but Quinn and I had never shared a class all through elementary. I've always wondered if my mom had something to do with that.

So. Lunch recess. Playground. I was minding my own business, following a garter snake through the bushes on the far side of the swings, and Alice came up to me.

"You know who that boy is over there?" She pointed to the wall of a wing against which a group of boys and girls were playing wall-ball with a big red rubber ball. "The one knocking the ball right now?"

"That's Quinn Halliday," I told her. Who cared?

"But, do you know who he is?" Alice Winterbaum was all blonde curls and pink baby-fat cheeks and tattled-tales and gossip. An evil Shirley Temple.

I shrugged. Like I said, who cared?

"He's your brother."

I turned, put my fists on my hips, and looked at her like she was some kind of idiot. "Quinn Halliday is not my brother. Lewis and Terry are my brothers, and they're in middle school."

Alice nodded slowly at me. "Quinn Halliday is your brother, too."

I looked at Quinn. He didn't even look like my brothers. Lewis and Terry were auburn-haired, like my mom. Quinn Halliday had jet black hair like me and my dad.

"If he's my brother," I challenged her, "then how come he doesn't live with me? How come he has a different last name?" I smiled, pleased with myself for having destroyed her claim with simple logic.

"Because *his* mom is different than *your* mom."

"Who's his dad, then?"

"*Your* dad."

"How?"

"Don't you know anything?" I did know anything, but my brain just wasn't going to put the pieces together. Alice spelled it out for me. "*Your* dad did it to *his* mom," she said. "*That's* how." She put her fists on her hips and smiled at me like *I* was some kind of idiot.

I beat her up pretty good.

The principal never found out what started the fight. Alice didn't tell, for the sake of self-preservation, I figure.

I didn't tell because I couldn't stop crying, which probably confused the shit out of him. There Alice was, pressing a wad of bloody Kleenex to her nose, and there I was, bawling my head off. My uncontrollable, abject misery most likely saved me from detention and a pink slip. They sat me in the nurse's station until I could get hold of myself, then after someone daubed that last tear from my eyes and asked if I was alright, they sent me off to finish school for the day.

On the bus home, I watched the back of Quinn's head. He sat across the aisle from me, two rows down.

I tried to read his mind.

I wondered if he knew he was my brother.

I wondered if he secretly thought about me.

A probable no to all of the above, which filled me with a sense of desperation, knowing he was inside me but I was outside him. I wanted to poke a hole in the back of his skull with a mental ice pick and pour my name into his head.

We shared the same stop, but depending on where one or the other had found a seat on the bus, either he or I would lead the walk home. We never walked together. He lived past me, and usually I'd leave him as soon as I turned to cross the threshold of my granite driveway. That day was a different story, though. That day I followed him on past my house. He must have heard the crunch of my shoes on the gravel shoulder, because he turned around once or twice to look at me. Finally, he said, without slowing, "Why are following me?"

"Is it against the law?"

"It should be for you."

God, he was mean. I kept following.

He turned back. "I already have a girlfriend, if you want to know."

"I don't want to be your girlfriend."

He screwed his face up at me, turned forward, and walked the rest of the way home without another backward look or another word. I followed him until my legs lost their will at the mouth of his driveway, then I just stood and watched his back as he set the distance between us, pointedly ignoring me the whole way until, at last, he climbed the front porch step and, finally, severed the link between us with the slam of the front door of his house.

I ran home.

I burst inside—no one else was home yet—and slung my backpack onto the dining room table, then swerved immediately back into, through, and out of the foyer, past the brace of staircases, one that lead up to the bedrooms and one that lead down to the TV room, on across the marinara-colored carpet in the family room that made Lewis and Terry and my Red River game, and right on back outside again through the French doors that opened onto the concrete back porch. I kept the pace across the first few ragged yards of our back-forty until I met the split-rail fence that guarded it—not so dilapidated then, but still easy to skirt—ducked between its splintery timbers, then, in just a handful of quick-scissor strides, hit the unpaved gravel shoulder of West Ludlow Road.

West Ludlow runs through a wide, low meadowlands, cleared of trees, except for copses of neglected sycamores, pines, and stands of bushes. There were maybe a dozen properties spread back-and-forth down its ten-mile length. Quinn was practically my neighbor. I made it to the bushes along the border outside his property in less than a minute. There I found a tight gap in the branches and nestled myself inside the leaves to spy on his house.

I waited a long while for him to come out again. I was half-convinced he knew what I was doing and was intentionally torturing me by staying inside. Actually, I didn't really think that at all; I just pretended he was to pass the time and make myself feel important. It was the only way I could stand sitting still so long. The leaves brushed my face and dry earth crunched under my Mary Janes every time I shifted to a new position when the old one became uncomfortable.

At one point, I felt a tickle on my calf and found a

55

spider crawling on me. I was never afraid of creepy-crawlies like girls always are, so I let this one go about his business so long as he stayed out of the folds of my skirt.

I tried to imagine what Quinn was doing inside the house. Was his mom in there with him? Did he have a stepdad? Did he have stepbrothers or -sisters? (I found out later he was raised an only child. Much later after that, I found out that Miss Halliday had had a fiancée when she got knocked-up with Quinn. Needless to say, the marriage fell through. She never picked up another man—which isn't to say you can't pick up men if have a bad rep in this town, just usually not the marrying kind. The house she lived in alone with Quinn was her parents'. They'd willed it to her. It was hers free and clear now, except for a nominal yearly land tax. I still wondered just how much she needed child support, and how much she used it as some sort of revenge against my dad.)

The house was a ranch-style on the western edge of thirty square miles of untended land. Miss Halliday would sell it off bit-by-bit over the next fifteen years. The house was painted dusty white and trimmed in blue-gray. A covered porch ran the length of the front.

When Quinn finally came out again, he was carrying a broom. He began to sweep the porch with it, working small mounds to one end or the other where he sent them off the edges in small puffs.

I watched him, fascinated. I'd made him into something like an angel since Alice Winterbaum had made her claim that he was my brother. I still didn't half-believe her, but now I was watching him, secretly, doing chores. Chores like ones I had to do. Didn't that make him even more of an angel?

It took until the next week to get the nerve to get close to him again. I spied on him over the following weekend, or spied on his house, really. Watched him do more chores. I saw his mom. I'd seen her before, but never really took notice.

She was slim and pale and pretty, with dark, brown hair, cut short. I tried to imagine her and my dad *doing IT*, as Alice Winterbaum had put it, but my attempts always got high-ended on all the things I didn't know about doing IT. I could only see my dad rising from a tumble of sheets in an early morning bedroom and facing away from Miss Halliday, who lay on her back and watched the ceiling. In this image, the both of them were fully clothed.

That Sunday afternoon, I asked Lewis whether brothers and sisters could have different mothers. He was slouched across the big recliner in the downstairs TV room.

"'Course they can, dork." Lewis was fourteen, a year older than Terry. The two of us and Terry used to play together all the time until I was about six or seven. As the two of them entered middle school, all the old games I still wanted to play began to bore them. I also think my mom's prickly temper around me was starting to get under their skin.

"Like," I prodded, "is there anybody that you know who has a brother from a different mom?"

He tapped the insteps of his Nikes together and thought. "Well, Mary Stratham's mom got divorced from her dad, then she married Mary's stepdad and had a baby with him. So Mary Stratham's little sister is from her stepdad, but it's still Mary's sister."

"Do we have any other brothers and sisters?"

His head snapped my way. His brow creased. "Me and Terry don't, but you do."

My heart skipped a beat.

"In fact," he went on, "you have tons of brothers and sisters."

"I do?"

"Yeah." His lips curled. "You know that big fat sow in the Ashbourne's pen? You dropped out of its ass-end along with all the other piglets." He turned back to the television and sighed. "So, if I was you, I wouldn't eat bacon anymore."

"Shut up."

"Could be chewing up a baby brother if you do, is all I'm saying."

I'd learned to stop showing I was shocked and miserable over shit like that about a year before.

Monday. Lunch recess. Quinn's back to playing wall-ball.

A line of kids waited on the sidelines for a turn. When I joined the line, I got some looks. I'd never played wall-ball before.

"What are *you* doing here?" said a short, blonde girl standing next to me, sneering.

"Holding my breath so I don't smell *you*."

The champion of wall-ball was an enormous, redheaded farm girl named Jerri Jansen. She was in Mrs. Thompson's class, wore overalls and black work boots, and she scared the holybejesus out of me because I'd seen her beat up boys before, mainly for making fun for her overalls and work boots. She was something like a monster.

Quinn held his own pretty well against her, but she got him out with a piledriver that sent the ball sailing over his head.

He got back into line and I watched him out of the corner of my eye. He seemed oblivious to me, spending most of his time talking with Beverly Trudeman, who was ahead of him. I wondered if Beverly was his girlfriend. Jealousy prodded the back of my head. I imagined how I would take my turn at wall-ball and beat Jerri Jansen, who would be so impressed with my skill, she would name me wall-ball champion. Then Quinn would sit next to me on the bus on the way home and admire me. We would walk down West Ludlow Road together. Maybe I could go over to his house for dinner.

I was less confident with my plan when I stepped up to take my turn. Jerri barely gave me a glance before she served, swinging her arm downward to hop the ball off the blacktop, where it jumped, struck the red brick wall, and rebounded back at me in a wide arc. I danced backward to let it bounce off the ground, then swung a sloppy fist at it. On the rebound, Jerri caught it in mid-air. She smashed the ball right back into the wall with her fist. The ball rebounded and smashed me dead in the face.

I was not going to be wall-ball champion.

Kids were laughing, and a mean, sharp pain was creasing the back of my head. I found myself on my back on the blacktop. Tears rolled down my cheeks, but I was a little too stunned to really cry. I blinked and saw Quinn crouching on his haunches over me.

"You okay?" That was the first time I really saw his eyes. God, his eyes! They were blue as the sky above him. Blue as the sky, lake-mirrored.

"Yeah." I cupped the back of my head gingerly. There was a knot there.

He looked over his shoulder at the riot of children. "Stop laughing. She's my neighbor."

His command didn't silence anyone, but I didn't care. No one had ever defended me before.

A playground monitor found her way over to us. "Are you all right, honey?"

I took my hand away and found blood on the palm. "I'm bleeding."

"Let's get you to the nurse." She helped me up by the arm.

I didn't bleed long, but the nurse asked if I wanted to go home early. I stunned myself by saying that I wanted to go back to class. Going back to class wasn't my true aim, naturally; I really wanted to ride home on the bus with Quinn.

He didn't stand in line with me while we waited to board. I kept stealing glances at him, but never caught him looking my way. The back of my head had kept up with a sick thump all day, and now it reminded me of lunch recess and my sad attempt at wall-ball. I suddenly felt stupid.

When the doors opened, I climbed on and took a seat as close to the front as I could. I decided I was going to get off before Quinn and hurry home. I looked at my knees as the other kids boarded. The engine rumbled to life, then idled. My eyes stung, and I wished I could just blink and find myself home.

The hairs on the back of my neck flared. I looked to my left. Quinn was leaning forward in the seat behind me. His arms dangled over the backrest.

"My name's Quinn."

"I know. My name's Nicki."

"I know." He looked at me for a while, then said, "We can walk home together today, if you want."

"Okay." I smiled. My head didn't hurt so much anymore. I twisted in the seat so I wouldn't have to crane my neck to look at him.

"Is Beverly Trudeman your girlfriend?"

"No. Pauline Wilson was my girlfriend, but I had to break up with her. She only wanted me for my red Sharpie."

Story of his life.

I don't remember what we talked about on the bus ride or the walk home, but I do remember thinking that if he really was my brother, then that meant he should come live with us.

We lingered at my drive. He wouldn't start to top me in height until we were fourteen. He said, "I have to do chores, but do you want to come over later?" Yes, I did. I dropped my backpack off at the house, and I left a note explaining that I was over at Quinn Halliday's, and when I got there, we watched TV together until his mom came home at four. She was wearing the uniform that the waitresses wear at Nick's Outback Diner, a restaurant we nearly never went to. She greeted me with a blank stare.

"This is my friend, Nicki," Quinn told her. "She rides the same bus as me and she lives down the road." He pointed in the general direction of my house.

Miss Halliday found her voice and said, "Hello, Nicki."

She turned to Quinn. "Honey, are your chores done?"

"Yeah, they're all done." It was almost a complaint.

"Nicki, your mom and dad know where you are?"

"Yeah, I left a note."

"Okay." She hesitated. "I think maybe it's time you should go home."

"Why?" Quinn wanted to know.

"Honey, I have to start cooking dinner. And we have stuff to do."

"Like what?"

"Please don't argue." Quinn made an unhappy noise. Miss Halliday turned to me. "It was nice to meet you, Nicki, but I think you should get along, now. I don't want your parents to worry about you."

I left Quinn glowering at the floor. He was too mad to even say goodbye to me. I walked home baffled and a little hurt, but I still held onto my dream of moving Quinn in with us.

It was dashed the moment I walked through the door.

"You are not to see that boy again." My mom grabbed me by the arm and pulled me to her. Her bangs flopped in her face, but I could still see her eyes. They got very dark when she was angry. Right then, they were vicious bullet holes. "Do You Understand?"

I had ceased questioning my mom's demands ages ago. She was mean and she hated me, and that was the only explanation I needed to understand her.

"I don't ever want to see you hanging with him again. If I find out you are, you are going to be in very big trouble, little girl."

I was in trouble a lot after that. It was worth it.

I started carrying the straight razor in my pocket when I was fifteen. It'd once been my grandfather's. I'd found it at the back of the hall closet in an oak shaving kit. The interior of the box was lined with worn red velvet. I took the razor and the strop—a strip of leather to keep the blade polished and straight—and left the box.

My razor has a smooth pearl handle. I don't know how often my grandfather used it to shave, but it fits my hand perfectly, like it was made for me to use.

I don't usually carry it to work, but I do on Mondays. Mondays are delivery days. I won't need it, but I like it in my pocket when I'm getting down to business.

Whitmouth Foods Services, Inc. is the supplier for Crenshaw's Bakery. Adam Crenshaw, the owner, takes lunch from one to two. I work in the oven room, and either Sheila Vargus or Michael Allens works the front. Adam keeps a skeleton crew in order to pay his employees well.

I work a forty-hour week spread over six days, Monday through Saturday. It sucks, but Saturday I come in at ten, which gives me an extra two hours in the morning if I stay out too late the night before, and I'm off by four o'clock, which lets me rest up for Saturday night. I'm the only employee with forty hours, which earns me a pretty decent health insurance package.

The other oven-roomer is Grant Sokoloff. He doesn't work Mondays.

Andy Fosse is the driver, and he's supposed to unload a little after a quarter to one on Mondays, but today he's fucking late.

I make a point of getting the breads out of the oven by one o'clock. Sheila or Michael, whoever's working that day, needs to stay up front for customers; neither ever comes back while Andy's here. I think they know what the hell's going on, but no one's ever said anything.

Today, Andy is fucking late. It's almost twenty-after, and I'm going to need to start putting another batch into the ovens soon.

The ringer sounds. He's here. Thank god.

I roll open the metal door in back. Andy's standing there in his blue-gray uniform.

"You're over half-an-hour late."

"The fucking warehouse guys. Loaded the wrong orders. Got everything in the truck, then had to unload and reload." He smiles. "I'm here now." He's skinny in a lanky sort of way. His cheeks are acne-scarred, and his dishwater blonde hair is a patch of cow licks, but he can be nearly as amusing as he thinks he is when he's on a roll, and, best of all, his cock is something like a wonder.

Proudly, he plucks from his breast pocket a condom in a dark orange wrapper.

"Mm-mm-*mango*."

"*Where* the fuck do you *find* these things?"

"Vending machine in a truck stop out on Wilmington."

"Were you born a romantic or did you learn the art of seduction from books? Come on, we got to make it fast today."

"We always got to make it fast."

"Faster."

He follows me to the corner behind the pallets of flour. "Get your pants down." I get on my knees and reach for the condom. "Here, give me that thing."

"Oh, I got a thing to give you." He hands me the condom. I tear the wrapper open and put the rubber in my mouth. Guys love getting wrapped this way. He pulls his pants down to his knees. His cock flips straight out like a bamboo switchblade. It ain't pretty, but it does the job.

With one hand, I take his cock by the root; with the other I set the condom between my teeth and lips and roll it on. My mouth fills with the very best mango-flavored latex to drop out of a truck stop vending machine. I work him awhile to speed things up. I'm probably not going to get mine today, but I suppose I can live with that. Maybe I'll have a little bathroom break after the supplies are unloaded.

I stand, flip my apron up, and hike my baggy white chef pants down.

"Let me see your tits."

"No time, come on."

This is the most awkward position I've ever done it in, with my pants around my knees, my apron held up with one hand, wooden pallets digging into my ass, but over the past year, Andy and I have made it our own. We are consummate supply room-fuckers.

I don't know if it's Andy's dick, the way he uses it, or our broken-mannequins pose, but somehow it just hits all my buttons. His entrance is honey-colored. When he gets his rhythm, everything goes cherry-pink, from my thighs to my waist and all the way up to my nipples. I'm lost in the both of us. The whole of the world collapses into the single point connecting us to each other.

I finish before Andy. It takes me by surprise. I guess I needed this more than I thought.

He surges and shudders a second later, then slumps gently forward onto me. I wrap my arms around him and hold him. I've wanted to hold someone since my blowout with my mom yesterday afternoon. And here someone is. I press my face into his shoulder. We tremble against each other and huff to get our winds back.

He takes a deep breath, eases away from me. "Let me take care of this," he says, "before it starts to leak." A romantic to the core, that Andy. He slides out and turns away. I wriggle my pants back up, fix my apron. When I finish, he's tied the rubber off and pinches it gingerly between thumb and forefinger. It hangs like a sad, bald, single-nutted scrotum. At least it's filled with the right stuff.

"Hey." I turn my back to him. "Brush me off."

"You're okay." He gives my shoulders and the small of my back a few perfunctory slaps anyway.

"Thanks. I got to get buns in the oven."

"Ain't my buns in your oven." He holds the rubber up. "I keep my dough sealed for your protection."

"Bitchin'." I move off to the oven room. In the refrigerator, trays of balled dough are waiting for the oven. As I'm opening the oven door and sticking the tray in, Andy wanders in from the storeroom. He's disposed of the condom.

"Shouldn't you be unloading?"

"I will."

I get an idea. "Do you get high?"

"What?"

"Do you smoke weed?"

"Are you a cop?"

"Yes, Andy. I am a cop."

I move the industrial mixer, shut it off, and lift the dough that's been churning in there. I'm going to need a Coke pretty soon. There's still the tang of mango and latex on my tongue.

"Yeah, I smoke," he says.

"Listen." I deliver the dough to the counter and start making balls out of it. "I've got an eighth of fabulous chronic I'd be willing to let go for seventy. I smoked some the other night. I can vouch that it's good."

"Seventy? I don't know. That's kind of steep."

We haggle down to sixty-five. I know, down to sixty-five from seventy. Fuck it. I got gas for the week. We'll make the exchange when he's done unloading.

"Hey, I was thinking," Andy says.

"Hm?"

"Do you want to go out sometime? Like Friday, maybe?"

"Out?"

"Out. Like to dinner?"

"Oh." I stop working the dough and look at him. My brain is misfiring. I understand the meaning of his question, I just can't make sense of it as it applies to me.

He stares at me. "Haven't you ever been asked out before?"

"Fuck you."

"So that's a yes, then? You'll go out with me Friday?"

"I..." What do I say? "Yeah, okay."

"Great. When can I pick you up?"

Shit, he means it.

"Um, well, where do you live?"

"Where do *I* live?"

"If you live in town, it might be easier for you if I met you at your place. I live all the way out past Cowen Road."

"Ha. Okay. I live on Stradtford and Alameda."

"Where? Landmarks, please."

"Um, around the corner from Craig's Mini-Mart and

the Neighborhood Deli?"

"Craig's? Oh, yeah. Gotcha."

"How about six?"

"Okay. Six. What's your address?"

"Can I text you?"

"I don't have a cell."

He snorts.

"Fuck off. I don't have a cell, okay? I'm broke half the time."

"Okay, you don't have a cell. You got a piece of paper and pen?"

I do. I'm going out on a date.

"I thought he was a dweeb," Quinn says, using a description I'd once applied to Andy against me.

"He is. But, he's funny, and, I don't know, he's a novelty."

"Huh?"

"Guys ask me out to get into my pants. A guy's never gotten in my pants to ask me out. I mean, he can't be shooting for anything. He must want to take me out just because, you know, he wants to take me out. Right?"

"Can't argue with that logic." It's an hour before closing at the print shop. Quinn's at a table in the workroom assembling some booklets. A hundred of them. His actions are pure muscle memory as he glides the pages between the clear plastic covers and runs the whole package through the levered machine that snaps the black spine into place.

I'm sitting on the edge of the worktable, my feet on the seat of a wooden chair. Every time Quinn cranks the lever, the table top jumps under my butt.

"You trust him?"

"Well ... sure. What do you mean?"

"You trust him to go out with him, but not enough to leave your straight razor home on Mondays." He reaches out and pats the pocket of my jeans. The way I'm sitting makes a perfect outline of the handle under the denim. I put my hand over it and shift into a new position.

"That's not—" What is he trying to do, talk me out of this? I would have expected more elation from my mom. "You know," I say, "I wasn't expecting you to click your heels or anything, but you could try to pretend to be happy for me. For my benefit."

He stops what he's doing and looks at me. "I am happy for you."

"No, you're fucking ecstatic."

"I just want you to be careful is all."

"Careful? This is safest thing I've done in ages. Shit, if I walk off with a trucker tag-team at the bar, you fucking high-five me. I go on a date and suddenly the world is all shadows and gloom? What are you afraid of? That I might end up disappointed? I might get my feelings hurt?"

He looks back to the booklets and starts working on them again. He's quiet. Is he just going to leave me sitting here in silence? He takes a breath.

"Just don't let your guard down." His voice is so small I nearly miss the words.

I trace the outline of my folded straight razor. Maybe it'd be nice to let my guard down for once.

What he's said proves it. Quinn's jealously guarding the tatters of my purity, like he always does. He's afraid of me going blind over a guy and getting myself into trouble. It kind of puts a sick pit into my stomach. I don't like the idea that Quinn thinks I'm destined for a nasty dose of shame and regret. It also brings back the old hurt, and all those election signs with Bobby James' name in red and white aren't helping me keep it packed away. Seeing Jonathan Garver the other night doesn't help either. Not knowing what he was up to kind of puts a sliver of ice in my chest.

"I won't let my guard down," I tell Quinn. "First thing I'll do is check his fridge for stacks of girl briskets."

He laughs. "Hey, I wasn't being *that* grim."

I still feel a little wounded about Quinn's opinion of me, no matter how centered it is in concern, but don't like how he and I have been snapping at each other lately, either. I want to make it up to him. I say, "Maybe after the shop closes, we can go to dinner. I'll buy."

Quinn gives me a double-take, bulges his eyes, and slumps backward in his seat as if staggered. "*Holy shit!*"

I stick my tongue out at him.

We go to Louie's. It's Quinn's choice. He's in the mood for pasta. We talk about the books we're reading. I like biographies. I used to read about rock stars when I was a teenager. Now I read memoirs by women from Manhattan or India or ones who grew up under the Khmer Rouge. Quinn reads novels, but a lot of them are about women, too. You wouldn't figure that if you didn't know him.

As we talk, I keep wanting to tell him about Saturday night. I haven't let the whole incident slide to the front of my head, but it's been there in the back since I woke up Sunday, rolling itself over and over like a disco mirror ball. I hate the angles it flashes at me. The only clear glimpse I've picked up is the obvious. I was set up.

Todd was in on it, but I think Ellis was Jonathan Garver's prime agent. I saw him at the Wheatpenny, and he saw me. I don't know about Parker. The way I figure, Ellis must have been scouting me out. When Quinn and I showed up at McNamara's, either Todd contacted Ellis, or somehow Ellis knew to contact him. I don't know; I can't figure it, but what matters more is what the holy hell Jonathan Garver wants with me. Well, I know one of the things he wanted, but did he really set up the whole thing to get me up to his house because he's still holding some perverted ten-year-old crush on me? What can I possibly have left for him that he hasn't already taken? Or is there something else going on? He said he wanted to talk to me. About what? What the hell could be possibly talk to *me* about?

If I talk to Quinn, he might offer me a new angle to consider, and I need a new angle. This whole thing's got me on edge. Strike that—it's got me scared shitless. Quinn would watch my back, if he knew what to watch for. Then again, if I tell him what happened, he might just flip right the fuck out and start shit. That's part of the reason I don't want to tell him. If this thing Jonathan pulled is some fucked-up, backward jab at getting with me after ten years, then I must have disappointed him. He might feel stupid, might just want to give up on me for good. If that's how it is, then all this is over now. More than anything else, I want it to be over.

Our dishes come. His is chicken alfredo rigatoni. Mine is spaghetti and meatballs. He splurges for two glasses of wine himself, handing the waitress a couple of bills from his own wallet on the spot.

Our conversation goes slack as we dig-in. Four or five bites in, Quinn chuckles.

"What?"

"There was this guy—" He holds up his hand, finishes chewing. "There was this guy who came into the shop today ..."

He launches into some customer shit-talking that cheers me up pretty quickly. He even gets me laughing so hard, I nearly shoot wine out of my nose.

After dinner, I drive back to the house and find the lights on in the bungalow.

Dad—

Goddammit.

Inside, he, Roger Hanlon, and Pat Saunders are sitting around the pool table in foldout chairs carried over from the back patio. Thank god they decided to play poker instead of pool tonight.

"Nicki!" they greet me.

I say hi and I go to my dresser, grab purple sweatpants that hang just below my calves and an oversized grey sweatshirt, and carry them over one arm to the bathroom. While I'm changing, Pat calls through the door, "Join us for a few hands, Nicki!"

Jesus fuck. I don't answer until I come back out. "Got to work tomorrow." I don't look their way as I shuffle a beeline toward my mattress.

"Aw, come on you wascally wabbit!" Pat nasals, sounding nothing like Elmer Fudd. He's making a reference to the image of Bugs Bunny on the front of my sweatshirt, who is flashing his patented wide-mouthed, bucktoothed grin as he dashes away after having clearly dealt out some richly-deserved comeuppance to Elmer or Daffy. Lewis and Terry were avid watchers of Scooby-Doo. Lots of kids at school knelt at the altar of Snoopy, or Mickey, or, dear lord—if a girl—the Disney princesses. They can have them. It's always been Bugs for me because that rabbit takes shit from no one.

"We'll make it interesting," Roger says. "We'll play strip poker." He guffaws. I glance sideways in time to see Pat shaking his head. He's on the far side of the table, looking bone-thin and lantern-jawed like always. I've never seen him without his red baseball cap. I think he's the youngest of the three, but he looks the oldest. Even Dad's twenty-case-a-day habit hasn't aged him like Pat's somehow aged himself.

Dad's in the middle of the two, on the far side of the table. He just sort of grins, blinks dumbly, and reshuffles his hand. It kind of pisses me off when he doesn't call Roger out on shit like that.

Roger's sitting on the end closest to the bathroom door. Couldn't have planned it, but the fact that I was naked ten feet away from him—forget the wall and the door that separated us—still strikes me as icky. He's round-faced, beer-gutted, and very pale. Even his hair, thick and flattened to the right, is blizzard white. With his black eyes and red nose, he's always reminded me of an unwholesome Frosty the Snowman.

I huck my work clothes on top of a shallow pile of laundry slumping against the wall between my mattress and dresser. "Rog," I say. "No matter what cards I get dealt, no matter how I fucking awesome I play my hands, for me strip poker with you will always be a lose-lose situation."

They laugh and *Oooh*!

"All right," I say, "give me some chips."

I clear off my night stand and drag it over to the pool table, dressing it with my pillow. God forbid anyone offers me a chair. Pat drags me a beer out of the cooler, though. I nurse it. It'll be my only one. Luckily, the three of them are more serious about cards than pool and hunker nearly quietly behind their poker faces. I win a little, lose a little, let myself lose a little more so can I say good-night without argument, then reset my nightstand, tap the earplugs in, and roll onto my mattress toward the wall.

I can't quite sleep, but I fade in and out until I open my eyes and realize the lights are out. Then the alarm shrieks and I wake up in morning light. The tail-end of a dream plays through my head as I shower. I remember spinning up and up and up, like I'm captured in some gentle tornado, and I'm thinking that I'll probably die, when it finally lets go of me, but I can't help feeling like I've finally found where I'm supposed to be.

I twist off the water and listen to myself drip, disappointed that I woke up before the dream was finished with me.

The next day at work I scan the phone book during my break. An hour earlier, Adam Crenshaw had barked back that we needed to whip up an order of cornbread for some guy named Raymond Forrest. I told Grant I'd start working on it, since he was in the middle of another order. As I was hefting a bag of cornmeal from the shelves, my mind kept repeating the name *Raymond, Raymond, Raymond*, until is sliced it in half to *Ray, Ray, Ray*, then finally dunked the name *Ellis* in front of it.

Ellis Ray.

Holy shit, I thought. Isn't that how Todd introduced that fucker? *Nicki, this is Ellis Ray*. Was "Ray" a middle name, like Joe Bob or Billy Budd or, shit, Bobby James? I didn't think so. Todd'd only called him "Ellis Ray" in the introduction.

I find six "Rays" in the phone book. Only one has an *E* for an initial in front of it. No address, just the name of the town and a phone number. I flip to find alternate spellings. *Rey*. Three, but the first names are all Filipino. There's a Reye, Anthony. There are no Reighs to be found. How else can you spell "Ray"? I don't know, but I'm sure Mister E. Ray must be Ellis. I grab a pen and tear a small corner off the bottom of the page to write the number down. I look at it. I have him. I'm sure I do. Now, what do I do with him?

Nothing. Not yet. If he or Todd or Jonathan Garver make another move, I don't know, I'll figure something out. I always have Quinn if I need him. If nothing happens, I'll give it six months, then I'll hunt Ellis and Todd down and key their fucking cars.

I can't quite let it rest that easy, of course. After all, I just got myself a sliver of power, a very small sliver, enough to *just* squeeze between my thumb and forefinger, and I want to play with it.

After work, I go to McNamara's. It's not even happy hour, but a few solitary barflies are slumped over their drinks and the bar already. Opposite end of the room, a couple about my age sit holding hands across an elevated table. She's a pretty blonde in a red blouse and he's tallish, dark-haired, and clean-shaven, in a dark button-up. The way their smiles are almost giddy, the way they lock each other in each other's gazes, like one blink too long might vanish the other, tells me these two are not supposed to be here together, holding hands. They either should be somewhere else with someone else, or they're caught inside some sort of Capulet/Montague accident of circumstance. Whatever they're feeling for each other may be real, but it's colored and swelled by desperation. It makes what they're feeling more exhilarating even as it's tarnishing every other part of their lives.

Hey, I get around, but it's not like I've never been there before.

I find a place at the bar where I can clear the late-afternoon drunks by a good two seats on either side of me. The bartender is watching sportscasters talk intently about some bullshit thing or another. When he bothers to pay attention to me, I order a bottle of Bud Lite and tilt my head so I can watch Romeo and Juliet out of the corner of my eye. I'm halfway through the beer when a commercial comes on and releases the bartender. He's tall and broad, in his forties, and has a bushy dark mustache and take-no-shit eyes.

I say, "Hey, I was in here last Saturday. There were a couple of guys I met. One's name was Ellis Ray. The other's was Todd. Don't know his last name."

The bartender shrugs. "Don't know any Ellis Ray. There's a Rod or Todd Keeling that comes in here. I don't know if he was here Saturday. There's also a Todd Frakes, but I know he wasn't here Saturday."

"Todd *Keeling*?"

"Rod or Todd. I thought it was Rod, but it might be Todd." He's getting bored and wary.

"What's this Keeling guy look like?"

He shrugs.

"Does he have dark hair, dark eyes, clean-shaven? Maybe about this tall." I raise my hand about six feet off the ground. "Kind of slim, but not skinny?"

"Sure." He shrugs again. "He doesn't *not* look like that, anyway."

"All right, thanks." Todd Keeling. Or Todd Frakes, who wasn't here Saturday, as far as the helpful bartender knows, who admits to the possibility of being mistaken about Keeling's first name. Well, it might be something or nothing.

I finish my beer and keep sneaking glances toward my two star-crossed lovers. Their hands never part.

About a month-and-a-half after we watched TV together for the first time, Quinn popped the question.

"Do you want to be my girlfriend?"

73

We'd been spending a lot of time together on the playground at school, in the open fields around our houses, and at the shore of the river about a mile downfield from his house. You know, that river has a name, but I never learned it. Anyway, by that time, my mom had only busted me twice for hanging out with Quinn. The first time I got an arm-twisting and a yelling; the second time I got the same plus a week's grounding. I'm sure my mom suspected Quinn and I were together more often than she knew, but since I'd been off playing by myself ever since my brothers abandoned me, she couldn't prove anything.

I'd have kept spending time with Quinn even if he bored me just to spite her. But he didn't bore me. He was a revelation.

See, when Lewis and Terry let me play with them, it was just that—they *let me* play with *them*. I was a broken training wheel dragging behind their bicycle. I followed their leads, I played the games they decided to play, which were the ones they invented. Any new games were their own. Any modifications were their own. Any ideas from Baby Sister were summarily shot down. "*That's* not how you play it, *Nicki!*" was the refrain.

One game we played was called Red River. Terry'd been crazy for dinosaurs at the time, and he had a shelf full of outdated books from the Fifties, Sixties, and Seventies he'd collected from the thrift shop on Alameda Street—you know, the ones with pictures of galumphing dinosaurs, all tail-draggers, and always placed in front of erupting volcanoes spilling channels of molten lava? He'd got the idea from those, and from the carpet in the second-level family room, which, back then, was the color of marinara sauce.

This is how it went: We scattered the throw pillows on the carpet between the three sofas that rested against separate walls. Our job was to jump from furniture to pillows to furniture without touching the carpet, the "red river," or losing balance and "falling in." Every so often, one of us would scream "Tyrannosaurus Rex!" or

"Pterodactyl!" or "Velociraptor!" and we'd have to fight the predator off by thrusting our arms, as if armed with spears. Typically, we won out, but my brothers would sometimes get eaten so they could make an hysterical performance of being carried off and chewed up. For that matter, whenever one of them slipped and fell onto the carpet, he'd wriggle and shriek in agony. Generally, when I shouted the name of a dinosaur, my beast was ignored.

With Quinn, I discovered equality. We followed my ideas and plans as often as his. I even adapted Red River to outdoors, and running in the fields was much more fun than hopping from pillow to sofa anyway.

We weren't playing Red River when he asked me. We were down by the river throwing stones into the water. The surface was too uneven and rocky to skip them, so we were just finding the biggest to splash.

I said, "I don't think I can be."

"Why? Do you already have a boyfriend? 'Cause, if you do, I'll beat him up." He didn't say it out of anger or jealously. He was simply offering a solution to a problem.

"No, I don't have a boyfriend," I told him. At least, I didn't think I did. I had kissed Vick Turner on a dare earlier that month, but I wasn't sure if that made him my boyfriend. Probably not. Anyway, we'd barely spoken to each other since.

"But that's not why."

"Then why?"

"Because you—" My voice caught in my throat. I'd never said it out loud, and it was still a wonder to me. "You're my brother."

He scrunched his face up. "*Huh*?"

I shrugged. "I think so."

"How am I your brother?"

I remembered the way Alice Winterbaum spelled it out to me and felt my face burn. There was no way I was going to say the same thing to Quinn. I ducked my head and shrugged again. "It's what Alice Winterbaum said."

"*Alice Winterbaum*? What does *Alice Winterbaum* know?" I was beginning to feel stupid.

"Where's your dad?" I asked.

Quinn's face dropped a little. "My dad left when my mom was pregnant with me. They were engaged. They were going to be married. But he skipped out on her."

"Oh."

"Was that *your* dad?"

My scalp tingled with the idea, but then I shook my head. "I don't think so. My parents have been together a long time. My brothers are way older than us." We had discovered earlier that month that we shared the same birthday.

"Well, see? I can't be your brother then."

I was a little disappointed, but I found a silver lining I could live with. I said, "If you're not my brother, I'll be your girlfriend for sure."

He smiled. "Okay."

"But we have to be sure."

"How?"

I shrugged. "Ask, I guess."

I waited until after dinner so I could corner my dad alone. Back then, he wasn't the dipshit drunk he is now. He used to keep me company when Lewis and Terry ran off without me. We'd watch videos or go for ice cream, play board games or card games. I'd been playing poker with him and Pat and Roger since I was eight. Roger, by the way, didn't start hitting on me until I was a teenager, after I became the fourteen-year-old slut who gangbanged three grown men in a Chevy Nova down by Lake Spring. That's when all the guys started hitting on me.

So, anyway, I'd got Dad cornered. Everyone else was downstairs in the TV room. Dad was in the kitchen mixing himself a drink. (I didn't say he didn't drink back then; I said he wasn't a fucking drunk.) I'd had butterflies in my stomach since I'd gotten home, which was earlier than usual. Quinn and I had called it quits right after we'd decided to find out once and for all our relationship to each other. I didn't want to take a chance of getting busted by my mom again.

Dad heard me come in. Without turning, he said, "What's up, Pixie?"

I'd barely touched my dinner, and now those soft, anxious wings were circling so fast inside me, I felt like tossing up everything I'd managed to get down. To settle my stomach, I tried to remember the words I'd repeated to myself all afternoon and evening. Now that the time had come, my mind was a blank. I looked over my shoulder to make sure we were alone and said, "Dad, you know what Alice Winterbaum said the other day at school?"

He turned to me. "Who?"

"Alice Winterbaum?"

"Guess I don't."

I told him. It all came out in a rush.

Dad was frozen when I finished. I had watched the color draining from his face as I spoke, but the words wouldn't stop. Now I wished I could tear myself from this spot in time and stitch my mouth shut.

Dad cleared his throat. He started to speak, then he drained his glass. Finally, he looked at me and said, "Um, I need to talk to your mom about this, okay?"

"No! *Dad*—" Dread sliced through me. I pitched my voice low. "*Don't tell her, okay*?"

"Honey." He put his hand on my shoulder. "I need to talk to her about this."

"Please, Dad, *please* ..."

"It'll be okay."

It wasn't going to be okay.

He turned away from me and made himself another drink. I wheeled and ran upstairs to my room. The door shut behind me. I sat on the edge of my bed, wanting to cry, not wanting to, not knowing what else to do. The immediate future was a solid, white wall. I had no clue what would happen once my mom heard what I'd told my dad. I couldn't imagine any good outcome, but I couldn't see why it should turn out bad either. This wasn't *my* fault, after all. True or not, I couldn't be blamed.

Really, I should have known better.

Dad should have known better.

What neither of us could have known was the shape and language my mother's fury would take. As much shit as I'd put up with from my mom over the years, beyond being grabbed or having my arm twisted, I was never physically abused. I can count on one hand the number of times I was spanked, and, honestly, each swat I'd got those times, I'd earned.

However, a quarter of an hour later, when my mom stormed through my bedroom door, I knew that the two of us were about to enter a private little place all our own, and neither of us would ever find the way out again.

She grabbed me by the collar of my t-shirt, I remember, and pulled me toward the mask of her face. By that expression that I saw, I was certain she was playing some sort of prank on me, a trick to shock me out of my dismay and bring me back down to earth, because no one could look like that and mean it. I was sure. I heard the material of my shirt shred under her grasp and thought the sound of it, the damage she'd done to my clothes, would bring an end to the game.

"*You little bitch!*"

The first sharp, white blow struck me just below and behind my left ear. It made me wail, "*I'm sorry!*" over and over. I was sorry. Really, truly, honestly sorry. From the bottom of my soul, I was sorry. I had done nothing all my life but make myself worth hating, and I was sorry. The best I could do was to be the cause of her fury, and I was sorry. I was sorry, because as much as I was convinced she hated me, I never hated her, really.

When I was small, I was prone to waking up at four or five o'clock in the morning. I'd creep into my parents' bed and snuggle between them. Once, my mom's hand was lying open, palm up, on a pillow. I slipped mine into hers. Even back then, she'd never touched me all that much; in fact, the only time she'd ever held my hand was when we crossed the street and she didn't have my dad or my brothers to pass me off to, and she usually just snatched me by the wrist. This time, her fingers closed around mine. Her breaths were still deep and even, so I knew she was asleep.

Today, I know the way her fingers curled was probably nothing more than an automatic response to the feel of my hand, or that in her dreams I was Lewis or Terry, but it didn't matter. I felt, I don't know, home, I guess. Pathetic as it may be, I still feel that way when I remember my hand enclosed in hers that morning.

Her first strike, palm flat, right across the cheek, is all I remember until I collected myself off my bed, in the dark, aching all over my shoulders, chest, and face, still bawling. I let myself cry until the crying sputtered to a stop, and I laid there on my stomach, quiet as a stone.

Don't think I didn't feel the throbbing in my face and chest, but the sensation was far away, useless, like pins-and-needles in your legs before you get a notion to walk somewhere.

Finally, I did get the notion to walk somewhere. I pushed myself to my feet, tiptoed to the door, and cracked it open. My breath was still hitching, but my emotions where spread out and hushed like static on a dead television.

Peeking into the upstairs landing, I saw a light under the door of my parents' room and heard voices on the other side, tense, but hushed. I leaned further outside and looked down into the stairwell. It glowed with the light from the TV room. Lewis and Terry were occupied. I crept out and hurried down the first flight to the foyer. I eased open the front door, slipped outside, and ran away from home.

All the way to Quinn's house.

I crept out from bushes bordering his property, across the dead grass of the lawn, to his bedroom window and was disappointed to find the room dark. I peeked in through a slim part in the curtains and saw light from somewhere down the hallway, a glow outside his doorway.

He couldn't have gone to bed yet, I was sure. It was only around six-thirty, and a blade of evening light hovered about the treetops in the west. I tapped on the window anyway, hoping he might miraculously appear on the other side of the glass, see me, part the curtains, and let me in.

No miracles came to greet me. I sat in the soil between the branches of the bushes that lined his house, hugged my arms to myself, and waited.

My brain has always spun a hundred miles an hour, but that evening, I don't think one single thought lit my head. I looked forward into the deepening dark, let my bruises smart, and listened for Quinn.

I don't know how long I sat there, but when a bright rectangle flashed over the patch of lawn before me, I popped up and wheeled toward his lighted window. Someone moved inside. I rapped frantically on the glass. I didn't have the presence of mind to hope for Quinn and not his mom.

It was Quinn. He parted the curtains and looked out. His face scrunched in bewilderment. It scrunched more the moment he saw me outside.

"*Let me in.*" I had started to cry again.

What are you doing here? he mouthed.

"*Quinn, let me iiinnn!*"

He pressed his finger to his lips. I mirrored him with my finger to my lips to show him I'd be quiet and he slid open the window pane. "What are you *doing*?" he whispered through the screen.

"Quinn, *please.*"

He looked back over his shoulder, then turned back to me. "Okay. Shh." He worked the screen out, then reached for me. The sill was chest-level to me, which made for one of the least graceful entrances into any place I've ever made.

"Nicki, what's wrong?" He guided me to his bed and

sat me down on the edge.

I was crying so hard I could barely speak, but I managed, "I can't be your girlfriend."

"I know," he said. Neither my mom or my dad had answered my question outright, but Quinn's response proved that what Alice Winterbaum had told me was the truth.

I said, "I want to come live with you."

He looked doubtful. "I don't know."

"If I'm your sister, I should get to come live with you."

"*Shh*. Nicki, you *have* to be *quiet*." His face was anxious.

I nodded.

He stepped back and looked at my ripped collar, then at the bruise under my jaw and the one on my chest. "Nicki, what happened? Did you get in a fight?"

I was too ashamed to tell him. All I could do was put my face in my hands and cry. Quinn sat next to me and patted my back.

After a while, his mom called to him from somewhere down the hallway. "Quinn? What's taking you? Come on!"

"Okay!" Quinn called back. He turned to me. "We watch TV in the living room while I do my homework. I have to get back or she'll come looking." He pulled me up off the bed, folded the blankets down, sat me back down, then kneeled and pulled off my tennis shoes. Gently, he guided my head toward the pillow.

"You can stay, but you have to be quiet."

I nodded.

"She can't find out."

I nodded. He covered me up, then walked across the room and gathered some text books and binders. He looked back once, then walked to the door and shut out the light. I listened to the muffled sound of the television in the living room, and watched the light on the wall in the hallway.

I don't remember closing my eyes, but when I opened them again, the room was fully dark and silent. For a moment I thought I was back in my own room. The bed felt strange, and the smells were odd. Not unpleasant, just different than usual. Then I realized there was someone lying next to me and remembered Quinn. He was breathing steadily and evenly. He was rolled on his side, facing away from me. I put the flat of my hand between his shoulder blades and fell back to sleep.

It was dim-to-bright when Quinn woke me.

"*Nicki ... Nicki, wake up ...*"

He was standing by the bed in pajamas. They were dark blue, and the color made his eyes snap. I wished he could be my boyfriend.

I giggled.

"What?"

"You're wearing pajamas."

He looked down at himself. "So?"

"I just never seen you wear pajamas."

He scrunched his face. He had no time for this. "Are you going to school?"

I didn't know. Did runaways go to school? It didn't seem likely. I shook my head.

"Well, I have to. My mom leaves for work after I go. You can wait in the spare room until she's gone. *You can't let her find you, okay*?"

"O-*kay.*"

"Come on."

My bruises were smarting something fierce, but I tried to ignore them. He led me to the end of the hallway where he opened a door to a small room cramped with stacks of cardboard boxes, a bookshelf lined with encyclopedias, dictionaries, and atlases, an exercise bicycle, and, leaned against one wall, a mattress, a box spring, and the disassembled parts of a bed frame. There were no curtains on the window.

"After she's gone you can come out. I'll be home first. There's bologna and Pepsi in the fridge, and peanut butter and jelly. Don't eat the leftovers."

"Okay."

He rubbed his nose and thought. I looked down at his toes. I'd never seen his feet before. They weren't blunt and wide like Lewis and Terry's. They were narrow like mine. I wiggled my own toes inside my white socks.

"Where are my shoes?"

"I hid them under my bed." He continued with the household menu. "There's cookies and stuff in the cupboard. Don't eat the ice cream, there's not much left."

"'Kay."

"I have to get ready for school, okay? 'Bye."

He closed the door behind him. I sat on the floor and looked around the room, doubts about this whole running away thing blossoming in the middle of my chest like the petals of an acid-blue flower, but I was unsure what else I could do. To calm myself for the time being, I slid over to the encyclopedias, pulled out the Q volume, and began to read about Quetzalcoatl, the Aztec feathered, serpent god.

Soon I heard movement and voices in the hallway. I lay still and silent on my side and tried not to breathe too loud. When I heard the front door shut fifteen minutes later, I knew I was alone in the house with Miss Halliday. I squeezed my eyes shut, expecting her to come barging in any minute, screaming, *What are you doing here? You little bitch*! with Quinn gone, unable to protect me.

Fifteen or twenty minutes later, the front door shut a second time. I let out a cautious sigh of relief. A minute after that, the motor of Miss Halliday's sedan revved in the driveway, shifted into gear, and faded into the distance. I kept still, fully expecting it to come back, or that the fading sound of the car was some sort of trick to lure me out of the room and into her clutches. Pretty soon I fell asleep again.

I had dreams of living in this house with Quinn, as brother and sister. We ate bologna sandwiches and Miss Halliday smiled at us. I was disappointed to wake from them.

I wasn't sure how long I'd slept, and was afraid Miss Halliday had come home without me hearing. I crawled across the floor, wincing at my bruises, opened the door, and listened. The house was dead quiet. I rose to my feet and crept down the hallway, ears pricked, peering into each room I passed. I reached the mouth of the hall and looked from the living room to the kitchen. I was alone. I felt like a burglar. My stomach rumbled. A hungry burglar.

I searched the cupboards and found boxes of macaroni and cheese, Top Ramen, and Rice-A-Roni behind one door, plates and glasses behind another, and cans and the peanut butter behind a third. I took down the peanut butter, but where the heck were the cookies? I found them in a separate cabinet by the refrigerator. There where packages of Chips Ahoy!, Oreos, and another kind that were like reverse Oreos, vanilla cookies with chocolate filling.

I took down those, because I'd never had them before, and the Chips Ahoy!, because they were my favorite, and ate a handful of each. Then I made myself a peanut butter sandwich and a glass of milk and went into the living room to watch TV. After two shows, I was beginning to feel less like a burglar and more like myself home from school on a sick day. That same boredom of a sick day was creeping in, but then I remembered that I wasn't really sick, which meant I could go outside. I found my shoes under Quinn's bed and headed down to the river.

I threw stones for a while, then took off my shoes and socks, rolled my jeans up to my knees, and waded into the water to chase the tiny frogs that swam near the shore. They all got wise to me and either swam away or hid until I couldn't find them anymore, so I climbed onto a rock. When my feet dried, I put my socks and shoes back on and returned to Quinn's house.

I went into his room and surveyed his toys. All he had was boy stuff, but I made do with it as best I could until the front door opened at two-forty-five. I rushed out to meet him.

"You're still here." Quinn dropped his backpack by the front door. He was smiling, and his voice was glad, but around his eyes, there was a hint of the doubt I'd seen last night.

"You didn't think I'd be?"

"I—" The doubt spread over the rest of his face. "They're looking for you."

"Who?"

"Your parents, probably. The school. I had to go see Mr. Skeenan. He asked me if I saw you last night after dinner time."

Quinn was called to the *principal's* office? Panic crept into my chest. This was getting way more hazardous than I thought.

"What did you say?"

"I said I didn't."

We stood silent, neither sure what to say or do next. Quinn turned and looked into the kitchen. "*Nicki*," he scolded and marched into the kitchen. "You have to clean up after yourself."

I had left the cookies, peanut better, bread, and the butter knife I'd used to spread the sandwich on the kitchen table.

My face went hot. "Sorry." I rushed in after him. "I'll clean it up. I promise." I snatched the cookies and took them to the cabinet. "I'll even help you with your chores." If Quinn told his mom I was pulling my own weight, she might let me stay.

"*Do* you think your mom would let me come live with you?" I twisted the lid back onto the peanut butter jar and put it and the bread away.

"Nicki, I don't know." He was washing the butter knife off in the sink. He turned and looked at me. "Why did you run away from home?"

My bruises hadn't bothered me since that morning, but now they started smarting again.   Quinn   came over and tugged at the torn flap of my collar.

"Is it because of this?"

I didn't say anything.

"Did you get in a fight with your brothers?"

"I just hate it over there, that's all!"

He recoiled and looked hurt.

"I hate it and I'm your sister and we should be

together!"

"I know." He looked at me. His eyes made my heart race. "I have a shirt you can wear."

He took me to his room and unfolded a burgundy pullover he took from a bureau drawer. I took my torn shirt off—our family was not shy; in the mornings my brothers and I roved around the house in various stages of undress. Besides, I was ten years old and might as well have been a boy from the waist up.

Quinn's eyes went wide. He pointed at my shoulders, my chest.

"Nicki, *what happened*?"

I quickly pulled the shirt on. Even though I was still an inch or so taller, it still fell around my hips.

I stood in silence and looked at my shoes.

"I'll ask my mom," he said. There was determination in his voice. "I'll ask my mom if you can live with us."

For the first time in a long time I felt something like bliss.

"But, maybe, you should go home for now."

My bliss deflated.

I put my face in my hands because I hated for him to see me crying again. He'd think I was a baby and change his mind about asking his mom. I hadn't even cried when I'd gotten beaned in the face by Jerri Jansen's return strike that first afternoon Quinn and I became friends. And now I'd ended up bawling in front of him twice in two days.

"I'm *sorry*, Nicki. It's just that I think that if you're a runaway, they're just going to make you go home, even if my mom does say you can live with us."

That made sense, I guess. I wiped my eyes and nodded. "But I want to stay here until my mom and dad get home."

"Okay."

"And I meant it when I said I'd help you with your chores."

I waited until a quarter after five to leave, shortly before the time Quinn said his mom was due home from work. The walk down Ludlow Road seemed endless, probably because my legs were so weak with dread, I could barely reach half my usual speed. I was still wearing his burgundy shirt. I carried my torn one wadded in my left hand. My heart was pounding so hard, I was nearly certain I'd pass out before I could step through the front door. Maybe that would be better. Someone would find me on the road, and I could make up some story that I'd fallen unconscious and had no memory of the night before.

No such luck; I reached the front porch still fully conscious.

I decided I didn't want to go in through the front door. There's a sliding glass door to the rear that opens to the downstairs TV room. I went around to it, found the curtains closed, but saw the lamplight and the shifting blue of the television. I slid the door open and stepped inside, the curtains trailing my shoulders. My brothers were on the couch, staring at me wide-eyed.

"Nicki ... !" Terry whisper-shouted.

"Oh, shit, you are *so* in trouble," Lewis informed me. His tone was half-admiration, half-sadistic anticipation.

I said nothing. The light from the kitchen was coming down the stairwell. I started to move toward it.

Lewis said, "Whose shirt is that?"

"Nobody's," I told him.

"What happened to your shirt?"

I stopped and showed him the torn collar, then I lifted the hem of Quinn's shirt up over my chest.

"Oh, shit!"

"Did Mom do that to you?"

I covered my bruises and started upstairs. I heard Terry ask Lewis, "What did Nicki *do*?"

My dad was sitting at the dining room table, one hand curled around a tumbler. He was slouched and looking miserable. My mom stood at his back. One hand rested on his shoulder. She smoothed his hair in a gentle caress with the other, over and over. She was speaking, her voice low and soothing. She wore a look I rarely ever saw, one of kind concern.

Now that I'm older, I know the reason my mom hates me. It's because she can't hate my dad. She loves him. She adores him, and he hurt her. He hurt her so bad she could never forgive him, but she could never hate him, either. She had to hate someone for his betrayal. And here I was, born the same day Quinn was born. I guess that made me her voodoo doll, her way to hate him without having to stop loving him.

My mom saw me first. She said nothing, but my dad must have sensed her movement, because he turned toward me a second later.

"Nicki!" He stood, barely allowing my mom the chance to back step out of the way, and hurried over to me. "Where were you, Pixie?" He went down to his haunches. "We were so worried about you." Sometimes I think I don't appreciate what I got. "Where did you go?"

I shrugged. My mom came up behind him and pinched the material of Quinn's sleeve. "She was at Quinn Halliday's house." She dropped the sleeve. "Weren't you?"

I didn't answer.

"Did his mother know you were there?"

I shook my head. "I snuck in Quinn's bedroom through the window. When I woke up, he hid me in a spare room until she was gone."

My mom nodded. My dad said, "Well, I'd better go tell the sheriff."

My stomach twisted. They'd called the cops? "Are they going to arrest me?"

He stood, chuckled, "No, Pix, they were looking for you. I can tell them you're home now."

He turned and went to the kitchen phone. I didn't want to be left with my mom, even if my dad was still in the same room, but it was too late.

She looked over my head, toward the stairwell. "You boys get downstairs and watch TV. I'll explain everything later. But this isn't any of your business right now."

I didn't turn around, but I heard disgruntled moans

and the clump of disappointed feet retreating down the staircase.

My mom looked back at me. "I'll run you a bath and lay fresh pajamas out on the bed for you. I want you to go to bed early tonight. All right?"

I had no complaints. "All right." Bed was exactly what I wanted right now.

"Hand me your shirt. I think we can just throw it away." I gave it to her. "Take off that boy's shirt. I'll wash it and you can give it back to him when you see him at school." I pulled the shirt over my head. I heard my dad suck in a sharp breath.

He was back from the phone and standing behind my mom. This was the first time he'd seen what she'd done to me.

"*Bette*," was all he said.

My mom turned. "*I'm sorry*," she told him. She really meant it. She meant it because she was apologizing for upsetting my dad, not for beating the shit out of me. I don't think either of them understood that, but I did.

I went upstairs to undress for my bath.

A social worker visited us for a month after that, twice a week for two weeks, then once a week for the last two. She was round and short, with big glasses, frizzy hair, and a mouth that looked the way Roald Dahl described the grandmother's mouth in *George's Marvelous Medicine*, small and puckered-up like a dog's bottom. She was nice and had a soft, patient voice, but she asked me questions I didn't want to answer and that exhausted me to hear. When I did answer them, I usually lied.

I don't have to say that I never got to go live with Quinn. My mom made me stay home from school the next day. It was Friday, and she probably wanted to give my bruises time to heal before I showed my face in public again. That meant I had an unscheduled four-day weekend ahead of me, but it wasn't going to be fun.

She brought me home my schoolwork at noon and

told me that I would work on it until dinner, then I would work on it all Saturday and Sunday until I was caught up. She called me on the phone every hour after that, to see that I was doing it, she said, but I thought she was just making sure I hadn't run away again. About two-thirty, I started watching out my window for the school bus. When I saw it, I ran out to meet Quinn at the edge of my driveway.

"Why didn't you go to school today?"

"My mom made me stay home. I still have to do schoolwork."

"Oh."

"Did you ask your mom?"

He looked at the road and nodded his head.

"What did she say?"

He crossed his arms, stood silent a moment, and he shook his head.

I thought I was going to start crying right then, but I didn't, because Quinn started to.

I moved close and wrapped my arms around his neck. "Don't cry, Quinn," I said. "Don't cry."

I hate to admit how excited I'm getting about my date with Andy Fosse on Friday, the guy who thinks he's adorable with his flavor-of-the-week condoms. It's getting to the point that if he manages to score chocolate mousse or Key Lime pie, I might just marry him.

I wish I had a girlfriend, because my best clothes are out of my fuck-me drawer, and I don't have the money to buy anything nice. I could ask Quinn to let me borrow some cash, but I feel like I'm walking on eggshells every time the subject of my date comes up.

Right now, I'm across the street at the Subway with Sheila. We have lunch at the same time on Thursdays, and sometimes we go out together. She's about my size, a little more full-bodied, bigger rack, wider hips, and I've seriously considered asking if I could borrow some of her clothes. She'd ask me why, of course, and with who, and I don't want anyone at work to know.

I'm pretty certain everyone except the boss knows I've been tagging the delivery guy every Monday for the last year, and I can just hear the sound of their snickering in my head. I don't know why it should bug me more that they'd laugh about me going out on an honest date, when I don't care what they think of my regularly scheduled ride on the skin baguette in the supply room.

Sheila's got short, dishwater blonde hair and a plain face with a weak chin. Guys seem to find her cute, though, because she always comes back and brags to us how one guy or another hit on her at the counter. We're not really friends; just co-workers who get along with each other.

She's my age, and although I don't remember her from high school, I think she must have known who I was. Once, I asked if she wanted to come out with me one Saturday night, and she got this look of dread on her face. "Oh, uh, thanks for the invite, Nicki, but I don't, um, you know, I'm not much of a bar person." Uh-huh. Bar person. Well, I suppose that's the most tactful thing I've ever been called.

Oh, and by the way, in case you're wondering, no, I'm not sitting over here at Subway in my whites. I only wear those in the oven room. I come to work in street clothes, change back into them if I go out to lunch, and change again when I go home. Just don't want you getting the wrong picture in your head. The place Crenshaw rents the coats, pants, and aprons from picks up the old ones every Tuesday and delivers clean ones for the week. There's a free-standing clothes rack in the pantry room, and Grant and I change into a fresh uniform every day. Not the sexiest ensemble in the world. I don't know what Andy saw in me.

Sheila's talking about her friends. I've never met any of them, but I know intimate details about their lives because of our lunches together. I guess I'm sort of a safe pair of ears for her. She seems to see more drama in their lives than I do. Today, I'm just nodding and giving polite *Mm-hm*s as she prattles on.

"You're really in la-la-land today, Nicki," she interrupts herself midsentence.

"Oh. Sorry. Just stuff on my mind." I shrug, look at her a moment, take in her size again. Oh, fuck it.

"Um, Sheila?"

"Yeah?"

"Do you think I could borrow some clothes from you? I've got this sort of function I've got to go to tomorrow, and I want to wear something kind of semi-formal. Well, nice, anyway."

"A function, huh? What's the occasion?"

"Um, a political rally for Mayor Loomis." I wince inwardly. It's the first thing that popped into my head.

Sheila flares her eyes at me. "Ooh, Nicki Valentine is political!"

"No, not really. I have a friend who's supporting the mayor, and she wants me to go to the thing with her, is all." I shrug. Sheila stares at me for a moment. I can tell her bullshit alarm is going off.

"Yeah, sure," she says. "You want to come over after work? There's got to be something in my closet for you."

"Okay. Thanks." I wasn't aware of the weight until it lifts off me. "Thanks a lot, Sheila."

"No problem." The side of her lip curls. "What?"

"What what?"

"You're grinning like a crazy person."

I can't believe how much fun this is. Sheila's got Violent Femmes playing on her iPod in the living room and we're drinking Merlot that comes in a box. Her cheeks flush before she's halfway through her first glass. It's cute. I can see what guys see in her. She's not gorgeous, maybe not quite pretty, but when she smiles, her eyes shine and wink at you, and the sound of her laugh brings out the laugh in you.

She's got a lot of nice clothes, and I've been modeling them for her, walking up and down the narrow catwalk that her bed and the three walls make in front of her closet. Right now, we're on dresses. I haven't worn a dress since I don't know when—skirts, sometimes, but not dresses—and she's insisting I should go to "the function" in one. That means I'd have to borrow a pair of heels, and since they're a little big for me, and since I can probably count the number of times on both hands I've worn heels, they make me totter a little bit.

She's sitting cross-legged on her bed. When she doesn't like what I'm wearing, she doesn't say it looks bad on me, she serenades me with Right Said Fred, crooning, "*You're* too sexy for that *v-cut, too sexy* for that *v-cut*," or "*You're* too sexy for that *sleeveless*, *too sexy* for that *sleeveless*."

I wonder if Sheila could be my friend.

I take off the last dress and lay it on the pile of discards—I was too sexy for that pleated shift—and move back in my underwear to the three final choices. I like the green, seamed A-line, but Sheila is adamant about the blue sweater dress. "You are *so* pretty, Nicki. And you have the most beautiful eyes."

Guys say that all the time to me. When Sheila says it, I suddenly get all shy.

"Thank you."

"That blue dress will bring out your eyes. And look. You could wear the Martini pumps with it and use a Croco wristlet instead of a purse."

"You think so?"

"God, you'll look gorgeous. Listen, I'm jealous as hell right now of how good you look in my clothes, so when I say you'll look gorgeous, you'll look gorgeous."

"Okay. I'll wear the blue one."

I get back into my polo and jeans, which suddenly make me feel ratty, and help her get her clothes back onto the hangers and into the closet. Sheila's not drunk yet, but another glass will probably put her over the edge. The Merlot's gone to my head a little, too. I only drink wine when I'm with Quinn, so I'm unprepared for its effects.

While I'm getting my socks and shoes on in the living

room, I tell Sheila, "You don't know how much this means to me. I was so afraid I'd have to go out looking like a slob." Or a tramp, but I don't add that.

"No problem. Mayor Loomis is sure to win by a landslide when people see you in that dress supporting him."

Holy shit. That may actually be the nicest thing anyone besides Quinn has ever said to me. I stand and collect the dress and accessories to make my exit. At the doorway, I turn and give Sheila a big hug. "I mean it, thanks a lot, Sheila."

"Anytime."

"Hey, I was thinking." My heart is racing. "Maybe we could do something sometime. Like, I know you don't like going to the bar, but maybe we could just, I don't know, hang out, you know?" God, but I am so fucking lame.

"Sure. Sure, Nicki." Her face is dumb with lies. "That'd be fun."

"It was an idea."

"No." Her expression sinks. "We'll do something sometime." She flashes a smile I can almost believe in. I won't believe it, though.

I, on the other hand, am a fucking champion of the fake smile. I give her a dazzler, squeeze her arm, and tell her thanks again.

All the way back to the house, I try to figure out how the fuck I can be such a fucking, dumbfuck idiot.

"Oh, please, guys, not tonight, I fucking swear to god."

I am not in the mood for the blank stares that swivel my way around the pool table as I step through the bungalow doorway. Shit, do I really need to explain myself?

"Listen. I've got to work tomorrow and I'm going out tomorrow night. I just want to relax. Please, guys, clear out, all right?"

Stunned silence. Then Roger says, "You always got to work tomorrow and go out at night." I bristle a little. I'm just in the mood to rip his throat out, like he's been asking me to do for years.

My dad takes notice of Sheila's dress hanging over my arm.

"What's that you got there, hon?"

I'm at my mattress. I drop the pumps and wristlet onto the covers, then carry the dress on to the bathroom. There, I hook it by its hanger over the top beam of the shower door. There's no other place for it in the bungalow. "It's a dress," I tell them when I come back out. "I borrowed it from a friend."

"Got a hot date?" Roger quips. I give him a look.

My dad catches it.

"You have a date, Nicki?"

My dad almost sounds excited. Fuck, I did not want anyone to know, but what am I supposed to do now?

"Yeah," I tell everyone. "I have a fucking date. Okay? Tomorrow I have a date." Stop the presses, the slut gets asked out, all non-fuck-like. Mark this day on your calendar.

"Really? With who?" Dad's voice is delighted. For some reason, his approval hits me the same way as Quinn's misgivings.

"It's a guy I met at work."

"Is it Michael? Or Grant?"

"Michael's married. It's not Grant. It's one of the delivery guys."

"Well, that's good, Nicki." He's beaming. "All right." I can't look at him.

"Good for you, Nicki," Pat says.

"Thanks." Jesus, it's like I've overcome some sort of a disability. I hate that they're making me feel like getting a date is an accomplishment for me. I hate that they're making me realize that I've felt that way since Monday.

"Okay, you two," my dad says. "We're moving it to the back porch tonight. We can play cards."

"Thanks, Dad."

"Hey, can I take a peek at that dress you got?"

"Sure."

He flips on the bathroom light and looks in. "Wow. That's really pretty." He's gloating. He turns to me and takes both my hands in his. His crow's feet crinkle. His breath is vented directly from the Budweiser brewery. "Hey, do me a favor." He sways a bit.

"What?"

"Before you go out tomorrow, come over to the house and let me see you in it."

"Dad ..."

"Come on."

"Okay ..."

"Promise?"

"I promise."

He kisses me on the forehead and heads out behind Roger and Pat. I watch the door gently clap shut and stand in the middle of the room, staring at it. What if I told you, Dad, that the guy who asked me out is a guy I've been fucking once a week with my back pressed against pallets of flour? What if I told you I can get a date with a guy like that, but I can't make friends with a nice girl I've known for two years?

I sit on my mattress and find some music on my clock radio because I don't want to hear my thoughts anymore. I wonder if, even with the guys gone, I'll ever get to sleep tonight.

Friday goes on forever. The bakery is busy, and Sheila and I barely have time for hellos in the morning when she comes in. She's bright and sunny as usual. I don't think she remembers snubbing me. I'm not mad at her. How can I be? Who I am isn't her fault.

Grant and I are hit with a last-minute bulk order for sourdough rolls that has to go out to one of the local grocery stores. You couldn't choreograph a tighter, more precise dance number than the one we move through in the oven room. We've been working together back there for over two-and-a-half years, and we know each other's steps like our own.

Still, all the activity doesn't make the day pass any quicker. I look up at the clock—it's not nine-thirty yet?

It's just past ten?

It's not eleven?

Isn't it lunchtime yet?

I brown-bagged it today and eat my pastrami, pickle and mustard on rye (left another one in the fridge at the house for Dad) at the little table in the pantry room that serves as the break area. I can only finish half of it. With nothing to do but anticipate tonight, a warm, pleasant knot fills my stomach, leaving no room for the rest of my sandwich. I wrap the remains and sip on my water. I shake my legs. The chef pants always feel funny after I've shaved.

I want to talk with somebody. Not my dad or Quinn, who see either too much accomplishment or too much lurking catastrophe for me to stand. Maybe I could talk to Sheila, but I'm afraid to; I don't know, I can just hear that snickering in my head. Maybe after tonight it won't matter. I won't care what people think. I'll at least have something to back myself with. A good story to tell, of how gorgeous I looked in Sheila's pretty dress, how Andy held the door open for me, how we had a good time, maybe we went dancing, maybe we might go out again.

My lunch break is only thirty minutes, and, of course, it flies faster than the morning has. That's fine. Sitting and doing nothing but waiting for the time to pass would drive me up the wall, and that's all I'll be able to do until I get back to the house and start getting ready.

Crenshaw pokes his head around the doorway and sees me. He's short and squat, all shoulders and forearms. With his steel hair, rectangular spectacles— you just can't call them glasses—and his ferrety face, he reminds me of Mr. Badger in *The Wind in the Willows*.

"Hey, Nicki." His voice is phlegmy. Always is. I don't know why; he doesn't smoke. "You got a phone call up front."

"A phone call?" Shit. It's Andy, isn't it? Calling to cancel. This is just it. This is just what Quinn was warning me about. What had I said to him? *Are you afraid I might end up disappointed? I might get my feelings hurt?* That pleasant knot in my stomach is tightening. I'm glad I didn't eat the other half of my sandwich.

"Yeah, a phone call." Crenshaw waves his arms to hurry me up out of my seat and toward the phone. "You got five minutes left on your lunch break."

"Thanks for having my back, Adam." I blow him a kiss. Before it can reach him, he purses his lips and slips away.

I pick up the wall phone just outside the doorway to the front of the shop. "Hello?"

"Hey, Sparks." It's Quinn! I haven't talked to him since Monday.

"Hey. What's up?"

"You excited about tonight?"

"I guess."

"You guess?"

"Yeah, fuck off, I'm excited."

"Okay."

"Is that all you wanted to know? My lunch is over in, like, two minutes."

"Yeah. Look. I didn't mean to piss on your parade the other day when you came to the shop."

"I know you didn't."

"Yeah. Well, I just want to say that I hope you have a good time. I *know* you'll have a good time."

"Thanks, Quinn."

"I wasn't trying to wreck it or anything."

"I know."

"I don't want you—I don't know—I don't want you thinking I don't want you to be happy."

"Quinn, you know I don't think that."

"Okay. Well, give me a call tomorrow and tell me how it went."

Everything I wanted to talk about comes bubbling out. "I borrowed a dress from Sheila. She's says I look gorgeous in it."

"Sheila? Really?"

"Yeah. I went over to her place last night and tried on

things. It was fun. She chose this one for me. I wish you could see me in it."

"Model it for me tomorrow. I'll sneak into your bungalow."

I laugh. "Okay, let's do it."

Crenshaw's eyeing me, then the clock. "Got to go, Quinn. 'Bye."

The rest of the day is a rocket.

I primp in the bathroom mirror, then walk out to my mattress. I still have to go to the house to show off to my dad like he asked, and the twenty yards to the side door is a morass of soft ground and weeds. I don't want to get Sheila's pumps dirty, so I slip on a pair of tennis shoes, hook the pumps on a finger each, slip on the wristlet (you know, my straight razor *would* fit in there—but I leave it), and head over.

He's sitting at the dining room table, a beer in hand and four dead soldiers spread around.

"Don't look yet," I tell him as he starts to turn from his newspaper when he hears the door.

"Why?"

"Just don't." I toe out of tennis shoes at the threshold and slip on the pumps. "Hold on." I clack the heels against the linoleum to tuck my heels in. "Okay. You can look."

I had kind of hoped he might go easy on the boozing until I came over. Those four dead soldiers on the dining room table must have six or seven brothers-in-arms that've already found their way into the garbage just this afternoon, because he has to steady himself with one hand on the tabletop to stand up from his chair. I move to the center of the kitchen floor, where all the light is, to give him a good pose.

He rounds the counter and stops. His eyes aren't quite half-mast, but they're heavy. He stands there, silent, mouth half-open. He says, "Oh, Pixie. Look at you."

I do a turn for him.

His face lights up. "Honey, you are so beautiful."

"Thanks, Dad."

"You were always beautiful. Oh, you're going to make this guy the envy of every other guy out tonight."

Jesus Christ, am I blushing?

"He's handsome, I bet," Dad says.

"He's okay."

"He's got to be handsome. Who is he?"

"His name's Andy Fosse. He's the delivery driver for Whitmouth Foods. That's Crenshaw's supplier."

He smiles at me. His eyes shine electric blue under the flat glare of the panel lighting and inside the depths of his beer. "Oh!" He digs into his pocket. "Don't want to forget."

"What?"

"Look what I found."

He pulls out a small ring that flashes in the light.

"Remember when you got that?"

I do. We went to Fairharbor for Aunt Ruby's wedding when I was six. I picked out this ring to wear to it. It has a small pink diamond, princess cut, set in a thin gold band. It was big when it got it, and I wore it until it wouldn't fit my ring finger anymore.

"You still *have* it?" I say

"Yup." He looks proud. "Thought you could wear it out tonight."

"Oh, Dad, it won't fit anymore."

"Bet it will." He steps forward to take my left hand and slip it onto my pinky. It's tight over the second joint, but it fits.

I hold it up so we can both admire it. "That's great."

He stands back and stuffs his hands in his pockets. "Is he a nice boy?"

"He's funny. Makes me laugh."

"Good, good. You know, I love that you're going out on a date like this."

"I know, Dad."

"I know you'll have a great time tonight."

"Thanks, Dad. Thanks for the ring." I step in and plant a kiss on his cheek. "I better get going." I step toward the threshold, bending to slip the pumps off as I walk; I still have to hike back across the morass to my car.

"Say, Pix ..."

"Yeah, Dad?" It's a good thing I used the tennis shoes to get here. Just in the short hike, they've gotten covered with blades of grass and streaks of soil. "Yeah, Dad?" I say again, because he hasn't answered me yet. I tilt my head to see him standing there, smile vanished, brows heavy. "What is it?" I want to know.

He heaves a breath like I've never heard come out of him. He swallows hard. With effort, he says, "You know ... I wish I would've said ... before ... when it might've ... mattered some ..."

"Yeah?"

"It's just that ... Pixie, I'm real sorry what Bobby James and those others did to you when you were a little girl." His lower lip is trembling. His eyes shine. "*Real sorry.*" His voice is thick.

My mouth is dry. It seems like I'm breathing, but I'm not sure air is filling my chest. I can't quite seem to remember what I'm supposed to do. The tennis shoes. I slip my feet into them and stand. I have to get going. I don't want to be late.

My dad is still by the counter. His hands are still in his pockets. His head is down, his face is turned away. His shoulders hitch.

I grasp the doorknob and twist it, bring the door open.

"It's water under the bridge, Dad."

I step out and close the door behind me.

My dad's right. I've never been on a "date like this." I've been out with guys, but I've never been asked out. I've grabbed a burger with guys, but I've never gone to dinner with them. I've drank with them, but never had drinks with them. These were guys who were looking for some action. Guys who were fighting with their girlfriends, or waiting for their girlfriends to put out. Or between girlfriends. We'd cruise around town, growling at cops and howling at people on the sidewalks. Sometimes there would be other girls like me along for the ride, hooked up with other guys like the guy I was with, but none of these girls had my reputation. I was a sure score, but I was the most valued treasure in town. At least for one hunt. I never knew what was coming next when I was with these guys, but I always knew how the night was going to end with them.

Andy's place is easy to find. I'm on Stradtford, just passing the cross-street Alameda. The sign for Craig's Mini-Mart glows red on one street, the sign for the Neighborhood Deli glows green on the other. The street number for his apartment complex is painted in big gold numbers down one side of the office door. I ease my car to the curb, check the slip of paper with his address for his apartment number, kill the engine, and get out.

He answers the door almost immediately. He's wearing an indigo button-up tucked into black khakis. His shoes shine. He looks to have worked on his hair for as long as I did.

"Hi," I say.

He's silent and wide-eyed. "Hi. God, you look great."

"Thanks."

"That dress is almost more flattering than your whites."

"Yeah, I was going to steal a suit from work so you'd recognize me when you saw me, but I decided to put on something a little more run of the mill."

"If that's run of the mill, I can't wait to see you dress up."

"Thanks. You look great, too." I reach up and gently pat the tips of the spikes he's raised his hair into. "Look at your *hair*."

He grins sheepishly. "Yeah?"

"I love it."

"Yeah, I clean up real good."

I keep expecting him to whip out a condom in a pink

wrapper and go, *Banana-strawberry*, ba-da-*boom*!
Instead he asks, "Like seafood?"

"Love it."

"Great. Come on, my car's down back."

He opens the car door for me. I start to climb in, then
freeze. On the passenger seat sits a fat brown paper
shopping bag with a pair of twine handles sticking out
like bee's wings.

"What's that?"

"Oh, shit, I forgot I left that in here." He grabs it out of
the car and moves aside to let me in.

"Okay," I say, and cuff the hem of Sheila's dress to the
back of my knees and settle into the passenger side seat.
He shuts the door after me, and I watch him round the
front of the car to the rear driver side. He carries the bag
in one hand, carrying it like a shopper by its twin
handles, then swings opens the rear door and sits the bag
at the crook of the seat and the backrest.

"What is it?" I call back, but he shuts the door. When
the driver side door opens, I goad him again as he's
sliding behind the steering wheel.

"*Well*?"

"It's a surprise." He swings the door shut.

"For me?"

He smiles.

"When do I get to see?"

He starts the car. "Just be patient."

I look back at the bag. He backs the car out. "Be
patient," he says. *Oh*, what a fucker.

"You're a fucker," I tell him.

"Hmm," he tells me.

"Whatever," I say, 'cause I don't care.

I can only see his profile, but I can still tell that the
curve of his mouth on my side is one half of a half-ass
grin.

His apartment lies about halfway between Cowen Road
and Briar Range Road. He heads the car east. I can only

imagine we are going someplace pretty snazzy. The restaurants up that way are more expensive than I can usually afford. My heart's pounding, and I feel I should start some sort of conversation, but I can't think of anything to say. The car radio is playing some new band I've never heard of. Andy asks if I like these guys. I say I don't know them. He tells me about their newest album, and by the time we're pulling into the parking lot of Ivan's Shore, we're in a rapt conversation about music.

The restaurant's nice. I was worried that I was overdressed, but the place supports it. There are some people in jeans, others in slacks. The way Andy and I are dressed, everyone has to know we're on a date. I want them to know.

Andy's made reservations. We sit at a table by a picture window that looks out onto the woods north of town. In the final pink of the day, I can see the flash of the lake beyond the treetops.

"You like wine?" Andy asks.

"Wine's okay. I drink it sometimes when I go out with my brother."

"Wine's *okay*. You like beer more?"

"I like beer more."

He orders us a deep amber Scottish ale that tastes like caramel. I think I might not have room for dinner if I finish it.

The waitress comes to take our orders. She leaves, and we meet each other's gazes. I can't imagine how our conversation is going to go.

So, fucking anybody else on your rounds?

Two or three. Fucking anybody else in the supply room?

No, but I'd bang my boss for a raise.

Really? Prostitute yourself out much?

Not much. It's not like it's a career choice or anything. Just when the money's good and the guy's nastier than I like.

How fiercely individualistic of you.

Andy says, "So, how long've you been at the bakery?"

I nearly choke on my beer, it's so close to my mental

conversation.

"That long, huh?" He chuckles.

I clear my throat. "No. No. It's a good job. I've been there since I was nineteen. I worked at Prucell's Grocery before it went out of business. I heard about an opening at the counter from one of the old oven room guys who'd make runs to Prucell's when Crenshaw's was low on ingredients. I think that was before Adam signed on with Whitmouth. So, I started on the counter, and a year later, the guy who told me about the job quit and Adam moved me back to the ovens."

"How is Crenshaw, anyway?"

"Adam's cool. He doesn't fuck around, you know? He wants you to do your job. Don't slack off and don't fuck up too much and he'll look out for you. Pay was good enough even at the start to get me out of my parents' house that first year." I don't mention I'm practically back in my parents' house.

A waitress brings a house salad in a single, big, wooden bowl. She tosses it at the table and serves us portions into our bowls. It's really good.

Andy tells me about delivering for Whitmouth's and how it frees up his evenings for practicing with his band. I had no idea he was a musician. He plays the drums and the guitar. He says they've mostly been performing covers, but they've written five originals and once they get the songs tight enough, they're going to try for a gig at one of the bars. He says maybe I should come to practice sometime. Maybe I should.

I wish I had some dream to tell him about. When I think of my life, all I see is Quinn's face, or the face of some guy trying to move on me and the thrill of the weight of the razor in my pocket that he doesn't know I'm carrying. I don't think Andy wants to hear about the second thing, and who wants to listen to someone talk about their brother? There isn't really anything else I'd want him to hear about: high school, my family, all the guys I've used while they thought they were using me. How pissed some of them were when they figured it out.

How, when they tried to fuck with me back, I made them pay one way or another. The only really good thing in my life is Quinn, and the best times we had were when we were kids.

Our food comes. I've lost my appetite a little. I don't think it's because of the beer or the salad.

With a mouthful of food, Andy starts up again about music. I'm sort of relieved. We talk about our favorite bands, our favorite songs, songs we hate, types of music we hate. He mentions Jefferson Airplane's "White Rabbit," which brings up how much *Alice's Adventures in Wonderland* scared the hell out of me as a kid.

"The Disney cartoon?"

"No, dork, the book."

"Oh. The book?"

"Lewis Carroll?"

"Uh-huh."

"You know—*Lewis Carroll.*"

"I don't think so."

"'Jabberwocky?'"

"Huh?"

"'The poem 'Jabberwocky.' You know, "Twas brillig, and the slithy toves / Did gyre and gimble in the wabe; / All mimsy were the borogoves, / And the mome raths outgrabe.'"

He stares at me blankly, then throws his head back and laughs. "Did you make that up just now?"

"No, it's—"

"'Cause if you did, you should write some lyrics for my band."

I throw a sautéed scallop at him.

He dodges it. "No, I'm serious."

We walk along the waterfront after dinner. Andy's driven us down to the lake, and now that we've reached the boardwalk, I take off Sheila's shoes. I'm really not used to heels. The cool wood feels good.

"You don't mind, do you?"

"No, that's fine."

I take Andy's arm. "This area has gotten really swanky since I've been here last. I mean, I remember the docks, but not all the rest of this." I gesture at *this*.

This is the half-dozen knickknack and antique shops and diners that line the boardwalk. They're all closed now—it's close to seven-thirty—but I can tell that on the inside, they'll all have that phony rustic style to them that probably costs bundles to get to look quaint and old-fashioned but still meet code.

"There are a lot of east-towners that got their fingers in this stretch," Andy tells me.

"I bet."

"Word is, they're trying to bring in some tourism to the lake."

"Couldn't hurt, I guess."

"I guess some people on the council are fighting it. Not because they don't want the tourism, but because they don't like whose hands the money'll end up in. Some property rights or zoning issue, I guess. That's why this upcoming election's so important. Could tip things one way or the other."

"Damn, so when can I catch you on *Dateline*, next?"

"Oh, it's my dad. He talks about this shit all the time. When you hear something long enough, it just sort of seeps in. Honestly, I don't even really know what the fuck I'm talking about." He taps the fingers of the hand I have around his arm, a motion that we're about to change direction. "Come on, let's go this way." We cross a soft, plush lawn to a lone gazebo on a slight rise. I see why it was placed here. In the daytime, I'd have a fantastic view of the lake.

I set Sheila's shoes down on the attached seats that ring the inner platform, take Andy's arm again, and gently place my weight against him. Even after dark, the view's beautiful. The lake is filled with stars. Boats are flying the night.

Andy says, "You know, we've never kissed."

"I *know*," I tell him, like it's some confounding

predicament I have no idea how to fix. It's fun playing coy for a change.

He's quiet. I'm smiling, waiting.

He says, "Hey."

I say, "Hmm?"

He reaches for my shoulder and turns me to face him.

I say, "Hi, there."

He says, "Hi, Nicki Valentine."

I say, "Hi, Andy Fosse."

He says, "Funny meeting you here."

I say, "Best joke I heard all week."

He encircles me in his arms, leans forward, lowers his face to mine. I taste his mouth, his tongue. I'm finished playing coy for now. I want myself lost in the touch and flavor of our skins.

Soon, he takes me away, away.

There's a thumping beat that brings me around. It's not our heart-beats. It's so low, I don't so much hear it as simply know it's playing. I ease away.

"Is there music playing somewhere?"

"No, that's the magic between us."

"Nice dream, Casanova."

"There's actually a club farther up the boardwalk. You want to go?"

"You dance?"

"I could be talked into it."

"Well, let's go."

Closer to the club, the boardwalk crowds with people. At a bench, I sit, brush off my feet, and put Sheila's heels back on. The club's called Lakeshore Lights. Meh. The architecture's pretty cool, though. It's all sudden plains and angles and looks like something Gary Cooper would have designed in that movie *The Fountainhead.* House and techno *thrump-thrump-thrump*s my ears, even outside. I hate the shit, but I'll put up with it tonight.

Inside, a bouncer checks our driver's licenses and straps green Day-Glo wristbands on us. That means under-agers are here. Wonderful.

Andy considers his wristband and hollers above the din, "I don't know why we have to be punished for being drinking age!"

I hold my arm up. "We didn't ask for it but we got it!" I shake my wrist. "Shake it like you just don't care! Think they'd give me enough to run all the way up to my elbow?" I throw both arms over my head. "That'd show 'em whose boss!"

Andy leans close. "I'm having second thoughts about you." His eyes are mock serious.

"Only second?"

"Would have been third if we hadn't gone to the gazebo."

"Well then, when we get a chance, let's get you back there."

The hypnotic thump of the music and the strobing flash of multicolored lights is enough to make your mind swim without the help of alcohol. Or Ecstasy, for that matter, as one little, blonde teenybopper is obviously on as she sways by, flushed and writhing to the music.

Andy says, "She's going to be making out with another girl for the first time by the end of the night."

We move through the crowd. "How do you know it'll be for the first time?"

"I just like the idea."

"Are all men pigs?"

"Yes."

There's an empty table in the corner. It's low and has wheeled cushioned chairs. I take a seat. Andy scouts the area. He leans to me. "I don't think we're going to have any luck with a waitress. I'll get us a pitcher at the bar."

"Hold on. Let me go the bathroom first. Maybe a waitress'll show by the time I get back."

I have to wander a bit to find the restrooms. The place can't be that big, but with the noise, the lights, and the sway and stumble of the crowd, it's easy to walk in circles.

I pause for a second to get my bearings. There's

laughter behind me. High and feminine. I'm not one of those people who thinks everyone is laughing or talking about them, but those voices are so clear, even above a flood of sound from every direction, I have to turn and seek them out.

Behind me, two girls, my age, sit at an elevated table. One's blonde, the other's a redhead. They're trying real hard to look retro-80's. They lean into each other in personal conspiracy. They catch me looking and laugh again to themselves.

The blonde waves. "Hi, Nicki!" I don't wave back. Not yet. They look familiar, never a good sign.

In unison, they pump their fists and chant, "Go, Nicki! Go, Nicki! Go, Nicki!" and collapse in laughter.

Fucking cunts from high school. Most likely, they're still pissed because I've beat their asses once or twice. I flip them off and turn to look for the restroom again. And there it is, right in fucking front of me.

I get back to the table and I'm still fuming. I shouldn't be. If I'd have seen them anywhere else, any other time, I'd have just given them a reminder of why they hate me in the first place. But why now, when everything was going so good?

Andy says, "You were right. Waitress showed up right after you left. Pitcher's on the way. You like dark ale?"

"Yeah."

"Something wrong?"

"No. Nothing's wrong."

"What's wrong?"

I sigh. "I just ran into some people who—" I almost say *who know me*. Instead, I finish with, "Who I didn't want to run into."

"There some problem?"

"No. Just didn't need to see them is all."

My hackles go up. Does Andy *know me*? I don't remember him from high school, but there are a lot of people *I* don't know who know *me*.

"Um," I say, "so did you go to high school here?" I don't sound casual at all, but I need to put my mind at ease.

He shrugs. "Yeah."

"What year did you graduate?"

His answer is a relief. He graduated about three years before I would have. He'd have pretty much missed the social shitstorm that was my higher education.

But he's giving me a troubled look, still thinking about the people I didn't want to run into. He raises his eyes and searches the crowd, brow creased. He won't find what he's looking for in there. And he doesn't. He looks back at me. The corners of his mouth turn up.

"Hey."

"What."

Andy puts his hand on mine. "*Hey*."

"What?"

He leans toward me. "Come here."

I lean.

He kisses me. "Who cares about them?"

I shrug.

"Right?"

I smile, nod.

The ale he's ordered is dark as coffee and shamelessly bitter. It takes a little bit to get used to, but when he asks if I like it, I tell him I do.

We watch people dance for a while, talk about small things. The pitcher's half empty. I say, "Ready?"

"For what?"

"To get your boogie on."

He's not a bad dancer. I'm no Rockette myself, mind you. But he seems to be having a good time. Sometimes, guys will dance just because they think you want them to. Sometimes they'll make a joke out of the whole thing; but Andy's not self-conscious at all.

A slow song comes on. I take his hands. We sway. His arms encircle my waist. I wrap mine around his back, rest my hands on his shoulders, my head on his chest. This is nice. This is so nice.

I've never had a boyfriend. Not really. I've been with one, single guy for a stretch of time, but that's not the same thing. I knew what they wanted me for. They knew what I wanted them for. It never left room for something else.

I can't believe I'm hoping that Andy and I have room for something else.

About ten-thirty we decide to escape. The music isn't getting any better, and its pounding is becoming unbearable for the both of us.

The ride home is comfortably silent. I don't feel the need to talk just to fill the quiet. Andy doesn't seem to either. I say, "This is a really good time, Andy." The streetlights sweep by. "Thanks for asking me out."

"Thanks for saying yes."

We're making the turn onto Wilmington. I hear the crackle of brown paper shifting. I'd almost forgotten.

"Hey, can I look in the bag now?"

"Sure, why not? Grab it."

I reach behind the driver's seat and pull the bag by the handles onto my lap. It's not heavy. I open it, look inside. The streetlight shines just bright enough for me to see what's in there.

The tightening in my stomach makes me swallow hard.

"Um, what's this?"

I don't have to ask. I can see clearly. It's a box of body lotion. A bottle of Gold Dust Body Powder. A rounded cylinder that can only be a fucking vibrator. And, of course, a box of condoms. A street light flashes by, and I make out the words *SIXTEEN DIFFERENT FLAVORS*.

I try to swallow again, but my mouth is cotton. My eyes burn.

He eases the car into his parking spot and brakes, kills the engine.

"Well," he says, "we always have to make it a rush. I thought it'd be nice if we could take our time for a change. We don't have to use all of that stuff, or any of it, if you don't want—except for the condoms—but I thought it might be fun to have some options to explore, you know?"

"Oh."

I deserve this. If anybody in the world ever deserved anything, I deserve this. And I'm too strong to let it hurt, so I hate how bad it feels anyway.

"You all right?"

"I just wasn't expecting ..."

I look at him. His face is eager. "You want to, right?"

My hand goes to my hip. My razor isn't there. I close my eyes.

Funny meeting you here. Best joke I heard all week.

Fuck. "Yeah. Okay." I find the release lever and open the door. "Let's go."

I was a slut in high school before I even knew it. Probably before I even earned the title.

It was Tony Garver who passed around the story about me and Bobby James Sounder and Ted Wells and Jonathan Garver, his older brother, and the time the four of us had in the back of Bobby James' Chevy Nova one evening down by the lake. He left out a real important part of that story, but in the end, it might not have made any difference. Sure didn't make any difference to my mom. Whether or not Tony Garver ever learned the truth from Jonathan, I don't know. He was probably just as ignorant as everyone else. I'll give him the benefit of the doubt. Not that he deserves it.

All I knew was that boys were suddenly very interested in me. I didn't appreciate their attention at first. It scared the hell out of me. I'd been as boy-crazy as any adolescent girl, and dreamed of my boyfriend— whomever he might turn out to be—and I played out in my mind how we would meet, and savored the instant we discovered we were in love.

But by the time the boys actually started flocking around me, I felt trapped and helpless in their presence.

It wasn't until I started packing my grandpa's straight razor, *my* straight razor, that I could start looking them in the eye, and talking to them, and tolerating their touch. In fact, with my razor in my pocket, I started daring myself to meet with them. Their company still carried a thrill for me. Being near them was like walking into the dark. I began to challenge the danger I was sure was promised by their proximity.

One day, Alan Brush said he wanted to meet me under the bleachers after school. I went to meet him and found him there, looking nervous and surprised. And when I took him, armed with my hidden razor, I found a way to kill my fear.

Oh, the shark has ... teeth like razors ... and she keeps them ... out of sight ...

And when I'd gotten my teeth into the guys, the girls started hating me for doing what I needed to do. So, I gave those cunts a show to let them know they could not beat me down. I took Steve Dasher into the girls' restroom during lunch and had him on the toilet seat in the third stall. Girls pushed and shoved to watch over the partition and peek over the door. And when Steve began to moan and gasp as he neared climax, they began to chant *Go Nicki! Go Nicki! Go Nicki!*

Oh, they loved it. They loved it as much as Steve Dasher loved it. But like the guys, the cunts had to protect themselves. From each other. From the thick roots that ran to their dark hearts. So, they kept on hating me; they needed to hate me as much as they needed me to keep on doing what I needed to do.

They still hate me. All of them. They still need me.

But I don't know what I need anymore.

It's nearly three o'clock when I get back to the bungalow. My straight razor's lying on my mattress. I drop the clutch next to it, step out of Sheila's pumps, pull off her dress, hang it up. I take the razor to the bathroom and sit on the toilet seat. There are lines running like faint white

114

barcodes down both of my inner thighs. Before I started carrying the razor, I used it to make those lines. I haven't made a new one in a long time. No guy has ever asked me about them, except my ObGyn. I gave him some bullshit story about a bike accident he didn't fucking believe anyway.

I open the razor and with its edge, dint the soft unmarked skin at the end of the barcode on my right thigh. I draw it up the skin to make a new mark. It doesn't hurt. It never does.

After work Saturday evening, there's a knock on the bungalow door around six o'clock.

It's my favorite person in the whole world.

"Hi, Quinn."

"Hey, Sparks." He steps inside. I close the door after him. "So, how was your date?"

"It was fun."

"Yeah?"

"Yeah." I sit on my mattress. "He took me to Ivan's, and we went down to the waterfront and walked along the boardwalk. There's a lot of new storefronts there now. And a club. We danced."

"Sounds romantic."

"He kissed me in a gazebo."

Quinn blinks slowly. "Do you like him?"

A quiet laugh escapes me. Once it's out, I can't stop. I keep laughing.

"What?"

I shake my head, put my face in my hands. "Nothing." I heave a sigh.

The mattress bows as Quinn sits next to me. "What?"

"He didn't want to get into my pants. He wanted to get me into bed." Quinn puts his arm around my shoulders. I lean into him. "I mean, fuck, did I actually expect anything else?" I can't tell him about the bag. I can't tell him how Andy wanted to go gentle and slow, and I riled him up. I made him want to just fuck me. Me without my

115

straight razor. I let him do anything he wanted to me. As penance. As a lesson. So I'd never forget again. The long and short of it is, I made up the rules, and he beat me at my own game. Shit, maybe I should send him a trophy and a card of congratulations. Or not. I always sucked at games, anyway.

"You had a right to expect more."

I shake my head. "I don't think so." I shrug. "I thought he liked me." I snort. "Listen to me. *I thought he* liked *me.* Fuck."

"There's nothing wrong with that."

I bury my face in his shoulder. "There's no one for us."

He hugs me tight.

Outside, a car passes by the bungalow.

"Where'd you park?" I ask.

"Up the road, on the other side of my old house. That your mom who just drove by?"

"No, it's the queen of England, dipshit."

Quinn and I got really fucked-up one night when we were seventeen. We'd gotten drunk together before, but that night we were just blotto. We'd smoked-out, gotten a bottle of Jack, the guy at Hill Point Liquor on Marigold sold it to us because I'd do him favors sometimes, and we smoked-out some more. His mom had gotten engaged a week earlier, and she was going to move to Idaho. Yeah, fucking Idaho. I don't know the whole story.

Anyway, Quinn was torn-up about it. He was happy for his mom, of course. He loved her a lot. And this night—we were out in the back-forty behind my house; it was summer and the night was warm and clear—he just unloads on me. Says his mom always resented him for chasing away her first fiancée. Kind of the same shit with my mom.

Quinn and I started out spermatozoa and ovum butting heads, following Nature's plan after someone else set the course, but we got blamed for all the heartache churning in the wake of our conceptions. We were born in bad fucking luck and it's followed us ever since. I've never seen Quinn cry like that. I'd never had anything against Miss Halliday until I saw Quinn cry. He's better without her if that's how she is. But she's still his mom. They keep in touch, but it's because he calls her. She doesn't call him.

What do they say? The only things you can't choose in life are your family and who you fall in love with. I think if you get dealt the fuck-you card with the first, the world owes a better hand with the second. Yeah, but the deck is all-round stacked against me and Quinn. Fuck it, we got some crazy shit up our sleeves.

Quinn says, "Let's go out."

"I don't want to fucking go out."

"No. Just you and me. Let's get some dinner. Then let's go to Jay's or some place with octogenarian barflies neither one of us would fuck for an indecent proposal. It'll just be a you-and-me night."

"Okay. Yeah." I hug him tight. "I love you so much, Quinn. You know that, don't you?"

"I know. I love you, Nicki. Don't you know that?"

We don't end up at Jay's. We find seats at the bar at the Line and Tackle instead. There are no octogenarians to be found here, but there is an astonishing collection of booze on the shelves behind the bar. The clientele has been sampling from it longer than Quinn and I have been alive. Believe me, it shows. There are no illusions here, not in the lines of the faces of the people sitting at the bar, or cast by the shadows of hanging lights over the empty pool tables, and not in the ring-shaped stains in the laminated wood grain. At least, not any that aren't at the bottom of a shot glass. The juke plays nothing newer that Manfred Mann's "Blinded by the Light," even though it knows a few ditties from later decades. (I get the idea to play Social Distortion's cover of "Ring of Fire" just to watch the confusion.)

Quinn's gotten us a couple of shots of Patrón and a pitcher of something-or-other. I'm not in it for the taste. I was feeling shitty all day, but I feel good right now, and it's not just the beer that's lifting me up. As little as I have, at least I have Quinn, and that's probably more than most.   I will never let myself forget how much I have in him.

Can't choose your family, right? If it meant losing Quinn, I wouldn't change a thing.

Quinn's cracking me the fuck up right now. He's the funniest guy in the world, I swear to god. He doesn't even know it. He doesn't try; he just talks. I wouldn't ruin the magic by trying to repeat it. You just need to hang out with him sometime. You'll see.

So, I'm having a good time, and who the fuck should show his face? Oh, take a wild guess. There's a mirror on the wall across the bar, and I just happen to glance its way, and I see a soul patch and John Lennon specs. Ellis' hair is dark, and the locks coil in and around so that the tips fall halfway down his forehead, over the curves of his ears, and touch the nape of his neck. Ellis Ray. Ellis-I-like-me-some-"Darling-Nikki"-Ray.

Okay, real quick, let me tell you about "Darling Nikki." After I put on the show with Steve Dasher in the girls' bathroom, "Darling Nikki" became my theme song. I have nothing against the song itself, and I have nothing against Prince. *Purple Rain* is one of my favorite records, but I was serenaded with that song on a weekly basis in high school. It'd blare at me from car stereos when I was walking to school. You can't think it was by accident how many times I heard that song. Honestly, more than likely, it was my theme song even before anyone started singing it to me. I'd gangbanged at fourteen, after all, and I was the only one who didn't know how much I loved it.

So, Ellis Ray is here. In the bar. With me. And Quinn. He's chatting-up some of the barflies. Quinn's still talking, but his words are going in one ear and out the next. Half of me wants to cut him off and say, *Let's slouch the fuck out of here. Don't ask questions Let's go*. The other half wants to tell Quinn the whole story of last Saturday night and rise from our bar stools and converge on Ellis Ray with fists of furious anger. But my eyes are fixed on the

118

image of Ellis in the mirror and his performance before the couple in the booth alongside the far wall. There's something peculiar about his attentions.

Let me explain. The Line and Tackle is on Condor Avenue. This street lies around the unofficial demilitarized zone between the west and east ends of town. Now this place is a dive, like I said, but it's a respectable dive. You won't find the shitkickers the Wheatpenny attracts. Line and Tackle understands that east-towners must slum, and in accordance with that, it waves a few west-enders through the velvet ropes to attend to appearances and to maintain a supply of party favors.

So, all these old drunksters who've filled their gills with booze for more years than Quinn and I have birthdays, most likely pull in a smart six-digit yearly income by way of the bank. That couple there in the mirror, yukking it up with Ellis Ray, are no different. Plainly said, they may not do so well socially, but their bank account is alive and kicking, through no fault of their own, I have no doubt. Back when "Blinded by the Light" was in constant rotation on the radio, and bellbottoms and sideburns had been the height of fashion, and pterodactyls still swarmed the skies above, these two might have been called trust fund kids. Now they're just dumb fuckers who've never had to work a day for a living.

Bitter? Oh, a tad.

But here's my point. That couple has working money. They're here because they have it, and Ellis Ray has to know this plain fact as clearly as I do. As much as I dislike Ellis Ray, I never disliked him because I saw stupid in his eyes. There's no stupid on him now, any more than there's chummy affection for some old friends. Because, right now, Ellis Ray's performing. I've seen happy glad-handing before, and I'm seeing it right now.

I've seen Crenshaw's badgery face go all Cheshire when regulars come into the bakery. Seen Willie Barber at Village Liquor, a quick five-minute drive from the folks' house, chat it up with my dad every single time I'm with him on a beer run. You'd think the two were best friends since birth even though on the street, neither would know the other from Adam. Seen politicians kissing babies, and so have you. It's what we're looking at right now.

"Sparks?" While I was paying attention to Ellis, Quinn was talking about some recipe he'd found on the Internet he'd been having trouble with. I can't remember what it was, and it occurs to me he's been quiet for a bit.

"Yeah?" I say without turning.

"What's up?"

"Nothing." In the mirror, Ellis has just leaned forward and held up a 'scuse-me finger. Now he's turning and making his way between the pool tables to the bar.

"Just a sec, okay?" I tell Quinn. Don't know if he answers.

The bartender catches Ellis bellying-up and dutifully breaks away from squeaking the inside curve of a glass with a towel. Voice deferential, he says, *Hey, Ellis.* Ellis goes, *Bottle of Heineken. And, hey,* he jabs his thumb back to the couple he's been schmoozing, *Larry and Josephine? They're on the house the rest of the night, yeah*? Bartender's not arguing. *You got it.* Ellis raps the bar top twice with his knuckles to close the conversation. He turns on his heels and make his way back across the floor to the company of Larry and Josephine. He never pays for his drink.

Son of a bitch. Quinn and I are supporting Ellis Ray with each pitcher.

"Nicki?"

I turn to Quinn. "Sorry."

"Something up?"

"Nope." He doesn't believe me. Why would he? Even I can hear the stress in my voice.

"What."

I shake my head. "Nothing, 'kay?" I knock an elbow against his. "Let's just ... This is the first time it's just been you-and-me in a while."

"I know."

I shrug. "Let's just have fun, Sparky."

"'Cause you look like you're having a blast, right now."

"Sorry, okay?"

"Is something wrong?"

"It's nothing worth worrying about."

"Come on."

"Later, okay?"

I've been looking at the bar top. Now I look at him. He's got his head tilted and a scrunched look in his eye.

I laugh. "You're such a dork."

Quinn rolls his eyes, swivels away from me, and takes a deep pull of his beer. Oh, the angst, you could cut it with a knife.

"So, tell me about this dish you're cooking up," I say.

"Whatever," Quinn mutters.

My eyes are already on Ellis in the mirror again. He leans into his clients, says something, and rises from his seat. He's heading for the bathrooms.

I tell Quinn, "I'll be back. I got to pee."

I don't got to pee. I hang out in the hall next to the men's' restroom. I stand with my arms crossed and I try not to sway.

Ellis comes out, hitching his pants.

I say, "*Ellis*." I'm drunk and I'm surly and I know it.

Ellis raises his head. "Nicki. How are you?"

"Fuck you. I want you to tell me what the fuck was going on at Jonathan Garver's house last Saturday."

"Well, if you'd stuck around you might have found out."

"I'll find out on my terms. Not Garver's. Sure as fuck not yours."

"Fair enough."

"Fuck your *fair enough*. You tell me, or I'll let your friends out there watch you get beat up by a girl. My brother's out there, too, and I'll let him have the scraps. Don't think he won't want to pound on you a little."

"Okay. I'll tell you everything you want to know."

"Let's hear it."

121

"Later."

"*Fuck*." I lean toward him, eyes deep in his. "*You*."

"Let's talk tomorrow."

"Fuck you, Ellis. Let's talk tonight."

"Listen. I'll give you my number—"

"I got your number." I recite it to him out loud.

"That's it. Call me tomorrow, we'll make a date, I'll tell you everything."

I'm the type of person who can talk loud, but knows when they've lost their big stick in the last pitcher. Right now, my big stick is lost, for sure. I can barely stand without my shoulder rubbing one wall or the other. So, I make like I'm going to do the motherfucker a favor.

I say, "Fine. Tomorrow. I'll call; you better answer."

"I will. I want this over and done with."

"Just tell me this."

"What?"

"Was Todd in on it?"

"Yes."

"Was Parker?"

"No."

"Okay. Get the fuck out of my face."

He bobs his head like he's making a shallow bow, then slips past, out the corridor and back into the bar proper. I lean out to make sure he's set his self down so his back will be to me. He has. I totter back to Quinn.

"Let's go someplace else," I tell him.

"Yeah, really?"

I shrug. "There are just some people here I don't want to see."

"Uh-huh."

"Don't worry about it."

He worries about it. He looks over his shoulder and scans the floor. I don't know if he finds anything. Probably not. He turns back to me.

"I got it taken care of," I say. "I just don't want to hang around here anymore."

He nods his head. "All right."

"All right.

"Let's go, then."
"Let's go."
"You going to tell me about it?"
"Yes."
"Yeah?"
"Promise."
"Okay. "
"Okay."
"Let's go."
We go.
We get *so* fucked up.

Quinn drops me off at the house around three. We're nursing a couple of mean hangovers. I tell him bye when I push myself out of the car and he goes yeah as I slam the door. I'll probably need one of my dad's beers to clear my head before I contact Ellis. I've got a pit in my stomach, and it's not from the hangover. It doesn't help that I'm starting to recall more clearly my encounter with Ellis the night before, and from this side of it, I'm realizing I probably made an ass of myself.

I should have told Quinn what was going on, but if we're at the end of this thing, whatever the fuck it is, if everyone involved wants it over and done with, like Ellis said last night, then I don't want Quinn starting shit. He'll usually do what I tell him to, but sometimes he just goes off his bean if he thinks I need protecting. He thought I needed a lot of protecting in high school, no surprise. Didn't make him exactly popular. He fucking beat the shit out of poor Steve Dasher after the story about the two of us in the girls' restroom finally made the rounds back to him. I told Quinn Steve didn't do anything. I told him it was all my idea. Didn't save Steve from a black eye, a bloody nose, a fat lip, and more than a few strategically placed bruises. I felt really bad about it and pretty pissed at Quinn for a while. I tried to make it up to Steve, but by that time, he was playing the same game all the other guys played. The rules were simple: first you fuck Nicki

Valentine; then you call her a slut.

The thing is, if he finds out these guys took me to Jonathan Garver's house, I know he will fucking lose it. I will tell Quinn what happened, because I promised him I would. But I'm not dropping names. Except for Garver's, and that fucker's high enough up the food chain to keep his toes from getting nipped off.

I somehow manage the key into the door of the bungalow, lay a path of peeled-off clothes to the bathroom, and rinse off in the shower, tie my hair back, and change into some fresh clothes. My razor's on the bathroom counter. I wince when I see it, wishing I hadn't put a new cut on my leg. It was a hard thing to stop doing. I don't want to start up again. I pick my razor up, but I don't slip it into my pocket. The pants I'm wearing, it'll be clear as day against my hip. I unbutton the top of my blouse and slip it into my bra, under my left tit. It's not comfortable, but it'll do.

I walk to the house. My mom's car is in the driveway. I peek in through the kitchen window. It's empty inside. I slip in the side door. The sound from the TV is drifting from downstairs. They're both probably down there. Good. I'm just not in the mood to see either one of them.

I pop open a Budweiser from the fridge and down it as quickly as I can without letting it come back up on me. It does the trick. That throbbing in my head fades, and that sick-all-over feeling lets off. Gently, I set the empty bottle in the trash, slip back outside, and get in my car. Glad I could fill-up.

I'm going to call Ellis from the payphone I found on Brook Avenue after I escaped Jonathan Garver's house last Saturday. I can only guess that the reason Ellis and Todd were hunting the bars is because they didn't know where else to look for me. I have no idea if they can track by a received phone number, but whether they can or can't, if they want to keep searching me out, it's going to be in bars.

East Brook Avenue is busy today. There are no spots on the street, so I have to pull into a McDonald's parking lot and walk a block and a half to the payphone in front of the bike shop. I feed the coin slot and dial Ellis's number.

"Hello?"

"It's Nicki."

He clears his throat. "Where do you want to meet?"

I hadn't thought about that. Some place public and with witnesses. "The park over by McGee Fields," I tell him. It's the first thing that shoots into my head, but I say it like I'd planned this meeting since birth. "At the covered tables by the barbeques."

"I'll be there in fifteen minutes."

I get there before him. At least, before I see him. McGee Fields is where Little League plays baseball and office teams play softball. There are a few games going on today, and crowds of people are milling around, sitting on blankets, and pushing their kids on the swing sets. A family of seven is using one of the barbeques, but they're sticking to one table, and that leaves me the pick of the other five.

I linger in the shade of a sycamore, my back against the trunk, and keep an eye on the tables. I'm starting to think Ellis is doing the same thing. I look around, but I don't see him anywhere.

Ah, there he is. Walking from the opposite end of the park toward the tables. I break from the shade. He sees me, stops at the far corner, and waits.

He starts speaking the moment I'm in range.

"This is how it is. Todd Keeling is Jonathan Garver's nephew. Mr. Garver contacted Todd to find you, and Todd contacted me to help. Me and a couple of others, but they don't matter now. We've all been at it for about a month now. Mr. Garver wants to meet with you on behalf of Bobby James Sounder."

The name sinks me. Even the sound of it is a humiliation. I fold my arms across my stomach. I try to keep looking Ellis in the eye.

"Bobby James ... ," I shrug and shake my head. "Why ..."

"Because you're a celebrity, Nicki. Around certain

125

circles, you are."

For this, I have no words. I shake my head no, the motion taking a life of its own in an act of denial, of comprehension, of disgust, of avowal, of bafflement.

"This election is very important," Ellis continues, whether or not he's seen my objection, "and Mr. Sounder doesn't want old lapses to bite him in the ass. And since it was Mr. Garver's brother who got the story circulating, Mr. Garver took on the responsibility of finding you." Ellis shrugs. "Jonathan also wanted to see you again." He says it with a half-ass smile.

"What does—" I tilt my gaze to the grass. I can't look at Ellis anymore. "—Bobby—"

"Mr. Sounder is willing to offer you a handsome sum just to keep a low profile during the race. Out of sight, out of mind, you know? Mr. Garver was going to hand it to you last Saturday, but you ran off."

"He wanted to do more than hand me some money."

"I think that was on his mind."

I press my fist to my mouth. I can't stand. I reach for the corner of the table and use it to guide myself down onto the bench. I squeeze my eyes shut and lean my head between my knees.

"Oh ... god ... oh ... god ..."

A few deep breaths, and the sickness passes. I sit up. Ellis has been watching me, head tilted to one side and curious.

"That story about the four of you. That's not the exact truth, is it?"

I shake my head. "What difference does it make? Truth is a game."

"Mm-hm."

I swipe my arm across my forehead. My brow's damp. I say, "So that's it, then? That's all? Bobby just wants me to be quiet?"

"That's about the size of it."

"And he'll leave me alone?"

"Yes."

"And Jonathan?"

"Oh, I'm sure Mr. Garver would love to see you again, but if you play by the rules, there's no reason why he should need to see you again."

It's over. That's all I wanted. "Sure. Fine. Okay. I'll do whatever he wants. I won't go out, and I work where no one ever sees me, except my boss and my co-workers. I don't even want the money. Just as long as he leaves me alone."

"I have to give you the money, Nicki. It fixes the deal. Helps ensure you won't change your mind about keeping up your end."

"Look. Why don't you just keep the money and tell Bobby James you gave it to me."

"Doesn't work that way, Nicki. Sorry."

"Fuck. Fine. Whatever. Just give it to me, then."

"I don't have it on me."

"*Jesus.*"

"I can get it for you."

"Fine. Get it. I'll wait for you."

"It might be easier if you'd just follow me back to my place. I can go in, grab it, hand it off to you there. You won't even have to get out of your car."

I shake my head. "Just bring it to me here."

"I don't want to argue."

I cut him a look. "Do not *fuck* with me, Ellis."

He rolls his eyes to the tops of the sycamores. Keeps his hands in his pockets. Watches the treetops.

"*Goddammit.*"

He shrugs. "Rules of the game. The sooner we do this, the sooner it'll be over and done, for everyone."

He's right, of course. If he's telling the truth. And truth is my worst game. Who the hell would I get home field advantage from, anyway?

"Let's go."

I trail his white Sequoia out of the parking lot and out east along Park Line Boulevard. The houses here are ranch style, with wide lawns and expensive cars in the driveway. The streets are lined with elms. If he lives here, he's no slouch when it comes to business.

He's not. He guides the Sequoia through a lane of groomed elms getting back their green after the winter. The houses here are two-storied, with solid green lawns and beautiful facades. Ellis guides the Sequoia into a driveway no less snazzy than the others. I park my car by the curb in front of his mailbox and keep the engine running. Ellis climbs out of his vehicle, quick-steps across a concrete walkway, raising his arm at halfway mark to let me know everything's peachy, and heads inside through the front door.

When the door closes behind him, I look around, check the rear view. There are kids with backpacks walking down the sidewalk across the street. A bow-legged old man in a fedora is strolling my way on this side, turtle-slow. I keep turning and checking the street until the kids have disappeared around a corner. The old man passes by. I shift my gaze to the rear view and I watch him dwindle down the sidewalk to the rear of my car.

Takes all of ten minutes. Time enough. So, where the hell is Ellis? Is he fucking with me? Setting me up? Why? Why would he fucking do that? He said everyone involved wants this over and done with.

Oh, yeah. The money. He wants Bobby James' fucking money. Fuck, he can have it. I fucking told him so.

But—what?—he's afraid I'll bitch later. Is that it?

Fine. I'll sign a sworn affidavit saying I gave it to him. If I have second thoughts, like he put it, that'll save him.

I twist in my seat and search the street. It's empty. No school kids. No old men. No scary guy stepping out from behind the trunk of a birch tree with a piece in his hand leveled at my head. I think about snapping all the door locks, but a fat lot of good that's going to do against a bullet through the window.

"Goddammit." I want this to be over. It's so close now. It's so goddamn close. Shit. I should just leave. But what if I drive off and Ellis leaves me hanging again? He said

Todd had gotten two other guys to go out gunning for me. What if they don't get the memo to lay off? Am I going to have to look over my shoulder every time I'm in a bar, or walking to my car, or walking through the aisles at a corner store? Am I going to have to second-guess every guy I see? I'll be goddammed if I'm going to be afraid of men again. Fuck Bobby James. He can't have me anymore. This is over. Now.

I kill the engine and climb out. Check the area. I'm alone out here. I cross the lawn to the wide picture window which must look in on the living room. There's a gap in the short hedge that borders the front of the house. I lean up to the pane, find a part in the windows behind the glass. Cupping my hand over my eyes, I look inside.

Ellis is inside, sitting on a sofa, his legs crossed, boots up on a coffee table. He's talking on a cell phone.

What. The. Fuck.

I rap on the glass with my knuckle.

He looks up.

I make a What-the-fuck? gesture.

He holds a hand up—*one second*—then rises from the couch and walks toward the front door.

You've got to be kidding me.

I hear the clunk of the latch and the hush of the door opening, the seal of air conditioning giving and sucking outside climates.

"Nicki?"

Good god. "What the *fuck* are you *doing*?"

"Come here."

I step to the edge of the threshold. He pokes his head half around the frame. I can't see it, but I can tell his cell is still pressed to his ear.

"Come in," he says. With his free hand he waves at me.

"Jesus Christ, Ellis, do you have the fucking money or don't you?"

"Step inside a second." His voice is hushed like he doesn't want the party on the other side of the line to hear. "I'm sorry, this won't take long." He gives me another quick signal to join him.

I do not step inside a second. I step backward. "I'm going back to the park," I tell him. "Just fucking bring it to me there."

I wheel to start back to my car.

That big motherfucker coming up behind me across the yard must walk on cat-quiet paws. He's bald and broad-shouldered and must weigh something like three-hundred. Fat and muscle, all mass. A yellow Billabong shirt.

I dodge right toward the street. He sidesteps and catches me with his arm. It's like running into a tree branch.

I dip. He gets me around the shoulders in a bear hug.

I send a knee into his thigh, but I don't have the range to make it hurt. He wrestles me forward onto the covered patio and through the doorway, spins me around to face Ellis.

The front door bangs shut behind me.

There's another guy in the house, stepping out of an alcove that looks to lead to a kitchen. He's slim, fit, about my age. His brown hair is high and tight. His jaw is heavy. A dimple dints his chin.

"It'll be only a little while longer now," Ellis says into the phone. He folds the cell and places it on the coffee table.

"You *fuck*," I tell him.

"God, you got some mouth on you. Give me your keys."

"Fuck you."

Ellis holds out his hand, palm up.

"*I said I'd be quiet.*"

"Give me your keys."

"Go fuck yourself."

Billabong grabs me around the front and pins both my arms with one of his. He jams his free hand in my pocket, fishes my keys out, and tosses them to Ellis.

I kick out. "*Goddammit, what the fuck are you doing?*"

Ellis puts my keys in his pocket. Billabong lets go. I fly

forward, cock my fist, and feed my knuckles across Ellis' jaw. He crumples sideways, falls to his right, and just manages to throw his arms out to catch himself before he sprawls all undignified across the floor, but he can't catch his John Lennon glasses as they go flipping over the carpet. I wind-up again to give him another taste, but Billabong catches my arm, pulls me backward, and locks me up against his chest. My feet are off the floor. I kick, try to dig my heel into a shin.

"*Goddammit.*" Ellis snatches his glasses from the floor, rights himself, and pokes the frames back over the bridge of his nose.

"Let her go," he tells Billabong.

Amazingly, I'm dropped to the floor. I stumble for balance, shocked by my freedom.

I barely catch Ellis out of the corner of my eye as he launches into motion and lunges forward to send a hard fist into my stomach.

I've been punched in the stomach before. This is far from the worst I've suffered, but it's still good enough to make me cough and double-over.

"*Don't pull that shit again*!" he orders me. "Get on your knees!"

"Fuck off ..."

"Get on your knees or I'll have Anthony knock your legs out! *Got it*? Get on your fucking knees!"

I get on my knees.

"Put your hands behind your head and lace your fingers together!"

"Shit."

"Do it!"

I do it.

"Cross your ankles one over the other behind you!"

I do.

Ellis takes a deep breath, touches his jaw where I decked him, and sits down on the coffee table in front of me. He rests his elbows on his knees. "Now let's get some things straight," he says.

"I told you I'd be quiet."

"Shut up. You'll be quiet because Bobby James Sounder told you to be quiet. There's no money, Nicki. Did you really think a man like Mr. Sounder needed to pay-off a two-bit whore like you? How much of a bother do you think you are? Sweetheart, Bobby James is just cleaning house. And you're nothing but a dead spider he's sweeping out the door." He turns to the third guy in the room, High and Tight with Dimple, and says to him. "Fill up the sink, Pete."

High and Tight—Pete—disappears into the kitchen. The hollow sound of water starts to drum into a stainless steel basin.

"You're going to do what you're told to do." Ellis turns back to me. "I'll show you why."

But Ellis shows me nothing, yet. Instead, he just keeps dead-eyeing at me, just keeps pursing his lips. The water in the kitchen's getting deeper. The sound of it gets thicker as its volume rises. Ellis doesn't say a word. His face is expressionless, but he's looking me up and down. The water in the kitchen shuts off.

"Get up," he says.

I stand.

"Go into the kitchen."

I shake my head.

Ellis gives an impatient signal to Anthony, the asshole formerly known as Billabong. I try to dodge. Anthony gets me by the right arm. He twists it and wrenches it straight out behind me. Ellis grabs my left and does the same thing. I cry out. I can barely fight as the two march me into the kitchen.

The sink is deep. The water's so clear and still, the basin might almost be empty.

"I said I'd be quiet, I *said* I'd be *quiet*, *I said I'd be quiet* —"

Ellis grabs my ponytail. "I'd shut up and take a deep breath if I was you."

Anthony and Ellis push me forward. My knees knock against the wooden cabinet door under the edge of the sink. My face is leveled over the flooded basin. I feel the coolness of silvered water at the tip of nose. I take a deep breath. Ellis shoves my head down. The water is *cold*. My heart is a jackhammer in my chest. It's burning up my air. I have to breathe. I can't take this. Water is going up my nose. My lungs are burning. I'm going to drown with my face two inches under water. I can't see anything. It's so dark I might as well be trapped under an ice floe in Antarctica.

Ellis yanks my ponytail and pulls my face up. The old, stale air bursts out of me. I replace it instantly with a fresh breath. "*Don't!*" I shout as soon as I can talk. "*Don't!*"

"Save your breath, Nicki."

My face goes under again.

I'm not going to make it this time. I just know it. Panic is racing my heart, burning my oxygen, and I'm going to have to blow out the old air and breathe in. And when I do, there will be nothing but water to inhale. I don't want to die. I don't want to die.

Ellis yanks me out. I can't talk. I can only take in air like there's barely enough left in the world.

"Nicki." Ellis's voice is in my ear. "Nicki, now listen. We can do this all day long. And it's only going to get worse every time you go under. But it can stop right now, this instant. All you have to do is say you'll do everything you're told to do. Do you understand?"

"Yes—"

"Good. This is what you're going to do. You're not just going to lay low and stay quiet. You're going to leave town for a while. Nobody cares where the hell you go. But you're going to clear out before nightfall. You'll do it, won't you?"

"Yes, I will—"

"Good. But first, you're going to be very nice to me, to Anthony, and to Pete. No cussing, no screaming, no fighting, no crying."

"She can cry a little, if she wants to." My eyes are still closed, but that voice came from my right, so it must have been Pete who said it.

"You'll be very nice to the three of us, and we're going to take a trip up to Mr. Garver's house, and you're going to be nice to him."

I don't want to cry.

"You'll do that, won't you?"

I don't want to cry.

"Nicki ... ?"

I don't want to cry. "Yes I'll do it ..."

"Good."

Ellis and Anthony release me. I wipe my face with my arm. My muscles are sore, strained. Both my arms feel weighted. Ellis gives me a hand towel. I dry myself.

"Now get into the living room and take your clothes off." I slump against the counter. To Anthony, Ellis says, "Go stand by the front door." Anthony leaves. Ellis turns to talk with Pete. His voice is low, but I can hear him say, "The cameras are in the garage ..." He pauses, turns to me. "Nicki, go into the living room and get ready."

I go. Anthony is guarding the front door. Big old Anthony in his yellow Billabong shirt. He's nearly as wide as the frame, and maybe two inches shorter. It's just me and Anthony now. I've got nothing on him. If he wants to take me down, he's going to do it without a second thought. But we're very close together now. We are one-to-one in a very small world. If I have any chance of getting out of this, I've got to take it now. I've got to take it right now.

Think fast, rabbit.

I can't give him a chance for a second thought. I can't give him a chance for a single thought.

I've got my breath back. I stand in the middle of the room trying not to look at any precise point. But I do watch Anthony out of the corner of my eye.

Footsteps behind me. I glance over my shoulder. Pete's turning the corner down a hallway. Don't see Ellis. Must still be in the kitchen.

I free the first two buttons of my blouse. Anthony is making a point of looking at the far corner of the living room. I free two more buttons. He tries not to notice. I step toward him.

"Just keep to the middle of the room," he says.

I don't keep to the middle of the room. I take two more steps up to him, straight as a blade so he can't see the depth I'm closing. I say, "I bet they're going to leave you with sloppy thirds." I take another two steps, my eyes on him, my stance steady, the last couple buttons open on my blouse to show him my bra. I breathe, "You want to get the first taste?"

"Just hold still," he says to me. "You're not going anywhere."

Oh, just keep thinking that, champ. Just keep thinking I'm holding still and not going anywhere as I slip my tit out of the cup and slink one last step forward. Don't stop me. Keep your gaze on my bare tit as I slip my fingers under the swell like I'm trying to offer my nipple up to you. Don't take your eyes off it. Go ahead and instruct me to "Just keep yourself to the middle of the—" because my straight razor is already out, flipped open, and slashing.

He bats my arm away, but his blood is already blotting the yellow of his shirt. He hollers, claps his hand over his chest. I snap my razor shut, close my fist around it, punch him across the jaw. He's too big for me to put down, but he's hurt, and he's shocked when his gaze tumbles down to see the amount of blood that's washing his shoulder, his chest, and from the parting lips of the wound riding the inside of his bicep. He stumbles backward, one loose heal tripping over the other as his hip slams against an end table, sending it crashing to the floor and cracking under the unstoppable force his of his weight.

There's a shout behind me. I wheel, snapping the blade out again just as Ellis comes within striking distance. He sees my razor at the last second, raises his hands to protect himself. I cut both palms wide open. He shrieks, pulls his hands back. "*Pete!*" I flip my razor shut, close it in my fist again, step forward, and use my fist on Ellis like I used it on Anthony. I get a good solid strike against his temple. Anthony was too big for me to put

down, but Ellis isn't. He flops flat onto his back. I drop
down on him, drive my knee into his chest, use my
weight to pin him to the floor. He's not out, but he's
dazed. I grab a fistful of his faux hawk and pull his head
off the floor. With the other hand, I flip open my razor
and pinch the tip of Ellis's nose between my thumb and
the blade. It takes just a bit of pressure, about as much as
to cut a grape in half. That brings him around.

I stand and look behind me to check on Anthony. He's
slumped against the couch. The left side of his shirt is
soaked. "Call an ambulance. Shit, call an ambulance."

Pete skitters out of the hallway into the living room.
He freezes. I show him my blade. He looks uncertain
about it. I spell it out for him. "You want to cry a little
bit?" He doesn't.

Ellis is thrashing, hollering, drumming his heels
against the floor, holding his face in his hands. He's a
bloody mess. So is his carpet. There's no way I can get my
keys out of his pocket. But his cell phone's still on the
coffee table. I snatch it up and back to the front door, my
blade still out.

Pete is saying, "Fuck. Fucking shit." I reach behind my
back and throw the deadbolt, twist the doorknob.

And I am gone.

I run across the street and cross every other street
after that parallel to Park Line. My bearings are off, but
I'm sure if I keep in this direction, I should end up
somewhere along Brook Avenue. My razor's clutched in
my right fist. Ellis's phone in my left. I meet cars in the
street. I hear people up and down the sidewalks on either
side of me. Pass people in their yards. My hands and
arms are streaked with blood. If Ellis and the others don't
call the cops, someone else sure as hell will. I'm not going
to make it to Brook Avenue, and, anyway, I don't need to
show up there looking like this.

I'm at least four or five blocks down, now. There's a
house ahead with a waist-high hedgerow bordering the
yard, and a copse of young sycamores in the corner
nearest me. I slow, scope the area out. No cars, no people.

I check the cross streets. Danish and Paola. I break into a run and hurdle the hedgerow. The toe of my tennis shoe catches a branch and I land on the other side less than gracefully. I lay down on my back in the grass and wriggle my shoulder against the hedge roots. I flip open Ellis's cell and dial.

"Yes?" is the answer to my call.

"Quinn, it's Nicki, I need you to come and get me. Please. Hurry."

"Nicki. Are you all right? What happened?"

"I'll tell you everything, just come and get me. I'm on the east side, south of Brook. Cross streets are Danish and Paola. I'm down behind the hedgerow of a white house with blue trimming on the corner. I can't read the address."

"Okay, I'm on my way."

"All right. Hurry."

"I am. Don't worry. I got you, okay?"

"Yeah."

"Don't hang up in case you need to get in touch with me." He's breathing heavy. Over the earpiece, I hear his apartment door close. "Nicki, what happened?"

"It's Bobby James. Quinn, it's Bobby James again."

Okay, here's the story. This isn't the truth. This isn't even the *exact truth*, as Ellis put it. This is what fucking happened. It'll take a bit of time to tell, so you might want to grab yourself a beer and a sandwich. And take notes, because I won't tell it twice.

Here we go.

I met Bobby James Sounder when I was fourteen. He was thirty. It was the summer right before Quinn and I entered high school. It was especially hot, and the two of us had been spending a lot of time down at the river to cool off. We'd moved downstream, where the water opened up and got some depth for swimming, and the current wasn't so bad. We'd make an afternoon of it. I'd pack us sandwiches and Pepsis and candy bars. Quinn'd bring his boom box. We'd listen to a station out of Portland that played Nirvana and Blind Melon, Bad Religion and Violent Femmes, Mother Love Bone and The Sex Pistols. Those were the best days.

There was an access road that ran along the opposite bank. The freeway passed by a little farther out, and some people used the road as a shortcut to the freeway to bypass all the streetlights and stop signs along the surface streets. We hardly ever saw any cars on it while we were swimming, or maybe there was more traffic than I remember. We hardly paid it any mind.

That day, the station played the rare purely rock-n-roll song. "Welcome to the Jungle." Guns N' Roses. Quinn and I had gotten out of the water for lunch and were lying on the rocky bank to wait out the required twenty minutes after eating. Because cramps were supposed to cripple or kill you if you went back in the water too soon after.

So G N' R came on and I hopped onto a granite bolder and started snaking my shoulders and swaying my hips like Axl in the video. I was wearing shorts and a bikini top and didn't have a lot to show upstairs at the time, but then again, I wasn't going to be passing for a boy from the waist up ever again.

I'd been frustrated by what my body was doing to me, forcing me to tolerate a new period every time I thought I'd just finished the last one, and the shock of a snapped bra strap and giggling boy faces over my shoulder. But that day, none of that mattered because I was with Quinn, and we were the same, and I could slink around like Axl Rose all I wanted.

"Come on, Quinn, dance with me!"

He huffed in frustration. "*No.*"

"Come *on*!"

"*No!*"

You'll stop heaven and earth in their tracks before

you get a fourteen-year-old boy to dance. Mosh? Maybe. Dance. Never.

So I danced alone on the rock, my eyes half-lidded, the sun warm on my skin, the stone getting hot under my feet. The more Axl sang, the more I swayed and worked my muscles to get my body to do what I wanted it to do, and the more I felt like I was finally starting to get a sort of mastery over its latitudes.

I heard somebody wolf-whistle. Drawn-out double notes. Unmistakable. It wasn't Quinn—he was up and looking around quick as me. The sound came from across the river. I squinted my eyes under the flat glare of noon to see who was over there.

A white pickup idled on the shoulder of the access road. I could just make out the chest, arms, and head of the man hanging out the open driver's side window. I shaded my eyes with the flat of my hand. I didn't think I'd ever seen him before.

With my other hand, I waved to him.

He waved back.

"Hey, sweetie!" he called, his voice thinned by distance. "Why don't you come over here and visit for a second! Your boyfriend can come, too!"

"He's my brother!"

"Even better!"

Quinn turned to me. "*Don't go, Nicki.*"

I knew the routine. We'd had seminars and watched videos in school. We were supposed to stay away from strangers. We were taught whole methods for dealing with situations like this. I couldn't remember any of it.

I was starting to feel very warm standing up there on that boulder, and it wasn't the sun or the stone under my feet. I wondered how long he'd been sitting there up in his truck. The idea of me dancing and not knowing he was there watching me filled my stomach with helium. I felt like I might start floating if I thought about it too hard.

I crouched and slid forward off the rock.

"*Nicki,*" Quinn warned.

The man in the pickup called again. "Come on, be friendly! Come across the river! You don't even have to come up from the bank! I'm in a hurry anyway! I got to get going pretty quick!"

"It'll be just for a second," I told Quinn. I started to walk toward the river.

"Nicki, no, come *on*."

"Come with me, then." I looked over my shoulder. "He *said*."

It didn't settle him. Quinn glowered at me, but stood all the same and followed me into the water.

We paddled across the stretch of water, our toes tapping its rocky bed with each shallow kick. I kept the lead, and we reached the shore and waded up onto the opposite bank a minute later. The access road sat a on a four-foot rise about six yards from the edge of the water. This had to be a safe distance, I figured. We could always jump back in the river if there was any danger.

I could see the man clearly now. He was wonderfully male in the way that only adult men can be to adolescent girls who are only a few steps up the path from discovering real maleness for the first time. I couldn't quite take my eyes off the arm he hung out the window, and the tight, defined cords of muscle that ran under the skin. No boys had muscle like that. His blond hair was kind of messy, but perfectly so. He showed me his blue eyes when he nested his sunglasses on his forehead. His jaw was square, his chin dimpled. And his smile was sweet and friendly. And he liked me. I could tell that just the way he was looking at me. He liked me.

"My name's Bobby James."

"Hi. I'm Nicki."

"Hello, Nicki. I'm pleased to meet you."

"Pleased to meet you," I parroted dumbly.

Bobby James turned to Quinn. "What's your name, big guy?"

Quinn crossed his arms and glared at Bobby James.

"He's Quinn," I said. I punched Quinn in the arm.

"*Knock it off*," Quinn hissed.

"Oh, don't do that," Bobby James told me kindly. "Your brother's just being careful. I don't blame him. There are a lot of wackos in the world. He's a smart kid."

"Sorry," I said.

"It's okay." He smiled at me. I suddenly felt the need to take a deep breath.

"You are a very pretty girl, Nicki."

"Thank you."

"I liked the way you were dancing on that rock."

"Thanks."

"Are you going to be a dancer when you grow up?"

"I don't know."

"I think you could be."

I smiled and shifted from one foot to the other.

"You two come out here a lot?"

"Not anymore," Quinn answered.

I clucked my tongue. "*Quinn. Stop it.*" His jaw tensed, his eyes narrowed. "*Quinn.*" He wouldn't look at me.

"Well," Bobby James said, "I do have to get going. I have to be somewhere and I'm already late. But I saw you two, and I always try to make time to meet new friends." He was looking directly at me when he said that. *New friends.* I played the words over in my head.

Bobby James slipped his sunglasses back over his eyes. I was sorry to see that happen. "I hope I see you again," he said. "Both of you. Quinn, I think you're a good man for watching your sister's back like you're doing. You keep on looking out for her. That's a brother's job."

I was getting a little irritated by how much Quinn had gotten Bobby James' attention, but Quinn only scowled and looked downriver.

"'Bye now," Bobby James said.

"'Bye, Bobby James." I felt my face go hot as soon as I spoke his name. I hoped he hadn't noticed.

Bobby James' pickup turned back onto the access road and sped away. I wanted to watch it until it disappeared out of sight, but Quinn was tugging at my elbow and saying, "Come on. Come *on.*" We waded back into the water and swam back to our day site on the shore.

Quinn was sullen the rest of the afternoon. He didn't want to go swimming any more, and he didn't take the Hershey's I tried to give him.

"God, Quinn, what's your problem?"

He was sitting just a foot from the water with his arms wrapped around his knees.

"I don't have a problem."

"The hell you don't." I sat down cross-legged in front of him. "What are you acting all butt-hurt for?"

He didn't say anything.

"You jealous or something?"

"What?"

"Are you jealous because some guy wanted to meet me?"

"Whatever."

"I bet if some girl with big tits pulled up and called us over, you wouldn't even wait around for me."

"Whatever."

"See?"

He dismissed me with a shake of his head.

"What are you being such a dick for?"

"What are you being such a stupid bitch for?"

My jaw dropped. He'd never called me that before. Never. I think he shocked himself as much as he shocked me, because he turned his head away, found a small, flat stone, and side armed it into the river.

I stood. "I'm going home."

I tucked my feet into my tennis shoes, pulled my over-sized t-shirt on, collected the cooler I'd carried our lunch in, and started walking back upstream. I'd just entered the tree line when I heard Quinn rush over the loose stones to catch up to me. I didn't look back at him, and he kept five or six paces behind.

We'd come out on the other side of the trees into the clearing where his house broke into view before he jogged forward and came up beside me.

"Nicki, I'm sorry I called you what I did."

"Whatever."

"I'm sorry I was being a dick."

"Uh-huh." I didn't stop walking.

"Nicki, I'm sorry, okay? I didn't mean it."

I kept walking.

He circled in front of me. I tried to step left. He cut me off. I stepped right. He cut me off.

"Get out of the way."

"Nicki, I'm *sorry*, okay? *Please*."

I stood holding the cooler in front of me with both hands and watching at the wild grass sway around our knees.

"Okay," I granted him.

"You sure?"

"*Okay*, I said."

"You want to do something tomorrow?"

"'Course."

"I can get my mom to give me some money and we can ride into town and get pizza."

"Okay."

"Okay." I raised my eyes to him. He had an uncertain look on his face. Then, very quickly, he leaned forward and kissed me, on the lips, turned, and dashed off toward his house. "I'll call you!" he called back.

I met Bobby James the second time two weeks later. His memory had hardly faded by then, and I had been spending some time imagining what our encounter might have been like if Quinn hadn't been with me at the river. Sometimes I used the detachable showerhead in the master bathroom to explore the possibilities. Like a magic wand, it made my wishes come true.

It was the middle of the week and I'd been biking into town by myself because Quinn had family visiting and his mom was simply not allowing Quinn to get away from home. The two of us talked on the phone in the evenings—he was bored and miserable—but that was the long and short of our contact with each other. I think Miss Halliday was probably trying to keep me away to avoid uncomfortable questions. I suspect now that as far as her family was concerned, Quinn was still the result of an ex-fiancée who had knocked her up and abandoned her, and not the love child of the guy down the road who she'd been diddling on the side. Well, let her sell whatever truth keeps her stocked in smiles and sympathy, I guess.

I was in the record store that used to be on Willow. It was on its last legs by the time it started receiving my patronage and had been dying a slow death before finally going belly-up thanks to Amazon. Not that I knew any better at the time. The world was independent places unto themselves as far as I knew. So, I browsed its CD racks thinking they'd be there forever; browsing only, because I had just enough money to buy myself some lunch, which I would have sacrificed if I could have found anything I wanted in the used-CD bin.

"Well, hi there, Nicki."

I'd been admiring the artwork of a Chili Peppers' album—it was *Blood Sugar Sex Magik*—and I turned with slow suspicion toward the voice behind me that had spoken my name. I was embarrassed to be caught with the CD in my hands; the cover showed a line drawing of each of the band members in profile, one projecting from the top, one from the bottom, the other two from the left and the right, gape-mouthed and extending a long, thorny tongue out to the center to embrace a red rose. I found the image inexplicably titillating, and since I could not pinpoint the reason it turned me on the way it did, I figured my arousal must be symptomatic of some unique personal pathology.

But I'd been thinking of Bobby James a lot lately, like I said, and even though I'd turned his memory into a fantasy love-puppet that was about as true-to-life as the lead singer in an 80's glam rock video, I thought the voice I heard was very much like the voice from the pickup I remembered back when me and Quinn were out by the river. Since I couldn't be sure it was him, and since any attempt to conceal the bewildering perversions of my inner life was undone by the CD cover art in my hands, I made myself aloof and suspicious, and turned very slowly to see who it was that had spoken my name, in a way that would make it plain to anybody watching that I couldn't give two good farts one way or the other whom it might be.

I beamed when I saw Bobby James' face and the smile I was sure he must reserve only for me.

"Hi, Bobby James!"

"How're you doing?" he smiled.

"I'm okay. Just looking for new music, you know." I wasn't about to admit I couldn't afford any of it.

He stepped forward—he was much taller than I'd imagined him to be in the pickup—and slid the CD out of my fingers. His fingertips brushed my skin, and the whole side of my hand tingled unbearably where he touched me.

"Red Hot Chili Peppers, huh?"

"Yeah." I watched his face for approval.

He turned to someone behind him. "You like these guys, right?"

Bobby James' companion stepped up and looked over his shoulder at the cover. "Yeah. This record's a good one." From what I could see of his face, half hidden by Bobby James', the other guy looked around twentyish, as far as I could judge such an advanced age as that at the time, but his voice was high like an uncertain teenager's.

Bobby James slipped the CD back into my hands. "You going to get it?"

I shrugged. "Probably not today." I put it back in its place in the rack.

"By the way." Bobby James stepped aside to give me a view of his friend. "This is Jonathan. Jonathan, this is Nicki."

"Hi."

"Hi." Jonathan was taller than Bobby James, though younger. He looked just older than the seniors I'd be seeing in high school. He was slightly stoop-shouldered and his jaw line was a little droopy. His middle was a little droopy. His dishwater blonde hair was combed carelessly to the side so that his bangs accidentally puffed at his brow. His eyebrows were too straight over eyes too round. The bulb of his nose was too round, too. There was roundness at his shoulders, his elbows, his abdomen. Lanky as he was, he couldn't escape from round. I was not impressed.

He extended a hand to me. I shook it, felt knobby knuckles under my fingers.

"Me and Jonathan were just about to grab some lunch. Do you want to come with us?"

"Oh, um, I don't know."

"Come on."

"My bike's outside."

"It'll be safe. Come on, lunch is on me."

"Okay."

"Your brother here?" He searches the store. "He can come, too."

"No. He's got family in town."

"*He's* got family in town?"

I tilted my head. I didn't understand the question.

"His family's different that yours?"

Oh. "Um," I couldn't figure out how to explain it, "yeah."

Bobby James bobbed his head. "Fair enough. So, what do you like to eat? Choice is yours."

I shrugged. "Um, I don't know." This was not going at all like the showerhead had promised. I was supposed to be taller, more confident. We were supposed to be by ourselves, not with some other guy I didn't know. I was supposed to be able to talk to him like I talked to Quinn. I was supposed to be able to make him laugh and look at me with admiration. I wiped my palms on my jeans.

"You like pizza?"

I shrugged. "Sure."

Bobby James smiled. "Come on. Let's go."

Outside, he lead me across the stout parking lot to a metal blue Chevrolet Nova.

"I thought you had a pickup?"

"Oh, that's what I take when I have to go out of town. This is my town car."

Bobby James had two cars? My mom and dad had two cars, but not each, and they only got the second one when my mom got a job.

"You want to ride up front with me, right, Nicki?"

... with me ...

He asked like he was really hoping I would.

"Yeah, okay."

"You don't mind riding in back, do you, Jonathan?"

"Sure, whatever."

He opened the passenger-side door and let me climb in, shutting it after me. Jonathan got in behind me. By the time Bobby James got behind the wheel, my heart was pounding so hard it hurt. I wanted to fling the door open and run; I wanted to stay in the car next to Bobby forever. I hoped no one would see us; I hoped everyone would see us.

Bobby James revved the Nova's engine and we cruised over to the east end of town. The place we stopped at was called the Stone Oven. I'd never eaten there before. It smelled like heaven inside the front doors.

Bobby James sat next to me in the booth. His knee touched mine. I didn't move my knee away. He asked me, "Is there anything you don't like?"

"I don't know. Anchovies, I guess."

"Great." He ordered a deluxe special.

At first, Jonathan and I talked more than either of us talked with Bobby. Jonathan knew a lot about music. I was beginning to think he was pretty cool. Not as cool as Bobby James. Definitely nowhere near as good-looking.

Halfway through my first slice, Bobby James asked me, "So, how old are you, Nicki?"

Shit. Should I lie? What could I get away with? I wanted to say I was eighteen, but I didn't think they would buy it. I thought I might get away with sixteen, but that might bring up other questions that would open up the lie.

I said, "I turn fifteen in February."

"You're fourteen?" Jonathan gawked.

"*Sshhh ...* ," Bobby warned. He turned to look at me.

I wiped my hands on my jeans and shrugged. I should have lied.

Bobby said, "I had you pegged for older."

"Really?" I smiled.

"So," Bobby James said, "you start high school next year?"

"Yeah."

"Are you nervous?"

"I don't know. Yeah, a little, I guess."

"Yeah. It's not so bad, really. Freshman year sucks." He laughed. I laughed, too. "I'm not going to lie. But after you start meeting people it gets better. Jonathan's brother's going to be a senior next year."

"Really?"

"Yeah. His name's Tony. I doubt you'll have any classes together, but I'll tell him to look out for you on the quad."

"Cool. Um, how's he going to know who I am?"

"I'll just tell him to look for your beautiful eyes."

My face burned. I finished my first slice. It was good, but I was too thrilled to be sitting next to Bobby James— even as much as he had just embarrassed me—to have an appetite. As I reached for a second slice, to be polite— the guys were already halfway through their third— Bobby and Jonathan got into an animated discussion, and I felt his knee leave my side. I was heartbroken. I wondered if he'd moved it because he found out I was fourteen. I wanted to scoot closer to him, but I didn't want to be obvious about it. So, I just picked the toppings off my pizza and sulked over my lonely knee.

When we got back into Bobby James' Nova, Bobby revved the engine and said to Jonathan, "Since we're right by your house, do you mind if I just drop you off now?"

There was silence from the backseat. I couldn't see Jonathan, but I recognized the bitter tang of sullenness.

"Jonathan? Is that okay?"

"Sure, fine, whatever."

Jonathan lived a block-and-a-half around the corner behind the pizza place. Bobby James braked at the curb and Jonathan leaned forward. "Thanks for the pizza, Bobby."

"Anytime, buddy."

"It was nice meeting you, Nicki."

"Nice meeting you, Jonathan."

He climbed out of the car and shut the door behind him. As we were pulling away, he looked back and waved to me. I waved back. He smiled and turned toward his house.

Bobby said, "What time do you have to be home?"

"I don't know. Before it gets dark."

"Okay. Because I want to take you someplace. Is that all right?"

"Where?"

"You'll see."

My stomach was tight. I didn't know why, but I wished Jonathan was still with us.

"It's not far."

I regretted not telling him I had to be back earlier. I considered making something up, like, *Oh, I forgot. My mom and dad want me home early because bullshit bullshit.* The problem was, I couldn't fill in the bullshit blanks.

"It's not far, Nicki. Come on."

I looked at him. There was that smile that he saved just for me.

"Okay. I guess."

The radio was on. The station was playing 80's music. That was okay. We drove for a while without talking. Bobby James pointed the Nova north of town and up into the woods.

Bobby said, "Do you have a boyfriend, Nicki?"

My chest got tight.

"Uh-uh."

"What about Quinn?"

I turned to him. "Quinn's my brother."

He was silent a moment. "Are you sure?"

"*Huh*?"

"Well, you said he had family visiting. But not your family. I don't quite understand that. I mean, I have a couple brothers and sisters and we all have the same family."

"Oh. Well, um, Quinn has a different mom than I do."

"*Oh*. So he's your half-brother."

"Yeah, I guess. But I like Quinn better than my other brothers. They're dicks."

Bobby James laughed. I laughed, too.

We followed a winding two-lane on an upgrade for ten or fifteen minutes. Bobby pulled the Nova off the road, and let it coast down an unpaved path through the trees for another two minutes. Then the trees opened before us, and a vista of the town, about a mile below, broke into view.

"Oh," I said.

"Great, isn't it?"

"Yeah."

He killed the engine and we sat in silence. The view was nice, but it could only take so much looking at. I wasn't sure what I was supposed to do.

Bobby James put his hand on my knee. "Nicki." My heart was in my throat. I looked at him. "I think you're very pretty. I like you." I took a deep breath.

"I like you, Bobby."

"Do you?" He took his hand away, leaned across the seat, and combed his fingers through my hair. My arms lay limp on the seat at my sides.

"Mm-hm."

He cupped the back of my head and I let him draw me to him. I wanted him more than anything.

Vick Turner was the first boy I kissed. Quinn was the first boy who kissed me. But Bobby James Sounder was not the first guy I ever made out with.

*   *   *   *

I shouldn't have, but I told Quinn. I had to tell somebody. I was on the phone in the kitchen. Mom, Dad, and the brothers were downstairs in the TV room. I'd been in a daze since I'd gotten home at five. I was caught up in the rush of the afternoon, and of how it finished. A whirlwind spun inside my head, throwing about the random flash of memory—Bobby's practiced hands on me; my hands on his hard muscle; his mouth open to mine; his mouth on my throat. Outside my head, I probably looked and acted like a zombie. I could hardly keep up with everyone else around me. Bobby James crowded them all out.

"*God, Nicki, you can't do that.*"

I bristled. In my head I heard him calling me a stupid bitch. He'd apologized for that, but the tone he'd used then was the tone he was using now. I was sure he was thinking *stupid bitch* even if he wasn't saying it.

"*God*, Quinn."

"This Bobby guy is like forty years old."

"No, he's not."

"He's old."

"He's not older than, like, Dave Grohl."

"Dave Grohl's too old to make out with, too."

"*God, Quinn, I knew I shouldn't have told you anything.*"

"Nicki, he's *not supposed to be taking you for car rides to make out with you*. It's illegal. I mean, he could go to *jail* for it."

We were getting into a whisper-shouting match over the phone line.

"He's *not* going to go to *jail*."

"He *could* because he's a *pervert*."

"*God*! He's *not a pervert*."

"*Yes, he is.*"

"*He's not a pervert*! *He just likes me. He said so*!"

"*He's not supposed to like you*!"

"*Why not*?"

"*Because he's a-fucking-hundred years older than you, Nicki*. God *damn it*!"

"You don't know shit about this. *You don't know shit*

about me."

"*Nicki, he could hurt you.*"

"*He won't.*"

"*He could kidnap you.*"

"*Oh, fuck, Quinn.*"

"*Nicki,* please *don't see him anymore.*"

But I had already made plans with Bobby James for Friday night. I wasn't going to tell Quinn about them. I didn't think he could do anything to stop me. Even if he tried to tell my dad or mom, neither was likely to invite him in for sugar cookies. Do you remember last Saturday night at The Wheatpenny when Quinn told Rudy Foreman that our dad had said fuck-all to him in twenty-three years? He wasn't kidding. Answering the phone and saying into the receiver, *Just a minute, I'll get Nicki,* doesn't count.

I did bring Quinn over to meet my dad once. His dad. Our dad. Still can't figure out the phrasing. It was about a week after we'd confirmed to ourselves that we were brother and sister, and the whole thing was starting to sink in for the both of us. Quinn had been asking me daily about Dad: What did he look like? What did he act like? Was he nice? What did he do for work? Did my dad ever ask about Quinn? (Quinn always referred to Dad as *your dad*.) Finally, I got it through my thick head that maybe I should introduce the two of them. My dad was as much Quinn's dad as he was Lewis and Terry's, after all, yeah?

(By the way, I'm not exactly sure what my mom told Lewis and Terry about Quinn. They never seemed especially interested in him, and never asked me about him. Sometimes they'd call him my boyfriend to tease me. And Quinn never seemed interested in them. They might have been Quinn's brothers as much as I was his sister, but, for him, Lewis and Terry might as well have touched ground in a UFO.)

"My dad comes home at four-thirty," I told him that day. "My mom's already home, but we can hide in the horse stalls until Dad gets here and meet him in the driveway. That way, my mom won't know." It would still be a few months up the road till my mom gave up punishing me for playing with Quinn; but at that time, if she saw me bringing him onto our property, she might very well have grounded me for life and figured out some way to take my birthday away.

"*Can* I see him?" Quinn pleaded.

"Yes, of course, silly." Even now it's touching, my confidence in my father.

We made a game of getting to the horse stalls. We circled eastward through the fields on the opposite side of the road, then, as we came to the edge of the neighbor's property, we crossed Ludlow Avenue onto my property. From there, we crouched down and headed toward my house, keeping low and always placing a lone tree or a stand of tall grass or a hillock between the two of us and the house, almost as if the house were a spider and the windows its dozens of eyes.

Thanks to other games we'd invented, we were, to our knowledge, experts in stealth. We took our time, planned our moves, and meticulously followed the courses we'd set, so when we finally arrived at the horse stalls, we didn't need to wait much longer for my dad to pull up into the driveway and park the car. I popped out from behind the slanting wood and jogged half the short distance to his car. He saw me through the windshield, and when he opened the door and stepped out, he said, "What's up, Pixie?"

"Dad, come here." I motioned him to follow.

"Right now?"

"*Yes.* Come *on.*" I was sure my mom would walk out onto the porch for no reason at all and ruin the whole thing.

He huffed. "Okay." He closed the door and followed me.

Quinn was standing, wide-eyed, nervously rubbing one arm, when I came around behind the stall. My dad was just a few steps behind.

"What'cha got, Pix?"

I took a position next to Quinn and turned him to face

153

my dad just as he rounded the side. My dad came to a dead stop in his tracks. The look on his face told me I had done something very wrong.

I tried to save the three of us: "Look, Dad, it's Quinn!"

Quinn said, "Hi."

At the sound of Quinn's voice, my dad's face drained of color. He stood silent, looking left, right, left, right; me, Quinn, me, Quinn, me. He reached out. I thought he might pull Quinn toward him in a hug. Instead, he snaked his arm past Quinn, clasped the back of my neck, and said, "Nicki," tugging me forward, "come here." My legs trotted under his command without letting me in on the plan. "Nicki," he said, still pulling me, "he's not supposed to be here."

"But he is."

"Nicki, you can't do this to you mother.'

"Mom doesn't care ..."

He drew me to him. "Come on, let's go to the house. It's time you come in, anyway." His eyes searched for anything besides me or Quinn. As the hand on the back of my neck slid to the middle of my back, he turned and began gently coaxing me away. I looked back at Quinn. The expression I saw on his face made me feel so ashamed of what I had done, I wriggled away from my dad.

"*Dad ...*"

He grabbed my shoulder and spun me to face him. "*What are you thinking*?" he shouted.

I started to cry. "*I'm sorry ...*"

His hand still clamped to my shoulder, he tugged me with him toward the house. When we got to the front step, he whirled me toward him again and said, "You better dry those up. I don't want your mother asking questions."

I looked back toward the horse stalls, but my dad took my chin and pulled my face away. "Don't look over there. Look at me and dry those tears up, understand."

"*Daddy, please ...*"

"Nicki ..."

154

"*He's my brother, please, please, please ...*" I don't know what I was begging from him. If it was acceptance, he didn't have any to give.

"*He's no one.*"

"*No!*"

We must have been making a commotion, because the front door swung open.

"What is going on?" My mom looked from me to my dad.

My dad stood up. "Oh, nothing, Bette. Nicki just got scared by a dog. A big one, out in the fields."

"A dog?"

"Yeah. She's okay, though, aren't you, Pix?"

I couldn't do much more than cry.

"Come on," my dad said. "Let's go inside and get you some ice cream."

I got it, but it was all for appearances. My dad had to finish what he'd served me. Strawberry. Loved the stuff, but I'd have never finished the mountain he'd spooned out, even at my most gluttonous. My appetite had vanished. My stomach was cramped and my chest hurt and I was getting a headache, and all this was the pain of making my dad mad at me and hurting Quinn so badly. I couldn't take the weight of my crimes.

By the look on her face, my mom wasn't buying the dog story, but she wasn't asking for any other explanations from either of us. She just watched me from the other end of the table with a kind of weird fascination. To this day, I cannot guess what she was getting from my tears.

Finally, my dad said, "Why don't you go up to your room until you can settle yourself down." I trudged off and cried into my pillow until after dinner.

Quinn forgave me, of course, and so did my dad. Over the next few days, I played the scene behind the horse stall again and again in my head. Every time I watched it, one certainty cemented itself in my mind: more than anyone else, *far* more, Quinn was mine, and I was his.

That day, that discovery, is why I argued so long with

Quinn over Bobby James; his resistance rattled me. He had never set himself against me before. I'd had him at my side for so long, after having no one there for even longer, his betrayal tipped me off balance. I couldn't understand where it came from. I'd have understood it from my mom, Lewis and Terry, even my dad. But not Quinn. I had to get him back by my side again. He'd seen Bobby's smile, after all, the same smile I knew, so it never occurred to me that Quinn was actually afraid for me.

Friday afternoon, I snuck my bike out of the shed behind the house and hid it on the far side of the bungalow. I'd told Bobby I wouldn't be able to head out to Cowen Road, where he was going to meet me, until ten. He said that was fine with him, we could stay up all night. I was so excited my stomach hurt all day.

Lewis and Terry had cars and were out of the house with friends. My mom and dad always went to bed early, but they'd stay up watching television in their room until as late as nine-thirty. When the dancing blue light of the set winked out and the murmured words went silent, I wrapped my arms tight around my chest to keep myself in bed for another full half-hour. At nine-fifty-four, I slipped out from under the covers and dressed in the clothes I'd laid out for myself. I crept all the way outside in my socks to keep myself soundless. I put on my shoes on the porch and sprinted for my bike.

The moon wasn't quite full, but it shed enough light to see by. The ride down Ludlow to Cowen Road took three minutes. I'd timed it every day since Wednesday. There are no streetlights down Ludlow, and only a few on Brown. As two of them came into view, I squinted to find the shape of Bobby's Nova. I didn't see it, and started to panic a little. Had I said I would *meet* him at ten, instead of leave the house at ten? Had he waited there for me and left, thinking I wouldn't show? I peddled faster.

There is a copse of trees on the left side, a few yards before the cross street when you're heading toward

Brown. Once I'd cleared them, I saw Bobby's car. I waved. I couldn't see inside the car, but I heard the horn toot two brief notes. I brought my bike to a stop, then wheeled it back to the copse and lay it among the undergrowth. Then I turned and sprinted to the Nova. The passenger-side door opened, and the dome light came on, and there was Bobby James with a smile for me.

"How you doing, beautiful?"

"I'm good." I slid onto the seat, pulled the door closed behind me, and when I turned back around, Bobby was leaning over to give me a welcoming kiss on the lips. I had never been happier in my life. When he started to pull away, I grabbed his shoulders and drew him back to me for another kiss.

"Glad to see you, too," he chuckled when I finally released him.

"I missed you so much, Bobby."

"I missed you, too."

"I thought about you all the time." I wanted him to know I wasn't taking him for granted.

"I thought about you a lot, too." He started the car.

"Where are we going?"

"We're going to take a trip over to my friend Ted Wells' house."

"What for?" I was disappointed. I'd thought we were going to be alone together.

Bobby shifted into gear and headed the car east on Ludlow, toward town. He said, "Ever gotten high?"

"Um, yeah." He looked at me quizzically, but I was telling the truth. I'd gotten high with Terry and Lewis and their friends a couple of times out in the back forty. They'd let me join them, not because they were trying to be cool to me, but because they thought it'd be funny to get their little sister stoned.

"Have you?" Bobby asked.

"Sure." I tried to use a tone that would make myself sound like an old hand at pot smoking, but my heart was pounding. When I was with Lewis and Terry, no matter how much they made fun of me, I knew I was safe. Our parents would have killed them if they'd let anything happen to me. (My mom hated me, but she didn't want the trouble of a dead or broken daughter on her hands, either.) I'd feel so secure I'd go slipping off, hand-in-hand, with Alex Sturgeon or Stuart Chandler, or whoever. But there was a mile of difference between smoking with my brothers and making-out with their friends, and the place I was heading to that night, way past curfew, in Bobby's car. I knew Bobby would never hurt me—despite what Quinn kept saying—but how could I know how far I could trust him to protect me?

"Will anybody else be there?"

"Shouldn't be. Ted has a roommate, but I'm pretty sure he'll be out all night."

"Oh. This Ted guy, is he all right?"

"Sure. Ted's one of my best friends."

"Okay."

Bobby put a reassuring hand on my knee. "Don't worry. You're with me."

I put my hand over his and entwined our fingers together.

Ted's house was a ranch-style in a neighborhood full of ranch-styles fronted by snubbed-in front yards behind short, chain link fences. A basketball hoop hung over Ted Wells' garage door.

Before we got out, Bobby took out a cell phone and dialed a number. He said into the mouthpiece, "Hey it's me. I'm right outside. Uh-huh ... Nicki. Yeah, she's with me. Yup." He folded the cell and looked at me and smiled. "Ready for a little partying?"

Ted Wells was narrow-faced and sharp-nosed, with a long chin under full lips. His cheek bones were high, like a Native American's or an Asian's. He wasn't bad-looking. I couldn't tell if he was Bobby's age or closer to Jonathan's. I was fascinated with his thick black hair that might have built itself into a natural pompadour if he hadn't kept his bangs swept to the side. I wondered if one day he might let me style his hair. I just kind of wanted to run my fingers through it.

He was friendly, though his eyes seemed to behold everything and everyone in the room through a pall of overfilled disinterest. At the time, I would have called him *mysterious*. With a skin-cap and some make-up, he would have made a great Count Orloff for Halloween. Max Schrek, not Klaus Kinskey.

Bobby introduced the two of us to each other. Ted shook my hand. "I've heard a lot about you."

"*Oh*." I was delighted. Bobby really was thinking of me while we were apart.

"Want a beer?" Ted asked.

"Sure," I said. I'd had a beer before—thanks to Lewis and Terry, again—but I'd never gotten drunk.

Ted went to the kitchen and Bobby and I took a seat together on the couch in the living room. I curled up against him. Without missing a beat, he put his arm around my shoulders. "I thought we were going to smoke pot?" I said.

"We are." Bobby kissed my forehead. "Be patient."

I was patient, and buzzed, by the time Ted broke out the pipe. It was better stuff than I'd ever had with Lewis and Terry. Ted warned me, "Take it easy," after I blew a double lunged-cloud after my first hit. The thing with pot is, for me, you don't really realize you're stoned until you fuck up. You know, word something the wrong way, forget what it is the hell you've been talking about for the last five minutes, or just realize for the first time that someone's in the middle of a conversation with you. Ted had put some music on the stereo, and that night my fuck up came when I said, "Oh, wow, I love this song," and sent Bobby and Ted into gales of laughter.

"What?" It occurred to me how much of a balloon I felt like. Or, not all of me, but my cheeks. And how heavy my eyelids were.

Bobby recovered himself enough to tell me, "That's the third fucking time you said that in the last two minutes."

"Nuh-uh."

"Yeah."

"Shit. Yeah?"

That sent them off again. I started to laugh, too. It was some funny shit.

Ted and Bobby started talking about people I'd never heard of. I started to become very aware of Bobby's arms, around me, and the shape of his chest under the palms of my hands, under his t-shirt. I wanted to kiss him very badly. I wondered if we were going to leave and drive up into the woods again. When a lull came in the conversation, I took the opportunity to crane my head toward Bobby's. He turned and kissed me; he started to pull away first, but I caught him and gave him a deeper, longer kiss. Then we started going at it. I was lost in the moment, but I became aware of how Bobby was guiding our bodies, and I realized that we were putting on a performance for Ted. I let him ride my body with his hands. It was exciting. I threw myself into the passion of the moment. I got my hand down between Bobby's legs. He was hard. I'd never touched a penis before. I had never even seen a live penis, except for those unhappy chance sightings of flopping Vienna sausages when Terry was peeing with the door open or Lewis was stepping out of the shower. Even Quinn's dick was a mystery to me. The two of us had never even so much as played doctor together. But after I'd started my intimate relationship with my parents' showerhead, I'd pulled out one of Terry's porn DVDs he kept hidden in the bottom draw of his bureau, as a study aid. (I'd caught him putting them away a year earlier and extorted fifty dollars from him to keep quiet.) I paid particular attention to blowjobs. It didn't look difficult. I thought it might be a brilliant way to get a look at Bobby's penis.

I stroked him through his jeans. He groaned and clutched me tighter. He was hurting me a little, but I didn't mind. I said, "Do you want to take it out?"

"Really?"

"Mm-hm."

He leaned back and worked the button and zipper on his jeans. And there it was. In all its glory. It wasn't nearly

160

as big as the ones in Terry's pornos, but I supposed that was sort of a relief. But now that it was out, I wasn't sure what to do. The dicks in Terry's pornos had always been two-dimensional. This thing here aimed itself straight at me; its blind socket hypnotized me like a puppy or a snake. I reached a hand toward it. I hesitated.

Bobby said, "It's okay. Go ahead."

I wrapped my fingers around it. It was warmer than his mouth. I squeezed it.

Bobby flinched. "Easy, easy. It's not like gripping the monkey bars."

"Sorry."

"It's okay. Have you ever done this before?"

Should I lie? "Uh-uh."

"Take your time."

I stroked it, leaned close to it. I was starting to have some doubts about the whole thing. I remembered how blowjobs ended in Terry's pornos. I said, "Um, when you ... You know ... When it happens, um, don't ... You know ... Don't do it. I mean, let me know ... Before ..."

"I will."

He didn't need to, though.

He said, "That feels really good, but it's just not going to happen tonight."

I must have given him some sort of look.

"The pot and stuff," he explained.

I was relieved.

Anyway, I bet Ted Wells got a pretty good show.

Later when we all took another hit, my second of the night, Bobby and Ted's third, I made my second fuck up.

Oh, it was a doozey.

I said, "Bobby? Can I be your girlfriend?"

Dumb silence followed. Then Ted snorted, and Bobby barked a short laugh before he could stop himself. He said, "Isn't there a blonde joke that goes something like that?"

I felt my face burn. I clucked my tongue and pulled

away from Bobby.

He caught me and pulled me back to him. "No. No."

I wasn't having it and told him, "Oh, fuck off."

"No," he said. "I'm sorry. We're not laughing at you."

"Yes, you are." I pushed against his chest, but he wasn't letting go. My eyes were hot. He said, "Sweetie, we weren't laughing at you. Okay? I promise." Ted Wells said, "Sorry, Nicki." He gave me a sideways grin that made me want to be unfaithful to Bobby James; he added, when he saw he had my firm attention, "I honestly wasn't laughing at you. It was just the situation."

Didn't really make me feel any better, but I allowed Bobby to settle me back against him anyway. Ted said, "I'll get us some more beers." While he was in the kitchen, I asked Bobby, "Do you have a girlfriend?" There was a pit in my stomach. My chest hurt.

"No. I don't have a girlfriend."

Years later I found out Bobby James Sounder had three girlfriends while he was picking me up around Cowen Road. There was one he went around town with. Her name was Cindy Beckett. She was twenty-three. The other two were Amy-Anne Rhodes and Karen Sellard. They were both sixteen. I've heard since that Cindy Beckett used to pull trains with Bobby James and his friends. I can't vouch for the truth of it—I don't know her, haven't even met her personally—but I can't help feeling some sort of solidarity with the poor girl. It makes me feel sick to my stomach that the thing he was going to do to me probably wasn't the worst thing he'd ever done. Christ, how does a girl get called a whore, when a guy can pull shit like that and run for mayor?

"But let's wait a little while, okay?" he said.

I was disappointed. I was still embarrassed and a little hurt. But then the pot started swimming in, and I put my arms around Bobby, and my head against his chest, and I decided that, with or without his permission, at least for the rest of the night, I'd be his girlfriend.

* * * *

Bobby James got me back to Cowen Road just after four in the morning. I collapsed into my bed about five minutes later. My bike was still in the copse. I'd had Bobby take me all the way to my driveway because there was no way I was making it down Ludlow Road on my own. He kissed me before I shouldered my way out of the Nova and said to meet him Monday outside the record shop at noon. I'd sort of worried that he wouldn't want to see me again, but now I could creep into the house bathed in a warm daze that only had a little to do with pot, beer, and exhaustion. Because Bobby James Sounder was going to be mine, pretty soon. How could I not be sure?

The other dates with Bobby over the next month and a half went progressively downhill. The best were when it was just the both of us alone. But sometimes Ted Wells was with us, and other times Jonathan Garver was. Sometimes a bunch of guys and girls joined us. Everyone was past high school age by at least a couple of years.

I went down on Bobby a few more times, but never in front of anybody again. I was so humiliated the next time I saw Ted Wells, I wanted to die, but he never so much as mentioned it, even on the sly. Anyway, the first two times afterward, I told Bobby to warn me, and he did. I cleaned him up with whatever cloth was laying around. The third and fourth time I told him not to say anything and he didn't and it was pretty cool, but only because of the moment. I liked him a lot, mind you. Maybe I even loved him; or, at least, loved the person I thought he was. I wanted to make him happy. Honestly. Can't help I didn't see he didn't deserve it.

Should I mention I was still a virgin at the time? Seems to matter now that I think back on all of it, but none of Bobby's friends ever bothered to ask whether or not I was. Bobby James sure as shit never did.

My parents had suspicions about my night jaunts, but

I was never caught. I'd only sleep till noon or two o'clock and crawl out of bed hung-over and surly. Lewis and Terry had been doing the same thing for years, so Mom gave me the lecture she'd given them: I had better not get arrested, I had better not get found with drugs or alcohol in my possession, and all the fun and games were going to damn well stop once school let in. Yeah, yeah.

My dad was well on his way to drunkhood by this time. He'd mix himself a VO-and-Seven or a Jack-and-Coke the second he stepped through the door after work, even before he changed out of his work clothes, and was blitzed on the recliner in the TV room by eight-thirty. His deepening alcoholism was wearing a hole in my mom, which meant straying over the edge and tumbling down right into her furnace was getting too easy a thing to do for me. Even Lewis and Terry got a snap from her now and then, but I got the brunt of her frustration. She never hit me again, but I got a lot of arm-twisting, which I had started to tolerate with less and less aplomb. I felt I was much too old for her to jerk me around like that. After all, I was drinking, smoking pot, staying out all night, hanging out with twenty-year-olds, and having oral sex; who the fuck was she to grab me?

During this stretch, I treated Quinn very badly. Doesn't give me any pride to say I was a shit to him. We'd still hang out, but what did he have to offer that could compete with Bobby James and the gang? I got him to smoke pot a couple times; the pipe and weed were gifts from Ted Wells. I think he did it just to please me, but his dopey eyes and his giggling just made him seem obsolete. I was so far ahead, and he could do nothing else but bore me with his new discoveries.

Me and Jonathan Garver, on the other hand—believe it or not—had started to strike up a real friendship. I had fun talking with him about music and movies. And books, too. He was a reader, like no one else I knew except for Quinn. His thing was science fiction, and we'd trade titles back and forth. Most of his stuff left me cold (like most of my stuff left him, I'd wager), but there were some good writers he introduced me to who I've followed, off-and-on, even to this day. The best thing about Jonathan was how he never made me feel like a child. When Bobby James was with everyone else, I felt dumb and young. But Jonathan was a buddy to me, without fail. There were times when he and I would just wander off from the group and talk. I would always hope for a night with Bobby James, but I never lamented if it turned into a night with Jonathan.

Problem was, he took these times too seriously. Once we were off in the corner and he tried to hold my hand. I pulled it away and giggled. He looked hurt, but I kissed him on the cheek and he blushed. A part of me thinks that if I had been free from my stupid crush on Bobby James, Jonathan would have been my boyfriend, and everything would have turned out differently.

A very, *very* small part of me.

The rest of me just fucking hates him.

I never asked Bobby James if I could be his girlfriend again, and he never asked if I would.

The afternoon before the lake, Quinn and had I rode into town to hang out at the strip mall on Rainard and Vine. There was a used book and record shop there, alongside an arcade and a sandwich place, as well as a second-run movie theater around the corner.

We'd planned to hit each one, one after the other. We only made it to the bookshop together. I'd slipped off to the bio section and was combing the titles for rock stars. The pickings were slim. I was thinking I'd have to make a trip to the library soon, which was disappointing since I was trying to build up the little personal library in my room. My shelf was lined with Roald Dahl and Judy Blume and Ellen Wittlinger and J. K. Rowling and whatever. Now I was trying line my bookshelf with all the shabbiest, unauthorized life-stories of the hip and decadent I could lay my hands on. Quinn was browsing the young adult section. We used to sometimes swap books with each other. He'd given me the John Bellairs books a couple of years ago, starting with *The House with a Clock in Its Walls*. I liked those. I'd gotten him to read a handful of Judy Blumes, which he liked more than he's ever admitted. Lately, he'd gotten turned on to Robert Cormier and had foisted *The Chocolate War* on me earlier that summer. I thought it was a weird and depressing book and refused to read anymore of Cormier's stuff because of it. Our personal literary tastes had started to stray from one another's.

Well, that's only partly true. I'd begun to resist nearly anything Quinn had to offer. He'd lost his glamour in my eyes. Everything he touched went a little gray in his hands.

Also, that day, I was feeling particularly surly. Summer's end was so close, I was starting to bang my head against it, and I knew my mom wasn't kidding about putting a halt to my nighttime roaming. I was afraid Bobby James might find another girl if I failed to make it out to see him anymore. He'd said he didn't have a girlfriend, but at the same time, he'd never said *I* was his girlfriend. How could I know he didn't have a lot of girls like me lined up, waiting for his attention? The idea dropped a desperate ache into my stomach that wouldn't go away and got heavier and heavier with each passing day.

In the bookstore, Quinn came around a shelf and walked down the aisle toward me.

"Find anything?" he said.

"No."

"Me neither. You want to go get something to eat?"

"I'm not hungry."

"Well, I am."

"So, go get something to eat."

"Well, what are you going to do?"

"I don't know."

"Are you going to come with me, or are you going to

stay here?"

"*I don't know.*"

"Well, can you make up your fucking mind?"

I glowered at him. "I'll fucking stay here."

He sighed. "Why?"

"Because I'm not fucking hungry."

"Why don't you just sit with me?"

"Why the fuck would I want to do that?"

"Because—" He threw his arms into the air. "*I don't know.*"

"Neither do I."

"*Fuck*, Nicki."

"*Fuck*, Quinn."

"Jesus Christ, when are you going to come off your fucking period?"

"When your nuts finally drop."

I was taking sadistic pleasure in this. I wasn't just trying to push him away, I was trying to unload a little of the dark, heavy ache in my stomach, trying to roll the weight over onto Quinn. If I was my mom's voodoo doll, then Quinn was starting to become mine. I had good reason to dread the end of summer: Bobby James was starting to get tired of me. When we were alone, he couldn't get enough of me, but when other people were around, he'd shift away from me, pull my arms off from around him, or, if Jonathan was around, send me off with him, my babysitter, I suppose, for those times when Bobby wanted to go play with the grown-ups.

Worse, I caught him flirting with other guys' girlfriends.

The Thursday before, he'd taken me to a party at a house I'd never been to before. There was a girl there, Brittany Drewes. She was a pretty blonde with a big rack. Bobby sent me off to grab us a couple of beers. When I came back, he was sitting on the couch with her, close, knees touching, the both of them speaking through big grins and staring with moon-eyes.

Jealousy is the worst place you can be. It makes you small and helpless. It makes you desperate and sick. It collapses all your thoughts into a single pinpoint. It puts all your self-worth up for sale, and the going-rate is cheap. A steal, really.

I handed Bobby his beer and made a point of sitting on the other side of him, and I wrapped my arms around his neck. Brittany Drewes needed to know her trespass, and I needed to show her. Bobby tolerated me for a bit, then he shrugged me off, flipping my arms free of him and hissing, "*Okay*, Nicki."

I let him go and threw my back against the couch and sulked. When that didn't kill him, I stood up and walked outside. I bummed a cigarette and smoked it with some of the boys out there while I waited for Bobby's desperation to build to misery and he came after me. There was a guy who wanted me to do shots with him, but I couldn't stand tequila at the time, which seemed to be the only shot in his world, so I wandered off.

I went back inside and caught Bobby James in the hallway. I thrust the flat of my hands against his chest and pushed him into a bathroom. I kicked the door shut behind me with my heel and dropped down before him. He batted my hands away as I tried to work his zipper. "*Nicki,* come on, *not now.*" He dodged around me, twisted the door knob, and slipped back outside, leaving me on my knees.

I turned all my dread and helplessness into pins and stuck them in to Quinn. I don't know why I chose him. Maybe because he would be the most hurt by them. Probably because he reminded me of who I was; a dumb little fourteen-year-old from the wrong side of Cowen Road.

So, anyway, that comment about Quinn's nuts dropping? I guess they did right then, because he turned and walked out the door. And can you believe how pissed off I was at him for leaving me?

Bobby picked me up the usual time; the two of us had gotten nervier since the first night—he drove right up to the end of my driveway, and I walked straight out the front door to meet him, regardless of who knew I was leaving the house. That night, Jonathan and Ted were inside the Nova with him. I climbed in back with Jonathan. Bobby barely bothered to ask if I wanted to sit up front with him anymore. My privileges had been on a dwindling course, slowly but surely.

"Hey, Nicki," Jonathan said.

"Hi," Ted called back.

"Hi," I said and shut the door. "Hi, Bobby."

"Hey there, sweetie." He revved the engine and squealed the tires.

"Hey, *sshhh*!" I warned. Just because I'd leave the house boldly, didn't mean I thought we were free to push our luck. My parents still didn't know who I was seeing. For all they knew it was Quinn I was running off to, or maybe some fourteen-year-old boyfriend I'd picked up. All that'd be fair enough as far as they were concerned, I figured. The sound of a car, though? Might start them asking questions.

Bobby pressed a finger to his lips. "Oh, *sshhh*." He rolled his eyes at Ted Wells. "Don't want to wake up Mommy and Daddy. Don't want Nicki to get grounded." Ted cackled.

"What's up with you?" I was still in a bad mood from Quinn ditching me that afternoon.

Jonathan threw me a warning glance and shook his head. I hitched my shoulders and mouthed, *What*?

There was a smell in the car. I'd gotten a whiff of it the second I shut the door behind me. I'd thought it was some new, bad cologne one the guys was wearing. But now I recognized it. After a shower, I'd sometimes smell it on my blankets following a night out with Bobby. It was a sour, beery tang.

"Have you been drinking already?" I asked.

"Yeah. *That's* what's up with me. That and *cunts* with asshole boyfriends."

Wide-eyed, I leaned back against the seat and put my hands in my lap. I had never heard anyone use that word

169

before, outside a reciting of that limerick about the man from Nantucket, and I'd never heard any curse word made to sound so vicious. Even the time my mom whaled on me and called me a bitch, she didn't put that hateful of an edge on it.

Bobby stabbed the stereo on with a finger. Something hard and fast came on. I was pressed back into my seat as he punched the gas. In front, Ted pumped his fist in the air to the beat.

"Check this shit out," Bobby said. We were still travelling west down Ludlow Road, away from town, and would eventually merge with the freeway six or seven miles down if we kept on. He must have raced the Nova up to sixty by the time he slammed on the brakes and cranked the wheel. The car went into a spin. The side of my head cracked against the window, and I was crushed up against the door, hoping it wouldn't fly open. I hadn't secured my seatbelt. If Jonathan hadn't had his on, he might have crushed me to death where I sat. As it was, the force of the spin sprawled him helpless across the seat. He'd managed to grab the strap to keep from tumbling free.

I could see nothing outside the car—the night blinded the windows except for the senseless zoetrope of trees, field, and dust in the headlights beyond the front windshield—but I sure felt the pop as the rear of the car jumped the asphalt, and heard the sound of spraying gravel, and knew it signaled the loss of the road under the back tires. I thought we all were going to end up rolled-over in the field, waking crumpled-up against the ceiling. But then the car skittered and came to a rest. Out the front window, the headlights found a split-rail fence. We were on the opposite side of the road, facing the land that had been to my right before the spin. We had nearly three-sixtied.

Bobby and Ted were hollering and whooping in the front seat. The music was screaming with them. I cupped the right side of my head. My ear stung. It felt hot to the touch, but I didn't find any blood on my fingers when I drew them away.

"What the fuck, Bobby ..." My voice mewled rather than scolded.

Jonathan pulled himself upright back to his side of the seat. "You okay?"

I touched my ear again. "Fuck ..."

"Might want to belt-up," Jonathan whispered. His tone was guarded, careful. It chilled me. I searched for the seatbelt's strap somewhere behind my back, found it, and wound it around my chest.

Up front, Bobby and Ted had settled down some.

"God, Bobby," I started, clicking the tongue into the buckle, "what're you—"

Bobby James twisted in his seat. So fast I flinched. "You got a lot to learn, little girl." He jabbed a finger at me. "First thing is when to *keep your mouth shut.*"

I blinked, hugged myself, and looked forward. My face burned. Bobby was still craned around in his seat, but I wouldn't meet his gaze.

"*Nicki.*"

I stared forward.

"Do you want to get out?"

I shook my head. I was hurt and humiliated, and I hated the tears that wobbled the world around me. I was a little afraid, too, but I was more afraid of losing a night with Bobby. Summer was almost at an end.

The music from the stereo wailed, but the keen silence between the four of us crowded it from my mind.

I said, "Could you just drive, please?" My voice trembled.

"Hey," Bobby said. His voice was gentler, but that made the slur of alcohol more pronounced.

"Hey," he said again.

"What?"

"I'm in a bad mood, okay. I didn't mean to snap at you."

I nodded, but didn't look at him.

"Hey." From the corner of my eye I saw him turn his hand, the one that had jabbed its finger, palm-up and offer it to me. "Come on."

I placed my hand in his and he gave it a squeeze.

"You ready to have some fun?"

I met his gaze and I nodded. He smiled. So did I.

He swiveled himself back around in the driver's seat, gripping both hands on the steering wheel.

The music was blaring its way back to my awareness. Its sound pumped love and crazy nights.

"Let's tear it up," Bobby wolfed.

My heart leapt.

We roared off.

Bobby spent a half-an-hour terrorizing neighborhoods on the west end. He and Ted rolled down the windows and blasted the music. They hooted and yelled at anyone they saw on the sidewalk or on porches. Tires screeched, taking turns too fast. I kept thinking of my mom's warning about getting arrested. I started to wish I had taken Bobby up on his offer to let me out of the car. I was too scared to ask him now.

I leaned over to Jonathan. "Bobby's drunk," I whispered over the noise, pitching my voice just low enough to keep Bobby and Ted from overhearing. "What if he gets arrested?"

"His uncle's the Chief of Police. He's got, like, three cousins on the force," he told me. "As long as he doesn't crash or kill anyone, we'll be fine."

None of that made me feel better.

The Nova swerved right onto another cross street, tires screaming. I hung onto the seatbelt strap with one hand and reached across the seat for Jonathan with the other. He clasped my fingers in his and we rode out the rest of Bobby's frenzy hand-in-hand.

The high dot of streetlights began to wink past more frequently until they lined the street in unbroken rows. We had crossed over onto the east-end of town.

Bobby brought the Nova to a stop in front of a liquor store. I peeked out the window at the storefront and the beer logos and posters of bikini girls lining its plate glass window, nearly wanting to hide behind the backrests in case a cop or the counterman or just some wandering adult spotted me and immediately identified me as underage and dragged me back to my parents.

Bobby turned in his seat. "You guys stay here. We'll be back in a sec." He and Ted climbed out of the car and went inside.

Jonathan and I were silent for a few seconds.

I had to ask: "What's Bobby's problem?"

Jonathan shrugged. "It's nothing."

"Looks like something to me."

Jonathan shook his head. "Ah, he got in a fight."

"A fight?"

"Well, an argument."

"With who?"

"With Mark During."

"What did they fight about?"

Jonathan shrugged, shook his head, and looked out the window.

I tugged his arm. "*What* did they *fight* about?"

He turned back to me. "Brittany Drewes."

My heart sunk. "What?"

He shrugged again.

"Why would they fight ..."

"What do guys ever fight about over girls?"

Yeah. What do guy ever fight about over girls? It should have been obvious. When I first climbed into the car Bobby's snarl about "cunts" and their "asshole boyfriends" should have clued me in straightaway but there was too much going on at every instant afterward to link the pieces together. Even then, I still tried to tell myself I'd misunderstood: Bobby couldn't be fighting some guy over a girl; I mean, he had *me*.

Didn't he?

"Is Bobby ..." My voice was thin, shrill. I couldn't help it. "Is Bobby seeing other girls?"

I knew it was a stupid question before I even I asked it, but I was desperate for my suspicion to be quashed and the tight, rock-hard pit in my stomach to be lifted, once and for all.

Jonathan's expression told me what I already knew— *of course* Bobby James Sounder was seeing other girls. He was thirty years old. He'd probably had more girls than I'd had birthdays. And who was I to him away? Some knobby-kneed, little pre-freshman in double-A's who was too eager to give him head?

My mind started playing a smear of clips of Bobby talking to other girls, holding hands with other girls, turning that smile of his on other girls, kissing girls, going down on girls, feeling them up, rolling in bed with them, the both of them achieving professional orgasms in tandem like experts. And when he was with them, was there any place in his world for me? Did I still exist? Or did I just fade away in his ecstasy?

Probably so. And since the end of summer was near, I was in danger of winking-out forever.

I turned away from Jonathan and wiped my eyes with the backs of my wrists. I tried to stop my breath from hitching, but I couldn't.

Jonathan said, "Sorry, Nicki."

His pity made it worse. I thought about flying out the door and just running. Running home. Running to Quinn's. Running until my legs wouldn't carry me anymore and just let me drop.

That's the thing about jealousy. It doesn't let you blame the object of your desire. I didn't hate Bobby James. I hated Brittany Drewes and all those other faceless girls—whoever the fuck they were—for stealing Bobby James' attentions. Boy, I did hate them. But I hated myself even more. I hated myself because I couldn't compete with them, because I had no idea what I was supposed to do to keep Bobby James. I hated myself for ever thinking I had a chance with Bobby James in the first place. Who the fuck was I to think Bobby James should be mine?

And it was all so unfair because—*goddammit*—I did

have Bobby James. Once. I *did*. Didn't I? I had him without even asking for him. Remember? When I was dancing on the rock by the river? *Remember that*? I didn't even know he was there. I didn't know and I *had* him.

I *did* have him, once, briefly and wholly, and *because* I did, it meant I could still *hope*. I was still *allowed* to *hope*.

Hope is the essential part of jealousy. Hope is the weight jealously uses to lock you into place. You know your hope is *dumb*, and *blind*, and *thoughtless*. You *know* that, but you embrace it. It's all you have left, so you wrap your arms around it and press it to your chest, giving to it all your desperation, all your promise, everything that should lift it into the sky, while only adding to the weight that presses you deeper and deeper down.

A hollow *ka-chunk* signaled the trunk opening. The car dipped as a small weight was added to the back end. A second later, Bobby was at the window and tapping the glass. The door panel had a crank roller. I'd never worked one before, so I started fighting with it. Jonathan said, "The *other* way." I twisted it in my direction and finally wound the damn thing open.

"Got us some beer." Bobby lowered his face down into the window's frame. "But here's something for the road." He held up a bottle of Jim Beam by the neck to show us the label and gave the door panel a light tap with the base. Ted joined him from around back on my side. Bobby's face disappeared as he stood up and twisted the cap off. The both of them took a swig, each bowing forward and coughing after a swallow. Bobby tipped the bottle through the open window to me.

"I've never had whiskey," I told him.

"Sip it, then."

I took the bottle and held the rim up to my nose.

"Don't smell it!" Bobby yelled, and both he and Ted buckled over and howled.

Ted swung toward the open window. "And don't breathe out through your nose after you swallow," he advised.

I held the bottle limply and turned to give Jonathan a helpless look.

"It's not that bad," he assured me. "Just take a small swallow."

I put the rim against my lips and tilted my head back. My lips caught fire. I let the whiskey roll over my tongue, down my throat. It burned like antiseptic on a cut. I jerked the bottle away and coughed.

"Shit, if you're gonna puke, lean out," Bobby said. The door opened. I shook my head, still coughing.

"You okay?"

I nodded.

"Sure?"

"Yeah." My voice was as raggedy as Mercedes McCambridge's in *The Exorcist—What an excellent day for an exorcism.*

Bobby was still chuckling at me. "Okay, we got a twenty in the trunk. We'll make sure you got a chaser for your next one."

"My next one?"

"*Yeah.* Hand the bottle to Johnny."

Jonathan hooked the bottle from me and took his swig with unwavering nerve.

We got back on the road. I asked, "Where are we going?"

"What's it matter?" Ted answered. "You get to go."

I hunkered myself against the backrest and stared at the back of Bobby's head. I wondered how many girls he'd been with. Was I the only one who'd ever gone down on him? If I was, did it make him think I was cheap or something? Is that what I did wrong? I thought of how he'd left me on my knees in the bathroom at the party the Thursday before and got sick to my stomach with the idea of it.

Maybe I could get some answers out of Jonathan when we got to wherever it was we were going. I rubbed my hands against my jeans.

The Nova dipped into a downgrade. We were heading

toward the lake. I leaned forward to look through the front windshield, but barely saw more than the flash of pine boughs in the headlights. Further on, the trees parted, and I saw the moon on the lake and the smeared reflection of camper lights across the water.

Bobby guided the car off the road. The music on the stereo wasn't as raucous as the soundtrack to his joyride around east-end neighborhoods. I heard grass whisper under the tires as the car shimmied over uneven ground. Bobby cranked the wheel and pulled up alongside a drop-off that tumbled down a steep bank. Except for the wobbling reflections of the moon and the camper sodiums jittering like firelight, the lake was as black as the night between the stars.

Bobby killed the engine, kept the stereo going. He and Ted opened the doors and got out. Jonathan and I followed suit.

It was a warm night, but the breeze blowing was almost cool. I shivered a little and walked around to the trunk. Bobby was already tipping the hood open.

"We used to party down here all the time," he said. "Me and Ted." He named off some other people, both guys and girls, a few I'd met that summer, the rest I hadn't. He peeled open the cardboard top of the twenty and passed us all a bottle from it as he kept reciting names, concluding the list by hoisting the whiskey and declaring, "*And Jim*."

"You could have afforded us some better whiskey, you know," Ted said.

"Ah, fuck it. You drink good whiskey after dinner. Whiskey you want to taste. You drink *Jim* when you want to remember *what* you're drinking *for*." He suddenly threw his shoulders back and his neck forward and his face collapsed into an ugly holler—"*To get fuuuuuucked uuuuuuup!*" It shocked me, made me step back a pace.

He turned to me, and I thought he was going to give me grief for my retreat, but he only held the bottles in each fist toward me. His face was still a little mad, lips skinned over his teeth.

177

"This," he hefted the whiskey, "is your drink. This," he hefted the beer, "is your chaser."

"Yeah, I know."

"Oh, ya do, do ya?" He reached the bottle out and gave me a curt bow. "Then you have the honors."

I took the whiskey. Bobby twisted the cap off in my grip and tossed it in the trunk. I looked at Jonathan. He mouthed, *It's okay*,

I pulled a swig from the bottle, swallowed—wasn't as bad as the one in the car, didn't shoot that lemon-juice-on-a-cut-lip-bite feeling like the first time, but still kindled heated needles in my stomach—then gulped at the beer after. The guys applauded and cheered.

"Now you're all growed up," Ted said. His black bangs were half-flopped over his face. His lips looked flush, full of blood. They made me think of *Nosferatu* again, same as the first time I met him.

A delayed whiskey burn rode up my throat and shocked a cough out of me. A sudden beer belch bubbled up with it. The sound I made went "*Kah*-uh-*uugghh*—!" I pressed the back of my wrist to my lips and might have been embarrassed—not for proper, ladylike reasons, to be sure; I was a world-class belcher in my age-group and gender—but it took me by surprise. So, when Bobby and Ted doubled-over, howling, I was just glad Bobby was paying attention to me and seemed genuinely pleased that I was there on the lake with him. I'd have kept on performing for him if I'd thought it'd do the trick. Shit, I'd have tried to pound the whole damn bottle if it'd kept his mind on me. I knew I had to be careful, though. I'd learned the perils of laying it on too thick. Lewis and Terry's friends were pretty open to me when I was the only girl in the group. I could lay it on thick for some boy I liked. But if there was as much as one other girl around, you'd find me kicked curb-wise. And Bobby James, he had his pick, yes he did. I knew I'd have to play a balancing act to keep his attention and leave him enough space at the same time. But I had an advantage because—just like in old times—as far as he could see, I was the only girl around. Ace in my hand.

Bobby took the whiskey back from me. "Good show," he said, and gave me that smile I'd been waiting to see again for so long.

The guys each did their swigs and chasers, and Blind Melon came on the stereo. "Galaxie."

"Oh, I love this song," I announced.

"Ah, don't start that," Bobby said.

"What?" That short gulp was whirling around in my head already. *Level out, dumb ass,* I told myself. *Level out.*

"Remember that first time we went over to Ted's and got high, and some song came on—what was it?" He tapped his forehead, couldn't recall it, then turned to Ted for help.

"I don't fucking remember," Ted shrugged.

"It was, like," Bobby pointed at him, "*Zeppelin.*" He shook his finger at him as if in admonishment. "Or something. Right?"

"Fuckin', like, 'The Rain Song?'"

"Yeah. It was slow like that. And kinda," Bobby raised his hands to his sides and swayed at the hips like a dazed airplane, "syrupy, like."

I knew what song he was talking about but I wasn't about to say because I didn't want either of them going on about it the rest of that night. It wasn't "slow and syrupy, like." It was The fucking Clash. London fucking Calling. Jesus.

The two of them kept going on about the story they already knew and I kept wishing for them to shut up, and Jonathan sidled up beside me. Under his breath, he said, "Don't worry. I won't get fucked-up. I'll get the keys from Bobby and make sure you get home tonight."

"'Kay. Thanks," I told him. I rubbed his arm with my fingertips to let him know nothing Bobby James and Ted could say was anything he should concern himself with, but kept my ears perked for any mention of my exhibitionist blow job. I had no need to worry—their conversation circled off onto tangents and they passed around the whiskey bottle a couple more times, Bobby handing each of us our own beer chaser, until, eventually, the two of them wandered away from me and Jonathan, over to the edge of the drop, and started hurling dead soldiers into the lake. Took Jim with them as they went. I didn't argue. The whiskey was creeping up on me faster than I'd expected. Bobby and Ted must have drawn at least double the sips I'd swigged, keeping the bottle tipped to their mouths for seconds you could count off on your fingers with some degree of accuracy. Jonathan looked to be keeping up with them, but he'd tell me on the sly that he was taking small sips. He might have been, but he was still pounding enough to slur his words for him.

The two of us finally felt dumb for being left behind at the open trunk of the Nova, so we walked off together to find ourselves a couple of rocks to sit on near the tree line. We made small talk about small talk and the weather and how the moon's reflection drifted in the lake. And I asked him, "Do you have a girlfriend?"

"No." His voice was alert. He watched me out of the corner of his eye.

"Did you ever?"

"Yeah, I had a girlfriend."

"But, you broke up?"

"Yeah. We broke up."

"Did you break up with her?"

"Um, well, it was sort of mutual."

"Oh?"

"Yeah." He chuckled. "She didn't want to see me anymore, so I broke up with her."

"Oh."

"Ha-ha."

"Oh. Yeah."

"No. No, she broke-up with me."

I rubbed my hands on my jeans. "Why?"

"She, uh, just wasn't interested in me anymore, I guess."

"She was interested in other guys?"

"Well, she wasn't interested in other girls, as far as I

know."

"Come on," I told him. "You know what I mean."

"Yeah." He looked to the stars. "I suppose she was interested in seeing other guys."

"She tell you why?"

"Shit, I guess. I don't know. No idea what I did wrong."

I got goosebumps. I watched Bobby's silhouette at the bank of the lake, sharply defined by the halo of the moon's reflection on the water.

Jonathan followed my gaze. "Nicki," he said. "You know Bobby James is thirty-years-old, don't you?"

I had known, but not in numbers plainly stated like that. Until then, he was only older than Lewis and Terry. He was only older than Jonathan. He was only older than Ted, probably. I'd been pretty sure he was older than most of the people he hung out with. But right then, it hit me that *thirty-years-old* was more than twice my age.

I fought to rationalize, but could only complain. "It shouldn't *matter*."

"Well ..."

"I didn't ask for him!"

"What?"

"*I didn't ask for him*. He called *me*. I didn't even *know* he was *there*."

"Oh."

"And, now, it's like he doesn't even know I am *there*, like I'm not *right in fucking front of him*."

"Uh-huh." There was a bitterness in Jonathan's voice. I can hear it now. I didn't hear it then.

So, I went on. "I want him so bad, Jonathan," I sniffed. I wiped my eyes with the heels of my hands. I wasn't ashamed. It was how I really felt. It was the truth. I was sure Jonathan understood. I was sure he was on my side. Jonathan was my friend. "Fuck!" I rubbed my fists against my knees. I hurt more than I had ever hurt before. "Fuck, fuck, fuck, *fuck*!"

Jonathan stood up.

"What are you doing?" I wanted to know.

"I'm going to get some more whiskey. You coming?"

"I thought you were going to stay sober."

"I'm not sober. I said I wasn't going to get fucked-up. You coming?"

I shook my head.

Jonathan turned and walked off to the drop to join Bobby and Ted.

"Where are you *going*?"

He kept walking.

I said to myself, "Fuck you, too, Jonathan."

I sat on my rock and felt bad for myself as the whiskey made mountains out of molehills.

I thought about what I'd told Jonathan, about how I'd had Bobby once without even asking for him. I'd been the only girl around then, too. What if Bobby just needed to remember how it was the first time he saw me? I could remind him. Remind him how I'd made him stop his pickup and watch. How I'd made him call me over. I hadn't even tried.

I got up off the rock and walked over to the Nova. My heart was racing. I was shaking a little bit, and it wasn't from the cool breeze on my arms and legs. All the Nova's doors were wide open. I crawled in through the front passenger-side on my hands and knees to the MP3 player in the middle of the console. I hadn't worked it before, but I'd watched Bobby fiddle with it a dozen times. I searched until I found Guns N' Roses, hunted down the song I was looking for, and hit play, cutting off the chorus of the current song mid-lyric.

I crawled backward out of the car, looked over the roof. The guys' silhouettes were up and standing at the edge of the bank. They were black cut-outs and I couldn't see by their angle if were turned my way, but I knew they must be.

"What're you doing?" Ted hollered.

"Do you remember this Bobby?" I called back.

"Remember it?" His face was flat and featureless over there, but I heard the hint of a memory in his voice.

I moved around from the Nova to the middle of the clearing, already swaying my shoulders and hips.

"Remember?" I swung around to face him just as the intro ended, and I shrieked along with Axl when he demands if you know where you are.

Bobby laughed. He and Ted joined me to shout the answer, and what was going to happen to you in the jungle.

The whiskey helped me slide right into Axl's serpent-dance. I don't think I would have been able to perform sober, not with the attention of three guys fixed on me. I closed my eyes and let the rhythm into my spine. I thought of dancing on the rock by the river, of Bobby James watching, of what he saw while he was still outside of me and while I was the only one inside. And the whiskey brought me back to that day again, and I had the night wind's chill instead of the sun's warmth, but it all felt the same, and I lifted my blouse over my belly and I didn't shiver, and I mouthed the words that Axl wailed, but I sang like it was a hymn, and I was just me again, and I wanted Quinn; I thought that if he was here with me, I would get him to dance this time. I would get him to dance with me. I would.

And I heard the grass whisper in front of me. And I looked up. And Bobby James said, "*Hhhhiiii ...*" And I said, "*Hhhhiiii ...*" And he took me under the arms and lifted me up over his head. And I laughed and wrapped my hands around the back of his neck and my legs around his waist. And I was above him. And we kissed. We swayed in cadence and Bobby James was mine. And he carried me to the Nova and he pushed my back against the back panel. And he set me down on the ground and he was hungry for me. And I was hungry for him.

And I said, "I want you, Bobby."

And he said, "Do you?"

And I said, "I want you so bad."

And he said, "Do you?"

And I said, "I do, I do, I do."

And he said, "Well, come on, then."

And I said, "What?"

* * * *

I want to stop. I don't want to go back there. I thought you might understand if I took you this far. Quinn knows as much as you know now—I told him, not in the same words, not all at once, but he still understood everything. But for you, all the same, there are still pieces missing, aren't there?

All right. Take my hand. We're going around that sudden sharp turn now. We knew it was coming, but we didn't know it was going to be so hard.

Take my hand, okay?

I wanted Bobby. I wanted him to be mine. I wanted to be his. I wanted all the romance that's fed to us on TV and in books. I wanted the true love that's promised us if we just keep our hearts open. But I couldn't have them, because none of those things are real.

The other kind of want is. And without everything else, that was all that was left for me.

Bobby said, "Well, come on, then."

"What?"

"Come on. Let's go." Oh, I had all his attention, now. There was nothing else in the world for him but me. He had a new smile for me. It was hardlined and toothy.

With both hands, he guided me by the shoulders toward the open rear door. "Let's do it."

I was excited. I *did* want him like that, too. Of course, I did. But ...

"Not here."

"Why not?"

"What about ...?" I looked over the roof of the car. Ted was on the other side, watching us intently. Jonathan was standing over by the drop-off, hands in his pockets, pretending an interest in the grass. But I could tell by the angle of his head that he was keeping Bobby and me in the corner of his eye.

Bobby set me on the seat. "Don't tell me you're going

to be shy around *Ted*."

My cheeks got warm. "God, Bobby, come on."

"What?"

"I was stoned."

"And you're sober, now?" He lowered himself inside and pushed my back against the seat. My legs still hung outside. He nuzzled his hips between my thighs and rested his knees on the seat.

"It's different," I explained.

"Yeah."

"Bobby, I've never ... done this before."

"Yeah, it's different."

He put his mouth around mine. I twisted away and craned my head and found Ted slouched inside, watching me.

"*Ted. Go.*" He didn't.

Bobby's mouth moved down my neck to my chest.

"Bobby, *I don't want to do it like this*."

"There's nothing special about it, sweetie." His hand was riding up my stomach, lifting my blouse. "It'll be the same no matter what."

I grabbed his wrists as his hands reached my breasts.

"Bobby, *stop*, okay?"

"Uh-uh."

"Bobby, *stop*." Ted was still lingering above my head. "Ted, *go* the fuck *away*."

Bobby raised himself, took me under the arms, hauled me up by the shoulders and slid me headfirst across the seat all the way inside, a sense of vertigo wheeling my senses when my feet left the grass.

"Bobby, *stop it!*"

His hands went down to my shorts and worked on the buttons.

I guess the best thing I learned growing up with Lewis and Terry was how to punch boys. I wasn't afraid to do it. And I wasn't afraid to get hit back. Repercussions are usually what stop people from doing what they have to do.

When I felt my zipper go down, I hauled off and

clocked Bobby James in the face. I think I got him in the cheek, just above the jaw. I heard Ted laugh. "*Holy shit.*"

Bobby reared back. "*Jesus* fucking *Christ*, Nicki! *What the fuck*?"

I threw another one, but he knocked it away, then grabbed my wrists and pinned them over my head. I screamed. I screamed for Jonathan.

Bobby pushed his face into mine. "Fuck you, you little cocktease!" He looked at Ted. "Grab her arms." Ted got a hold of my wrists and hoisted my arms behind my head. I fought him. I fought both of them. But Bobby still got my pants off.

I screamed for Jonathan again. I screamed for Quinn. And I just screamed. After he got his own pants down, Bobby clapped his hand over my mouth. I lost my virginity to the outro of Guns 'n' Roses "It's So Easy."

A lot of people say they're outraged, but they're all full of shit. I'd never felt real outrage before, and I've never felt it since. But I felt it the instant the pain hit me. It was a miserable, uncomfortable pain. It was sharp and blunt at the same time. I was sure Bobby had done something wrong and damaged me. I screamed against the palm of his hand. *You called me over, Bobby! You called* me! *I didn't even know you were there!*

Bobby got done. There was a slickness down there. I was sure it signaled broken insides and blood. His hand came away from my mouth, and he settled his full weight on me. He pressed his forehead into my neck as he got his wind back. He said to Ted, "Towels in the trunk. Get one."

"Bobby, get off me ..."

"Shut up."

"I think I'm hurt ..."

"You're fine. Shush."

Ted let go of my wrists and Bobby took hold of them. I told him to get off me again, started my fight up again. Ted handed a white towel over Bobby's shoulder. To take it, Bobby had to let go of one of my arms. I pressed my free hand against his shoulder and tried to push him away.

"Settle the fuck down, goddammit! Lift your ass up!" I didn't make it easy for him, but he slid the towel under me. "Jesus, would you quit crying." Did I know I was?

He slid out of me and staggered backward out of the car. I grabbed the backrests and tried to pull myself out after him, but Ted was already there in front of me, his pants around his knees. I started screaming again, and Bobby was already around the other side of the car. He swung inside over my head and pulled me back down flat onto the seat. He wrestled my arms back behind me and held them there like Ted had done.

I didn't really feel anything this time. I don't remember if I did. I suppose it doesn't matter. I do remember the cream-colored ceiling of the Nova, washed aqua in the light of the MP3 player. For some reason, that color made me want to throw up. I squeezed my eyes shut.

Ted finished and pulled away. Bobby let go of my arms. I felt slick and wounded. I reached down, grabbed the corners of the towel and folded it over my crotch. I was disgusted by what was leaking down there and wondered how I'd clean myself up.

I slid out of the car and collapsed onto my knees in the grass. My shorts and panties lay in a twisted heap just out of arm's reach. I cinched the edges of the towel with my fingers and swallowed hard, trying not to gag as the stuff seeped out of me.

Bobby and Ted were talking somewhere in the distance. Their voices wavered back and forth from low to raucous.

There were footsteps on the grass behind me. I flinched and turned to find Jonathan coming around the back end of the Nova. He bent over and picked up my shorts and panties and handed them to me. I hugged them to my chest. He crouched down next to me.

"Take me home."

"'Kay."

I slid the towel off from around me and tossed it to

the side. I sat down in the grass to put my clothes back on.

"Wait," Jonathan said. He placed his hands gently on my shoulders and pushed me onto my back on the grass.

"*No* ..." My fight was gone.

"It's okay, Nicki. I'll make it nice. It'll be nice for us, okay?"

"Take me *home* ..."

"Just let me do this. I'll make it nice, I swear. I'll pull out."

"You promised to take me home, you promised to take me home, you promised to take me *home* ..."

Jonathan did take me home, after. Bobby gave him the keys, and we left him and Ted lying in the grass by the drop-off with the last few bottles from the twenty. The empty Jim Beam had been cast off into the lake with the other dead soldiers.

Bobby James never even said good-bye to me.

Jonathan was silent on the trip back to my house. He'd been pretty talkative in the grass with me. As he nuzzled his face against the hollow of my throat, he'd told me that he'd been in love with me since the first time we met in the record store, and, even after everything that had happened, he thought we could still work it out. He said he'd wait for me, until I was eighteen. Other stuff. But after he shot his load into the grass, he got all quiet and shy. Now, as he sat behind the wheel, he said nothing at all. I did catch him in the tilting illumination of passing streetlights sneaking glances at me out of the corner of his eye. I kept my eyes straight ahead, but I could tell he was looking by the way he cocked his head.

Jonathan brought me all the way to the front door. We sat in further silence as the engine idled. I wanted to get out and go to bed and sleep forever, but my brain was locked to the view through the windshield and my body was locked to the seat.

"Nicki?" Jonathan shifted in the seat. "Nicki, I hope ... I

hope ..."

When he touched my arm, I squealed and started to howl and cry and scream. I shook my hands at him to ward him off, but he wasn't coming near me now. I swore at him and told him I hated him. I told him I thought he was my friend and demanded to know how he could have done that to me. Then I flew across the seat at him and started pummeling his shoulder and arm, and when he squirmed against the closed door, I threw punches at his chest and face. He crossed his arms to defend himself, and I kept swinging. He didn't try to stop me.

I twisted and wrenched the release and shoved myself out the door. I saw that the porch light was on and the front door of the house was swinging slowly open. Behind me, the Nova's door slammed shut and I heard the engine rev and the tires scatter gravel. The car faded down Ludlow Road.

My mom was standing in the doorway. Her arms were crossed. She had her white terrycloth bathrobe on. Her hair was sleep-frazzled. She said, "What happened to you?" and made it sound like an accusation.

My breath was hitching, and my voice was still thick from screaming and crying. "I want to go to bed."

I stomped and staggered toward the open door and the dim light inside from the upstairs landing. She moved out of the way and let me inside. I twisted past her. She hooked a hand around my shoulder.

"Mom, *please*—!"

"Don't wake your brothers." She followed me inside and shut the door behind her. "Just stop for a second."

I stood in the middle of the foyer and covered my face with my hands and cried.

"Did something happen to you?"

I cried harder. I felt like I did the day after Mom beat the shit out me and Quinn saw my bruises.

"Go to the downstairs bathroom."

"Mom, please ..."

"Nicki." She gently pulled my hands away from my face and looked me in the eye. When she had my attention, she nodded toward the staircase. "Go to the downstairs bathroom."

I took the stairs and she followed down after me. I followed the short hallway on in through the bathroom threshold in the dark. The lights snapped on as my mom entered and closed the door after us. She turned me around by the shoulders to face her.

"Okay, let me see."

"*No*, Mom ..."

"Nicki, I am trying to help."

I was numb, but I still felt an ache that made me ashamed of myself and a tightening in my throat when I tried to beg, "*Please* ..."

"Nicki, look at me."

I did.

I'd never seen her face set quite the way I saw it when I looked up at her that night. I couldn't explain what it was I saw, except that I saw nothing threatening in it.

I unfastened my shorts and let them drop to my ankles. I had tried to clean myself as well as I could with the dry towel, but dried streaks still smeared my thighs and clumped my pubic hair. I looked like a finger-painting turned into a scab.

My mom crossed her arms and took a breath. "Was it your first time?"

"*Mom!*"

"Okay. Are you still bleeding?"

"I don't know."

"Okay." She swung the shower door open and turned the water on. "Wash-up. We need to take a look."

I pulled myself out of my clothes and shoes and stepped under the warm spray. I lathered the soap up in my palm and began to clean myself.

"It hurts."

"Just do the best you can. And wash the rest of you, too. You smell like a bar mat."

The white tile of the shower flashed ice-white. I braced my palm against the wall and threw-up. It tasted and smelled like bile and foam and whiskey and ran down the drain all brown.

The shower door latch clicked and my mom leaned in and caught me by the chest with one arm and hooked the other around my waist.

"Nicki! Come on, now. Stay with me. Come on."

The spray was splashing all over her, but she stayed in with me until I knew my legs would hold me.

"Okay, that's good enough." She twisted the water off. "Okay, step out. On the rug." She helped me. "Can you stand? All right. Hold on to the counter." She ran the faucet, cupped her hands under the stream and held water to my lips. "Rinse. All right." She dried me with a towel, then wrapped it around me.

"All right. Sit down on the toilet seat." She guided me to it. I winced. It was cold against my bare ass. "Okay." She went down on one knee. "I need you to spread your legs." I started to cry. "Nicki, I need to look to see if you're hurt badly. Come on."

I stared at the ceiling and parted my knees. My mom sucked a breath in through her teeth. After a moment, she said, "Doesn't look like you're bleeding anymore." I looked down at her. She met my eyes and gently drew my knees together.

"Was it that boy in the car that did this do you?"

I nodded.

"Do you know his name?"

"Jonathan Garver." My breath hitched. "And Ted Wells." I could barely get the last name out. "Bobby. Bobby James Sounder."

"God ..."

I started to cry again.

"Okay, listen." She put her hands on my knees. "Listen. This is what we're going to do. I'm going to get you in to see Dr. Patel tomorrow. She'll make sure there's nothing ... *really bad* wrong with you. We'll get you on birth control. Get you checked for STDs. We'll eventually have you do a pregnancy test."

I put my hand over my mouth. My heart felt like it might give way right then and there.

"We'll figure out what to do after that."

"It won't be Jonathan's," I said.

"What?"

"It won't be Jonathan's. He pulled out."

Her voice was small—"… *oh … Nicki* …"—and she squeezed her eyes shut, bowed her head, and pinched the bridge of her nose between her thumb and forefinger. For nearly a minute-and-a-half, she struggled against the pity she felt for me.

My mom hated me, but she wasn't a monster. She just wasn't a mother.

When she collected herself, she rose to her feet and helped me to stand.

"*Bobby James Sounder*," she said. "Barry Sounder's boy." I had no idea who Barry Sounder was or that I'd been running around with the son of a city councilman, a businessman who owned a quarter of the town and had his fingers in another quarter, and who regularly threw the Christmas party for the PD at his house. "Jesus, Nicki, you really know how to pick your trouble, don't you?" With one hand on my shoulder, she aimed me gently toward the bathroom door. With the other, she opened it to the hallway. "Come on, now." I stepped forward; she moved with me and I stumbled trying to find her pace. "Easy, now," she said. "Take your time."

We climbed the stairs together to my room, arm-in-arm.

I had no STDs, and Dr. Patel found nothing *really bad* wrong with me. I have no idea why Child Protective Services wasn't called in; Dr. Patel asked some no-nonsense questions: Did I have more than one partner the night before? Was I forced? Was I sure I didn't want to make a report to the police? I told her that it just got rough, was all. I told her I wouldn't be seeing that boy again. I told her the things my mom coached me to say before we got to the hospital. I wasn't dead or broken, so, when, blissfully, the pregnancy test two weeks later came out negative, Mom was finished with the trouble I'd picked for myself.

I never knew exactly what she told my dad, not until the night of my date with Andy Fosse, when I modeled Sheila's dress for him. But the evening after I came back from the hospital, he started to get very shy with me, and refused to look me in the eye. I wasn't his "Pixie" any more, either. That hurt as much as the distance he dropped between us.

Lewis and Terry treated me the same. They didn't know any more than any other half-assed fucking dipshit in town. But that week—the last week before school—I could barely get out of bed. I lost six pounds, and I really didn't have that many to spare to begin with. When Mom cut me loose from my chores for the rest of the week, they bitched liked their civil rights had been violated, but laid off after they got a load of me. Shit, Lewis practically did me a fucking favor one day.

It was three o'clock Thursday afternoon. I was in bed, a book laying on my chest. I couldn't read more than a paragraph at a time without losing my train of thought. I'd been keeping my door closed, but not latched. I was staring at the ceiling without really seeing it, without really having a thought cross my mind, when the bedroom door swung slowly open. I looked. Lewis poked his head inside. "You awake?" I shifted. "Uh-huh." He leaned away, said to someone in the hallway, "Folks'll be home at four-thirty. You got till four." The door swung open a little more. And Quinn was standing there in the threshold of my room.

"Oh," was all I could manage. I hadn't seen him since he'd walked out on me in the used bookstore; the day Bobby James called me a cocktease and Jonathan professed his love for me. I was glad he was with me, happier to see him than I had been about anything for as long as I could remember, but my joy only came out in a dumb, low *oh*.

"Hi, Nicki," he said.

"Quinn." His name was cool water.

193

He looked at the floor and shifted from one foot to the other. He said, "I'm not, um, I'm not mad at you." He brought his eyes up to me.

I snorted. I cackled.

He said, "Are you sick?"

I started to cry.

"Nicki?"

I reached my arms out to him. "I need you here with me, Quinn."

He stuffed his hands in his pockets and shifted, brow furrowed.

"Quinn, I need you with me. *Please.*"

He came to me. He sat on the edge of my bed. I took him in my arms. I'd never held him like that before. I'd never held anyone like that before. I cried on his shoulder.

He said, "Nicki, what's wrong?"

"I'll tell you, Quinn. I'll tell you everything."

"I'll kill him," Quinn says.

"Quinn, shut up."

"I've been waiting for this, Sparks. I'll fucking kill that fucking—"

"Quinn, shut up, calm down, and just come get me."

"I'm on my way." I hear a car door slam on the other side of the connection. "*Fuck.*"

"Quinn, I'm just going to lie here quietly until you get here, 'cause if you stress me out anymore, I'm going to throw up on this nice family's lawn. I'm still dealing with a hang-over."

"That's the name of our clubhouse, ain't it?"

"Talk to me again when you hit Danish Avenue."

"Yeah." The earpiece belches the sound of his engine cranking. "Tell me if you get more trouble before I get there."

"You'll be the first to know. Promise."

I lie on the grass and focus on breathing. I really do

feel like I'm going to puke, and if I have to, I will, but not yet. I have made some bad decisions in my time and ended up wearing ounces of yack that were never meant to be a part of the evening's ensemble.

I listen for the tap of hard soles on concrete, search the air above the top of the shrubbery for the sudden appearance of a hostile face.

Something's crawling across my temple. I swipe at it with the back of a wrist. My skin comes away slick. It's only a drop of water. Not sweat. My bangs are still damp from Ellis' sink.

Christ. I thought people who *forgot* the past were doomed to repeat it. I haven't forgotten it a day and here it's nearly driven off with me *twice* in a little over a week. And Bobby James is at the wheel, as always. And Jonathan is waiting his turn in line to finish me up. And there's blood again.

"Nicki?"

"Yeah?"

"You okay?"

"Sure."

"Are you crying?"

"*No*. Just waiting, Quinn. Just waiting for you." I pull the phone away from my mouth and keep waiting.

I listen to Quinn curse out a few fellow drivers. I wipe my eyes and smile. He's so funny, and he doesn't even know it.

Quinn talks into my ear. "I'm on Danish."

"I could make multiple jokes out of that."

"Where the fuck are you? Paul-something?"

"Paola."

"Don't see it."

"Honk."

In the distance I hear something.

"Keep driving. Two, three blocks. Honk again."

I wait. I hear a car horn. It's not far.

"Okay, I heard that. Um, go two blocks. Honk again."

I wait. There's a honk.

"That's pretty close. I'm getting up. I should be close

to you. You got the door unlocked?"

"Door's unlocked."

"Here I come."

I clear the top of the shrubbery, half expecting to see Ellis leering at me on the other side, his damaged nose streaming blood over his lips and down his chin, making him a skull-faced vampire, but no one is in sight; no idiot citizens, no hostile faces, no monsters.

I hurtle the shrubbery and start sprinting south down Danish. There's a car up the street. I can't make the model out. It's got to be Quinn. I press Ellis's cell to my ear. "You see me?"

"Couldn't miss you."

"Pull over to the curb. I got you."

The car I see swings to the curb and parks a half-a-block down. I pocket my razor and Ellis's phone. The car door opens. I slide in and hug Quinn.

"Close the door," he says.

I yank it shut. He wraps his arms around me. "Where're we going?"

"Your place."

"Where's your car?"

"They got it."

"Are we going to get it?'

"They got the keys. I can hotwire it later if I need to." A little skill I learned from some Trenchcoat Mafia malcontents I hung around with in high school. Just add grand theft auto to my résumé.

"What the fuck is going on?"

"I'll tell you everything." I slouch down into the foot well. "Let's just get off the street."

He grabs my wrists and turns my hands palms up to look at the blood on them. "You okay?"

"Yeah." My breath hitches. "Not mine."

"Whose?"

"Couple of guys'." I press a knuckle to my forehead. "Oh, Jesus, Quinn. I hurt them. I hurt them really bad."

He heaves a breath. "They alive?"

"I think so. I hurt them, though. *Oh, shit, Quinn.*"

"Okay. Okay. Relax. Tell me when we get to my place."

"Yeah. Yeah. Oh, fuck, Quinn. I did not ask for this. I swear I never asked for this."

"Did we ever?"

Quinn's place is a three-room, one-bathroom apartment on Four Seasons. He pays as much as I do and he gets a living room, a kitchen, and a bedroom. The door to the bathroom is opposite the door to the bedroom at the end of the hall. Turn left and you're pissing on his bed.

At the kitchen sink, I use blue dish soap from a bottle to wash my hands. When they're clean, I join Quinn on the couch in the living room and fish Ellis' cell phone out of my pocket, toss it on the coffee table.

"Where'd you get that?"

"I'll get there." I consider it a moment. "I think we ought to ditch this. I want to cut all our links."

"That bad?"

"Quinn, I fucked those two guys up. I don't know what they'll do."

"You're worried about the police."

"Yeah. I mean, they'll have an awful lot of explaining to do." I shrug. "But it's their word against mine and they're bleeding."

"Tell me what happened."

My head starts to throb. "You got a beer?"

"Yeah." He rises from the couch and heads to the kitchen. "I think we both need one."

We twist our lids off together. I take a deep swig. It's medicine. I tell him about last Saturday night, after Todd, Ellis, Parker and I leave McNamara's.

Quinn's face is blank while he listens, but he can't stay seated, so he stands and crosses his arms and paces around the room. Toward the end, he finally settles down by the front window. His back's to me. His eyes are fixed outside. Probably not seeing a damn thing.

"You should have told me," He says when I finish. He doesn't turn to face me.

"I didn't know what was going on. I thought it was just some sick plan. Thought Jonathan Garver just wanted to get me up to his house. I thought it was over."

"You should have known better."

"Twenty-twenty hindsight, Sparky."

He looks at me. "If you thought it was over, you wouldn't have met with this Ellis guy."

"I had to be sure. Plus, I needed to know whose car to key."

He gives a wry snort. "What happened today?"

"Well, last night I saw Ellis when we were at The Line and Tackle."

"Jesus, Nicki, you should have—"

"I didn't, because I didn't want you starting trouble if there didn't need to be trouble."

He shakes his head and turns back to the window.

"You can't tell me you wouldn't have flipped out."

"I wouldn't have flipped out."

"What about Steve Dasher? You sure flipped the fuck out on him."

He faces me. "Who?"

"Steve Dasher. You know, the guy you beat up freshman year? Guy I fucked in the girls' restroom? '*Go, Nicki. Go, Nicki.*'"

"I remember." He takes a seat in a wooden chair in the corner. A wounded look crosses his face. "You know, you made it awfully hard, Nicki."

"What's that supposed to mean?"

He shakes his head. "Just tell me what happened today."

"Wait. What are you talking about?"

He bows his head so I can't see his face, presses his elbows to his knees, and folds his hands together. His fists are so tight the knuckles are turning white.

"Quinn?"

He shakes his head. I think of our battles in high school. Sometimes we were back-to-back, Quinn taking on the guys, me the cunts. I think of the rage he'd fly into whenever someone sang "Darling Nikki" under his breath, or when some cunt called me a slut to my face, or brought up my gangbang at the lake. He never told anyone what really happened that night. I told him not to. I made him promise. He kept it. I never realized it had left him with nothing else to defend me with besides hate.

He snaps his head up like he can't bear the silence any longer. "Let's just get through this, okay? Tell me what happened today when you met with Ellis."

"Quinn, tell me—"

"Doesn't matter now."

"Yes, it does."

"What matters now is what we're going to do about Ellis and Jonathan Garver and Bobby James Sounder. Because if we fuck up, they're going to come down on us. And if that happens, then nothing will matter anymore."

"Okay. Okay, Quinn. We'll get through this."

He nods, closes his eyes, and waits for me to start.

I'd forced that promise onto Quinn. My mom never forced it on me. But I understood my responsibility anyway. The night I walked into the house after the lake, I could have fully expected her to beat the shit out of me again. But she helped me. In her own way, she helped me. She saw that I got washed up, made sure I'd stopped bleeding, gotten me an appointment with Dr. Patel. But she'd also acted like my pain mattered, like the hurt I'd suffered needed healing. So, when she coached me before we left for the hospital the following day, I understood the silence I owed her. I let the silence seep inside until I believed it was the thing I wanted too.

I call it "silence," but it was awfully noisy at the center. Sometimes it was all I could hear. When I claimed my grandpa's straight razor and started using it on myself, it was just to let the sound out. Sort of like lancing a blister, almost. More like prying open your mouth and screaming. I remember how much the blood terrified me that night at the lake, but when I let it run again from the neat little lines I drew on myself, the memory of it didn't scare me anymore. It's just blood, I'd tell myself. It's just blood, and it's beautiful in its own way.

My mom was civil to me for almost half a year. Of course, after my fights started sending me home once or twice a month, her patience frazzled. And when I learned to control boys—itself, another kind of beauty—in the same way I controlled blood, *that* got around to her too, probably by way of the same mysterious channels that ran the news of my paternal connection with Quinn straight into Alice Winterbaum's vicious head, and I guess my mom must have decided that whatever happened at the lake was more than just chosen trouble, that it was something I'd willingly orchestrated for myself. And whatever paper-thin sympathy she'd carried for me that she couldn't quite shake, pressed like it was to the side of her furnace by the cross-currents of wind drawn between the lick of the flames and the white frost outside, finally fluttered loose and seared right into ash. Then it was just like old times, except she had a new word to add to her insults.

If I owed my mom silence, I owed Quinn everything I could bear to speak. Everything he could stand to hear. It was hard. I thought he would be mad at me. Disgusted with me. Call me a stupid bitch. (And how could I shout at him for saying that, now?) But he never did. He cried a lot. We cried together. Once, he even told me he was sorry. I still can't figure out what he was sorry for. It doesn't matter though. When he said it, he meant it, and it helped to make me feel like I was alive in this with someone.

I found strength in him as much as I found strength in blood, in sex, and in my razor. I was so wrapped up dodging the memory of hurt, of weak flesh, I never noticed how defenseless I'd left myself. How defenseless I'd left Quinn.

I guess that explains why I have to wrap my arms around myself, why I have to fight to speak through wracking sobs, when I tell Quinn how Ellis held my head underwater, and when I tell him the thing he had planned for me afterward, and how I agreed to do anything he named.

Quinn moves to the couch and takes me in his arms. "What did you do to them?" His voice is as thick as mine.

"I cut the big guy. Chest. Up across the neck. He was bleeding bad."

"What did you do to Ellis?"

I shake my head. "I can't ... I can't ... It was bad." I press my face against Quinn's chest. "I've never done anything like that before." I pull away and palm my cheeks. "I wish I hadn't. I wish I didn't have to do any of it."

"I know."

He draws me tight against his chest. My arms are folded between us, my hands still fisted, my head on his chest. His arms are around me. I feel like I'm almost inside him. I feel like, if we tried, we'd slide into each other and become one and never be alone again, and never misunderstand each other, and never mistake ourselves because we'd know each other inside and out. I'd hear his heart all the time like I hear it in his chest now.

"I wish it never happened."

"I want so much to take it away," he tells me. "I'd die if I could take it all away from you."

I feel like I've lost my wind. I can't speak. I can't think. I wish Quinn could take it from me, like he says. I wish he could, but ...

"Don't ever leave me, Quinn."

"I won't, ever." He presses his cheek to the top of my head. "I never would have stood in your way. I want you to know that. If you'd've found someone, if it'd worked out between you and that Andy guy, or whoever, I wouldn't have gotten between you."

I shake my head. "I don't need them. I never needed them."

I crane my neck to look at Quinn. He pulls back to look at me.

Funny meeting you here.
Best joke I ever heard.

My fists go loose and uncurl so that my hands are crossed over my chest like a dead person's in a casket. Or are they like a vampire's at rest? Both, I think.

I free my arms and reach for his shoulders. I pull myself up over him, swing a leg over, straddle his lap.

"They won't let us," he says.

"Joke's on them," I tell him. I fold my hands around the back of his neck. "Joke's on them. They only left us with each other." He wraps his arms around my waist.

I'm still breathless. I draw my face close to his so he's the only thing I see, so he is the only thing in the world, so I can lose myself in the beauty of him.

My mom never wanted Quinn to be my brother. Miss Halliday never wanted me to be his sister. My dad never wanted him for a son. We'll give them what they always wanted. Joke's on them. And when we laugh, we will shatter the world they cupped over us. I never knew it could break so easily. A single crack in its brittle truths and it's shattered.

Quinn smiles. "What?" He starts to laugh, too.

Our lips are close, a lap-dancer's tease. My fingers are in his hair. Our mouths taste the slender red blade between us. We're not afraid to kiss it. We will. But we like the way the silvery cracks spread in crooked lines. We like to think they'll find their marks and work their way inside like shivers up spines.

I can't take it anymore. This is for us. I crush my mouth against his. I take his hair in my fist. He takes mine. We open ourselves to the other. This is what he tastes like. This is what he feels like. It's like I've always known. It's like I've never known anything else. I want to hurt him. I want him to hurt me. I want us to feel together the sick, healthy ache of our wounds as they heal. I want the both of us to live under the same scar.

I grab fistfuls of his t-shirt and pull it over his head. His chest and abs are smooth, white, flat, hard. I run my hands over the skin, taste it, bite it. With a fold of his flesh still pinched between my teeth, he yanks my shirt over my head. I laugh as he unhooks my bra in a single deft motion. He pulls the straps forward off my shoulders, but I catch the cups and hold them to my breasts. I give him a wicked smile, then scoot off the couch backward onto my knees and across the carpet out of his reach.

"Show me yours, I'll show you mine."

He grins at my game. "I am showing you mine."

"*Uh-uh* ..." Keeping my breasts covered with one hand, I twirl a finger in the air at the general area below his waist. "Show me yours. Come on."

His grin spreads even as a dark sound, like a mad chuckle or a dizzy growl, rumbles his throat. He leans forward off the edge of the couch and pulls off his shoes, his socks. He stands. He releases the fly of his jeans, taking his time with the buttons. He parts the fly just enough to let the light catch his bunny trail. I lower the cups of my bra to give a hint of the pinkness of my areolas. I can judge how much I show by the force of my nipples pressing against the underside of my arm.

He pushes his jeans lower, down below his waist, below the flare of his pelvis, to show his pubic hair, and the root of his cock nestled inside. The outline of the shaft and head bulges against the front of his jeans.

When I get turned on—really turned on, not just wet-'n'-ready—I feel a sensation like a sudden, pleasurable vacuum filling my chest right as a fullness balloons between my legs. It nearly drives the air out of me, but I'm not suffocating, because air is no longer what I need.

I feel that now.

"*Show me.*"

I've seen Quinn grin like this before, but never while he was stepping out of his pants. Never with his cock out and hard as a dare. Never while he's standing naked before me. God, he's beautiful.

"*Hmmmm* ..." I keep the bra pressed to my breasts.

"What's that?"

"I said, *Hmmmm* ..."

He strides over to me. I lean backward, coyly, giggling. He laughs. I laugh. He goes to his knees, straddling me, pinning my waist with the weight of him. His hands go to my hair. He bends over me, his mouth presses against mine. The bra slides sideways to the carpet. I let it go and move my hands to work the buttons on my jeans. I toe my shoes off, slide my jeans and panties over my hips. "*Help me.*" Quinn rears back, stands, and yanks the waistband down below my knees and ankles and my jeans are off. One sock goes off with them. I spread my legs and he returns to his knees again, between my legs, spreading my thighs.

I run my hands through his hair, but he shakes me off and lowers his mouth to my right earlobe. His teeth take the flesh. He's biting me. Biting me hard. I hiss between my teeth. My earlobe flares. Hot. Slick. I fight to not push him away. I spread my fingers open over his shoulders but I do not allow myself to touch him, do not allow myself to stop what he's doing. He draws his head away. His lower lip glistens. My ear's burning. He takes me by the back of the head and kisses me. I taste copper. I wrap my arms around his shoulders. He's sliding on his knees, lowering himself. His stomach touches my stomach. His cock bats against my inner thighs. I wonder if he feels the scars there. He pushes himself forward. I open my legs and rotate my hips to find him. I'm so wet he won't need to guide himself in. His head parts my labia. Electric pink-and-blue delight flowers at my center and rolls out in waves to my giddy limbs. I draw a hissing breath between my teeth. He moans. He draws out, pushes himself in again, a little further. Just a little. He draws himself out again.

"Come on," I say.

He does it again. A touch, just a touch.

"*Come on.*"

Just a touch.

"Please."

Just a touch.

"*Please.*"

Just a touch.

"Oh, fuck you."

I press my hands against his chest and push him backward. He's laughing. I get up on my knees and force his shoulders against the foot of the couch. He grabs my shoulders, still laughing, and I shake him off. I don't know if I'm laughing or not, but I'm sure having a good time. A warm rivulet runs from my earlobe down across my jaw line. Red dots speckle his chest. I straddle his lap, lower myself onto him, take him inside. And I fuck the holy hell out of him.

I don't know if we're at it for thirty seconds or thirty minutes. It doesn't matter. We're going to come together. I've reached mutual orgasms before (once while a guy was eating me out and jerking himself off at the same time, if you can believe it—true altruism in action; a beautiful thing, that). But those were all accidents of movement and excitement (and maybe a dab of blow or alcohol). Each one was special and memorable in its own way, I suppose. But this is confirmation. Quinn and I are attuned.

We watch each other's throes through hooded eyes. My moans are his. His hands are belted around my hips, and his thrusts match mine. We call each other's names. We tell each other to *Fuck me Fuck me Fuck me*! And words are no good anymore and we croon an ecstatic glossolalia. His back arches and his shoulders slide down the couch to the carpet as he goes rock-hard and surges inside me just as my spasms grip him and buckle me forward onto his chest.

Our breaths are heavy and our sweat mingles. We are a heap on the floor and not much else. A buzz runs through my head. I shiver. Quinn's hands, still clamped around my hips, relax and slide up around my back in a gentle embrace. I curl my arms under his shoulders and press my cheek into his chest. We breathe in cadence.

I get my wind back and sit up, keeping him inside me.

His eyes flutter open. He smiles, strokes my arms. He looks down and snickers.

"What?"

He points at my left foot. I twist and look. The sock is still on it. I snort. "Yeah," I turn back. "That foot's bashful."

"Look at you." He strokes my face with the backs of his fingers.

"What."

"Your nose. Your cheeks. Your chest. They're all rosy."

I touch my cheek. It's warm. My fingers find a rough line down the edge of my jaw. I look at the sticky red spots smeared over Quinn's heart.

"You fucking bit me."

"Yeah."

"Did you bite Annabel Planter?"

"Annabel Planter? Oh, shit. Fuck. No. I didn't bite her. I'd never be with someone like Annabel Planter like I'm with you."

"Someone like Annabel Planter?"

He shakes his head. "That was a grudge-fuck, Nicki. You know, she had her boyfriend in high school write *Nicki Valentine takes it three ways* in the boys' bathroom. Turns out Annabel Planter'll take it three ways. And a couple other ways I came up with on the fly."

"Am I different than her? Am I different than all those other girls?"

"Am I different than all those other guys?"

"You're not all those other guys. You're my Quinn. You're always my Quinn. Always, always, and forever."

He rubs my arms and smiles. "So, what are we going to do?"

"About what?"

"About Bobby James Sounder and Jonathan Garver and that Ellis guy and your boyfriend Todd."

"You got to talk about it now?"

"Mind's as clear as it'll ever be."

I moan and lower myself back down to him and bury my face in his chest. "Haven't really given it much thought in the last couple hours, Quinn." I hope he'll just drop it and let the both of us bathe in each other.

"Here's what I think."

"What?"

"If they want you out of town so bad, let's give them what they want."

I crane my neck to look at him. "What?"

"What do we have here that we can't find someplace else? A crappy job? Some over-priced place to live? We have nothing to hold us. Have a lot more pushing us out. Especially now. So, let's pack and vacate."

"Where?"

"Who cares? North. A city. Someplace big. Someplace that'll lose sight of us the second we pass the Welcome To sign. Someplace where no one knows us. Seattle. Tacoma. We have different last names. Who's going to know any better?"

"Been thinking on this long?"

He shrugs. "Since I was twelve, I guess."

"Quinn ..."

He pulls me toward him and kisses me. He's gone half-soft, so the shift flops him out of me.

"Whoops," I breath against his teeth. He snorts.

I sit up again. "Okay." My heart feels the truth of it. "Okay, but there are a few things that need to get finished first."

"Like what?"

"Well, listen ..." The endgame of our wonderful love-making is starting its final, messy slouch toward Bethlehem. "First. We can spare ourselves a little time before we start talking about Bobby James and the rest. So right now, what you're going to need to do is slide your ass to the left, real easy, and get me a towel, Sparky."

We shower together and play under the spray until the water stops steaming and goes lukewarm. Quinn washes my face, and we step out and towel each other off. He dabs Neosporin on my bitten ear. If it gets infected, I tell him, I'll Van Gogh his ass.

My brain's starting to click, finally, and I start to springboard ideas off Quinn about what I want to do, what scores I want to settle, before we light out for the territories. I don't know what to do about Bobby James; I don't know if could do anything even if that particular light bulb flashed on in my head. As far as Ted Wells goes, that fucking drug-dealing piece of shit, he's just a bad dream bogeyman now for me. But I want to see Jonathan Garver again. Quinn asks me why. I don't know. It's just that the last time I saw him, and since telling you about that whole sad summer of my fourteenth year, things have been rising to the surface I hadn't realized I'd buried.

"I think our best bet is Todd," I decide when we're back in the living room climbing into our clothes.

"Why's that?"

"Ellis told me he was Jonathan's nephew. Jonathan went to him to search me out. I think we stand a good chance of getting the drop on Jonathan if we use Todd. Besides that, I'd just as soon avoid the fuck out of Ellis for the rest of my life. He'll kill me next time he sees me."

"Not if we kill him first."

"*No*, Quinn. You just drop that. Ellis is paid-in-full with me. Payed-in-full with interest." My stomach twists and I rub my hands against my jeans. My right palm runs over a lump in my pocket. I fish out the straight razor. Completely forgot it was there. I stuff it back in, and remember Ellis's phone on the coffee table.

"Let's see who Ellis has been calling." I pick up the phone, but all I know how to do is dial and send. I hand it to Quinn. "Here, work this."

He takes it from me.

"Todd's last name might be, fuck, what was it? *Keeling*. See if a *Todd Keeling* is listed in Ellis's contacts."

Quinn thumbs the keypad, squints, says, "Bingo. Todd Keeling."

"Well, holy shit. Got a phone book?"

Quinn does, and, lo, Todd has his address listed in the white pages.

"Okay." I close my eyes and pace a tight circle around the middle of the living room. "Okay. This is what we do."

This is what we do.

We collect everything Quinn has that can be used for packing and transportation. That amounts to two suitcases, two duffle bags, a backpack, and half-a-dozen cardboard boxes of various sizes. Quinn packs light, using the suitcases. I tell him I don't have much more than two duffle bags worth of shit. We fill the backpack with stuff from the bathroom, leaving room for a box of pads. My period's coming up next week. Into the boxes we load a loaf of bread, peanut butter, two sixers of V-8, crackers, chips, a can of cashews, instant coffee, six cans of tuna fish and Campbell's tomato soup, apples, oranges, a box of Cheerio's, Spam—yes, Spam; these are desperate times—a can opener, paper plates, and flatware.

Quinn says, "How are we going to get into your bungalow? Ellis still has your keys."

"I'll jimmy the lock. You got a screwdriver or something?" Those guys that taught me to hotwire a car? They taught me the finer points of home invasion, too. I'm a bad, bad girl.

Quinn goes to a drawer in the kitchen and pulls out a fat, red Victorinox Swiss Army knife.

"You're kidding me."

No, he's not. He flips out the screwdriver implement.

I go, "Have I ever told you that you're my hero?"

"What about your car?"

"Car's not a hero, silly."

"No, stupid. Are we going for your car?"

"Fuck it. Ellis can use it to burn me in effigy for all I care."

We load the trunk of Quinn's car and drive out to the house. I hunker down in the foot well because I don't know if the cops are looking for me or not. The more I consider how Ellis made me go down on my knees and lace my hands behind my head, the more I think he might have some connections with the police. That Pete guy, with his neat haircut and his nasty show of self-confidence, who I scared with my straight razor and my bloodying-up of his friends, he was cop material, all right.

Quinn drops me off at the end of the drive then U-turns back into town. He's going to clear out his checking account. He's got about three-grand at the bank. Not a lot, but it'll go farther than the ninety-eight bucks I have in a tin in my bureau.

The door lock opens easy. I throw the duffels onto my mattress and start packing them with clothes from the bureau, working them into tight rolls. I load all four drawers into the two bags, throw in the three library books. The ninety-eight bucks I stuff into my left pocket. Toothbrush and a razor from the bathroom. Oh, yeah, the pads. They fit, too.

I take off my tennis shoes and slip on my boots. The shoes take up less space in the duffle, and, really, boots are much better for stomping.

I put on my black leather jacket. It's been getting colder at night lately. And, actually, paired with the boots, it just makes me feel brutal.

I drop the duffle on the step outside, draw the bungalow door closed behind me for the last time, and look at the dimming sky. What is it, five o'clock? I look toward the drive. My mom's car is gone. She must still be at work. I wonder if my dad's still coherent.

I should just make a clean break, should just slip off the face of the earth, but I feel like I owe my dad something. He never defended me against my mom or Lewis and Terry, but he acted like he gave a shit about me. He was torn up when I ran away after Mom boxed the hell out of me. He watched movies with me, took me out for ice cream. He called me Pixie.

I look down Ludlow Road. No Quinn yet. It didn't take long to pack. I've still got some time while Quinn's busy screwing around at the bank. I go to the house.

The television is nattering downstairs. I follow the din, find my dad in the TV room, in the recliner, a collection of dead soldiers on the end table next to him. A live bottle's steadied between his legs.

"Hi, Dad."

He swivels his head to face me. His mouth his slack, his eyes dim. He says, "Oh, hey, honey." He pops the beer to his lips and takes a swig. "How're you doing? How was your date?" His words are slow, not quite slurred, but each one loses itself in the one that follows.

"It was good." I nod in confirmation and cross my arms. "It was fun."

He gives an open-mouth smile. "Well, that's great. You going to see, ah ..."

"His name was Andy."

"You going to see Andy again?"

"No. I'm not."

"Oh?"

"No, um ..." What do I tell him? That his son and daughter just had passionate sex and are running off as lovers to some nameless city? It kind of hits me for the first time that, from a certain angle, that'd be the whole truth of it. That'd be the only thing worth knowing. Weird world.

I clear my throat and continue. "Dad, I'm leaving."

"You're moving out?"

"No. I'm leaving. I'm going away. Um, you probably won't see me again."

He draws himself up in the recliner, his face full of bleary questions.

"Are you ... are you in trouble?"

"Um, trying to sidestep some trouble."

"What's wrong?"

I shake my head.

"Anything I can help with?"

"Got it all taken care of, Dad."

211

He holds a dumb gaze at me. "You'll be all alone?"

"I'm going with a friend."

"Oh?"

"Yeah. We'll make it together."

"Do I know your friend?"

"No." I kind of sound bitter when I say it. I shape up. "No, Dad. You don't know him."

"A boy, huh?"

"Yeah, a boy."

"A boyfriend?"

I nod. "Mm-hm."

"You going to get married?"

"I don't know, Dad."

"I hope you do." He shifts in his seat. "I hope you're happy. Will you let me know sometime that you're happy?"

My hands are curled into fists. By way of answer, I tell him, "I appreciate how you looked out for me."

"Oh, yeah?"

"Yeah. Like how, you know, when we went out for ice cream and watched movies together?"

His jaw is slack, but I can tell he's trying to show me a smile, trying to get thoughts together in his dumbed-down head. He manages, "All I ever wanted for you was the best. I just didn't know how ... you know ... to get it to you. I hated how you were with all those boys all the time. Especially after ... you know. I just didn't understand that. All I wanted was to see you with somebody special, is all."

"Yeah." I wondered what I might have said to him if I wasn't pressed for time, and if he hadn't given Quinn to me. Probably wouldn't have been much more than *yeah*. Anything else wouldn't have mattered in the long run.

"I'm sorry you and your mom never got along. Wish I'd did something about that."

I don't have the energy to say anything anymore. I don't have the energy to look at him.

"You want a beer before you go?"

"I'm okay. I should get going."

He hefts an arm out to me. "Gimme a hug."

I step to the recliner, bend down. He throws the outstretched arm around me. I give him a pat on his shoulder. He squeezes me with his single arm.

"Gonna miss you, Pix." His words are breathed, full of an emotion I can't start to appreciate.

"Yeah." I break away. "Goodbye, Dad."

His eyes are glistening. He raises a hand in farewell. I back step to the stairwell, not turning to see where I'm going because I'm thinking I might find something positive to offer him as I go, but then I reach the bottom step and turn and climb the stairs.

Quinn is right. There is nothing holding us here.

I sit on the duffle bags on the bungalow step and wait for Quinn, wishing I had a cigarette. Wishing I had taken my dad up on a beer. Or a shot. A hit, even, if I had anything to hit. I don't need the last three, but they'd go down real nice right now. Ellis's cell is in the pocket of my jeans. We'd decided I should hang onto it for the time being, while we're separated, in case things take a sudden turn to fucked. I take it out now. Flip it open and closed. Open and closed. I hope my mom doesn't come home before Quinn picks me up.

Sun's down behind the tree line, but its glow still pinks the sparse clouds near the horizon, and blues the sky that frames them. It's dark enough for headlights before I see a pair coming up Ludlow. They slow at the mouth of the drive, and I tense, but they don't turn in, so it must be Quinn. I reach out, heft the duffels in both hands, and sprint out the drive.

"What took so long?" I ask as I climb in and close the door after me.

"Paperwork. Bank hates parting with money."

"Quinn?"

"Hmm?"

I lean over the console and take his face in my hands. "I'm glad I have you."

He throws the car into park and wraps me in his arms and kisses me. "You've always had me."

I take him and hug him. "I didn't know I was so lost."

"I was there for you, Sparks. No matter what, I'd have always been there."

I squeeze him tight.

He says, "We could be on I-5 in, like, ten minutes. Five if we take the access road."

It's tempting. I say, "I want to do this. It's a risk, a big one, I know. I'm sorry."

"Don't be sorry. I kind of want this, too."

"Why?"

"It's been hard from the outside, Nicki. I don't know if you can understand that. It's hard trying to back you, you know, and cutting myself off from what doesn't seem like my right."

"Doesn't seem like your right?"

"I know what happened can never touch me like it touched you. It still hurts, though, Nicki. It still tears me up. And I never knew what to do for you."

I remember all the times I had to talk while he sat and listened. Then we'd cry in each other's arms.

I say, "You're exactly what I needed."

He hugs me tight. "I'm glad."

"I love you, Quinn."

"I love you, Nicki. I love you so much."

We drive to town in silence. I put my hand on his leg. He laces his fingers through mine. I think that if things go down bad, I wouldn't mind this being the end. I wouldn't mind this being our last day. At least they'd never be able to take it away from us.

We find Todd Keeling's address. The curtained living room window is bright. Even the front porch light is on. I point at the white, double-cab Tacoma parked in the driveway.

"That's his," I tell Quinn.

Quinn wheels the car alongside the curb on the

opposite side of the street, brakes, kills the engine. The blacktop and sidewalk illuminated by the headlights snap black. He says, "You got the Swiss?"

I fish it out of my pocket and show him.

"Okay."

We open the doors and head to our positions. Mine's around back. I'm assuming Todd's place has a back door I can jimmy. If it's a sliding glass door, well, we're winging it.

At the side of the house, I turn to make sure Quinn's taken his position at the front door. His cell's pressed to his ear. As I disappear around the corner, I hear his voice through the earpiece of Ellis' cell, which I have pressed to mine. He whispers, "See all right?"

"Yeah, shadowy," I whisper back. "Can see enough, with the streetlights and porch lights. There's a gate." A wooden one. I reach over and find the latch. It's not locked. Is that a sign that he doesn't have a dog? I slip through, peeking into the windows as I pass them. They're either dark or curtained. I have to move more carefully; the backyard is sunk in darkness. I whisper into the mouthpiece, "Hold on," and turn the cell outward like a flashlight to find my way. I spot a door, step up to it, test the knob. I nearly giggle.

I put the phone back to my ear. "Happy hala-fuckin-looyah, it's open."

"Okay. Let's hang up. I'm going to knock at the count of five. One—" His phone goes dead.

Two—

Three—

Four—

Five.

I twist the knob and step inside. I enter a bathroom. Weird. The door's open and the hallway's a straight shot to the front door. We must have timed it right, because I see someone move into view down the hallway—male, by his shoulders and stance—just as he reaches for the knob. Is it Todd? I think so. I pocket the phone and exchange it for the straight razor. I start to creep down

215

the hallway as I hear Quinn's voice, muffled by the short distance and the hollowness of the hallway.

Hi.

He's real casual.

I don't know if you remember me. My name's Quinn. We met last week at McNamara's?

I pass an open door.

Oh, yeah.

The guy's voice is familiar. I'm sure we got Todd.

You went off with my sister, Nicki.

I'm almost to the threshold of the hallway.

Remember?

I cross the threshold.

Um ...

"If you don't mind," Quinn says, his voice clear now, "could we talk about that?"

I can see Quinn's eyes in the porch light. His gaze never flickers from the guy in the doorway.

A quick survey of the living room shows empty couches, two empty recliners. We've got a private party. There's a plasma screen TV with the picture on pause. A guy in a white doctor's coat is gaping his mouth and waiting to finish his line.

"Right now?" Todd says. It's his voice. It is, without a doubt.

"Yeah, if you don't mind."

I move quietly up behind him and stop a foot away. The razor's open, ready to threaten.

"Um, now's not really a good time." He starts to shut the door. "Maybe later."

I slide the razor under his throat and press the edge of the blade against the hinge of his jaw. With my free hand, I grab a fistful of hair to keep him steady. He goes tense.

I say, "What's up, doc?"

He starts so say something along the lines of *The fuck is this shit?* so I give his head a good shake by the hair to make him behave.

"Later's no good," I tell him. "We've got to leave town

tonight. Per the request of Bobby James Sounder. So, if you think you can find a smidgen of time for us right now, we'd really appreciate it, yeah?"

I catch my foot around his and swing him into the living room. He's stronger than I am, and heavier, but I have the persuasion of a razor to his neck, so he's cooperating.

"Look," he's saying, placating, "look, look—"

I take the razor away and punch him just under his ribs. Behind me, the front door snicks shut. Before me, Todd twists and stumbles. I kick him across the back of his knees and he goes down. I give him another kick to the ribs. He yelps, twists toward the pain and tumbles onto his side, back to me. I hook my heel over his shoulder and roll him onto his back. He hollers, twists against me. I stab my heel down, he shouts. I bend and grab him by the collar and heave his face close to mine. "Next time you plan on whoring me out"—I give his a shake—"have my money up front." Another shake. The back of his head thumps the carpet.

Quinn's around the other side of Todd now. I lean back, out of the way. Quinn leans in, positions himself over Todd, then drops down with a knee onto the center of Todd's chest.

Todd huffs, buckles his knees, but finds himself pinned to the floor.

"Nicki." Todd blinks, rolls his eyes, finds me, fixes on me. "I swear, I *swear*, I wouldn't have let anything happen to you."

"What *did* you think was going to happen to me?"

"Look, look. Listen to me." He pleads with his hands. "Jonathan wanted to see you. He asked me to look for you, and I did."

"Just wanted to chat about old times, right? Maybe braid my hair, give me a pedicure. 'Cause if Uncle Johnny's anything, it's a gentleman."

"Please. Yes, okay I know what he wanted but ..." He squeezes his eyes shut, opens them, flits them from me to Quinn and back again, nervously; he thinks he might be getting on thin ice. "I didn't know you. I'd only ... you know ... *heard*." He swallows, waiting to get decked in the mouth, probably. When he doesn't, he continues.

"But, but, when I saw how scared you were, when Jonathan came out, I wouldn't have let anything happen. Nicki, I swear. I'm not like that."

"Not like Ellis?"

He freezes, his eyes go wide.

"Ellis?"

"Your buddy?"

He says, "What did Ellis—?"

"Shut up."

"You should have come to me—"

"Don't you two swap rape videos?"

"Nicki, no, okay? No. Please."

He's really scared. His voice is high, and his pupils are yawning. What's he so afraid of? What does he think we're going to do to him?

Oh. Yeah. Probably that.

"Heard what *happened* to Ellis?"

"Nicki, please ... I don't know about Ellis ... Nicki, I just, it's just—"

I crouch next to his head, bring my mouth to his ear, and sing softly, "Chest-*nuts* roasting on an open fire. Jack Frost *nipping*"—I snap my finger in front of his face—"at your *nose*."

"Oh shit ..."

"You heard about Ellis?"

"Yes, okay? Yes, I heard about Ellis."

"What happened to him? And that other guy?"

"You cut them."

"What happened after?"

"What?"

"They ended up at the hospital, didn't they?"

"Yes, okay, *they ended up at the hospital*."

"What happened to them there?"

"What?"

"Are they okay?"

Todd's eyes roll, focus; a look of tentative

comprehension crosses his face.

"Anthony's stitched up," he says, "lost a lot blood but he's out of critical."

"Ellis?"

His eyes roll in panic. "Oh, Jesus Christ, Nicki ..."

"Play a stupid game, win a stupid prize," I tell him. "What was Jonathan going to talk to me about?"

"Leaving town. Just until after the election."

"Is Bobby James really that afraid of me?"

"I don't know. I guess."

"Did he want me gone by tonight?"

"Yes. I mean, before tonight. Tonight was the deadline."

"Why?"

"The debate's at City Hall."

"Tonight?"

"Yeah."

"Fuck me running." I look at Quinn. "Isn't *that* interesting." Back to Todd. "Did they call the police?"

"No. But, um, they don't really need to."

My heart sinks. "That Pete guy. He a cop?"

"Still in academy."

Uh-huh. Story like that, no matter how you slice it, comes up career death. There are probably some pals on the force sniffing for me, but no APB.

"Okay," I say. "This is what's going to happen. You're going to take us to see Jonathan. But make sure it's a surprise for him. Where's your phone?"

"Uh, on the kitchen table, I think."

I get up, walk over to the table, find the cell. "Jonathan in your contacts?" I shout, picking it up.

"Yeah."

I deliver the phone to Quinn. He takes it, knee still weighed against the center of Todd's chest, flips it open, thumbs the buttons, and sends a call, handing it to Todd.

"What do I say?"

"It's your hide. Think fast, rabbit."

Todd closes his eyes, jams the cell to his ear as if it'll speed him ideas. A moment of pause. His lids flutter open. "Jonathan," he says. "Hi. Look, um, you know that thing that went down at Ellis's ... ? Yeah. Well, I got news on ... her. Might want to hear it. Yeah ... I probably just ought to come over. Is that okay? All right ... See you in, like, ten." He shuts the phone. "Okay. Now what?"

"Now you get to chauffeur. Get up."

Quinn releases him and Todd stands, crookedly. "Nicki, listen." He's rubbing his chest, looking miserable. "I want you to know, I swear I wouldn't have let anything happen at Jonathan's."

"You got duct tape?"

"Wha—"

"*Duct. Tape.*"

His face drops. "Nicki, I'll help you all you want."

"*Duct tape.*"

It's in a kitchen drawer, he tells me, right of the oven. That's where I find it. I come back into the living room unwinding a length from the roll, relishing the menace of the operation, and tell Todd, "Get your keys and your wallet."

In the Tacoma, Quinn tapes one of Todd's hands to the steering wheel, rounds the front of the cab, and climbs in shotgun. I climb in back, behind Todd, and shut the door.

"Did Parker have anything to do with this?"

"Parker? No. No, not Parker. He just happened to be there. He came along because we couldn't get rid of him without making you suspicious, is all."

"Yeah?"

"*Yeah.*"

"What'd he do after I was gone?"

"He was drunk and stoned. I don't know if it even registered what was going on. I haven't talked to him since." His voice pitches. "*Parker's got nothing to do with anything.*" His insistence is almost whiny, so stripped of dignity, so desperate to make me believe him, that I do. He might just be a good actor, might be trying to hide some ace he's got up his sleeve, but ...

"Okay." I glance Quinn's way. Quinn doesn't look so

convinced. We'll worry about who's the better judge of character later. "Let's get going," I tell Todd.

Todd cranks the engine to life.

"Drive."

We ride to Jonathan Garver's house in silence. Quinn twists in his seat and drapes an arm over the backrest. I take his hand. Grip his fingers.

I'm scared. Fuck, I'm scared. I've been angry at Jonathan, I've hated Jonathan, I've felt a sick, low shame over what he did, but I never thought I'd be afraid of him. God, what he did to me. What he did to me. I will always be that girl. Some part of me will always know her. I wish I could comfort her. I wish I could scream with her. I wish I could take her face in my hands and make her look at me. I wish I could tell her what's happening is terrible, tell her what's happening matters, tell her she didn't ask for it, tell her she's better than it, tell her she's more, tell her she's somebody else, but no matter how loud I call to her, I think she'll always be alone.

We're past Briar Range Road. It goes dark outside the windows. Porch lights flash by on either side, winking on and off inside the tree line. There are more than a few of Bobby James' signs that catch the headlight beam. I don't know if the one I smashed has been replaced. Probably it has.

The Tacoma slows, turns, brakes. Out through the windshield is a cast-iron gate. We're at Jonathan's.

Quinn says, "What're the numbers?" Todd tells him. Quinn opens the passenger door and makes for the gate, leaving the door open and the dome light shining.

Todd speaks. He doesn't turn to me. His voice is low and his words are full of breath. He says, "Nicki. I'm sorry."

We watch the gates part in the headlights.

Quinn climbs back inside, slamming the door behind him and killing the dome light. The Tacoma pulls forward. Its tires crunch gravel. The Jeep I saw last Saturday comes into view. It's parked in the same spot it was last Saturday. Todd guides the Tacoma next to it, brakes.

"Kill it," Quinn tells him. The engine shutters to silence, the headlights die. Quinn gets out, rounds the grill in silhouette and opens the driver's side door. I rise and lean over the backrest, the straight razor open in my palm. With the blade, I free Todd from the steering wheel.

"Out," Quinn tells him. Todd swings his legs almost drunkenly and slips out. Through the open door I hear him say to Quinn, "Come on, please. You don't need to." I open my door and slide to the ground. Gravel under boots. Quinn's got Todd twisted at the waist, his shoulders swung around and his hands duct taped behind his back. I step forward and take one of Todd's arms by the elbow. Quinn takes the other. We walk him to the front door.

"Numbers," Quinn says. Todd tells him. Quinn punches them, then works the door handle with his free hand.

Inside, I give Todd a nudge with my knee.

Todd calls out, "It's me, Uncle Jonathan."

A voice creaks downstairs from the loft.

"Up here." We climb the stairs, Todd in the lead, Quinn and me guiding him from behind.

Jonathan Garver's in a recliner, feet up. Blue button-up. Gray khakis. Black socks. Tumbler, cupped in hand, balanced on the armrest. Brown contents. Coke-and-something, I figure. On the rocks. His gaze is directed dully in our direction. His eyes flit, flit, flit. He blinks.

"Nicki?" We crest the landing and Quinn pulls Todd to the side of the banister.

"Get on your knees," he tells Todd. Todd does. Jonathan's gaze flits to Quinn, lingers. Flits to me. "That your brother?" The razor's still in my hand. I've got it gripped so tight the tang is pressing a hole in my thumb. I skirt the coffee table and stand before Jonathan.

Jonathan lowers the footrest and sits forward. Ice tingles against glass. "Nicki." He's smiling. The fucker is smiling. "I missed you. I didn't remember how much I missed you."

"Fuck you, Jonathan. Fuck you."

His face drops. He shakes his head, pleads with his eyes. "Don't."

"Why are you helping Bobby James against me?"

"I'm not, I'm not doing that."

"What was that shit you pulled last Saturday? Creeping out of the shadows like that?"

"I was afraid you wouldn't see me if I asked."

"Fucking right. I'd have dodged you like a rancid cock."

"Nicki, I wanted to *help* you. I still do. I have a place set up for you. Money."

"And I can head right off after you fuck me."

"Nicki ..."

"I got a question. Last Saturday, did you have dibs on me, or were you going to take a number like usual?"

His face crumbles. "I love you, Nicki. I've loved you since that first time you went for pizza with me and Bobby James. I told you I'd wait for you, remember?"

That sick pit in my stomach is making me keel forward. I put an arm around my stomach.

"I don't care about all those other guys, Nicki."

"You don't *what*?"

"I don't care about Bobby and Ted."

Oh, god, my stomach hurts.

Nicki Valentine likes it three ways.

"I called for you, Jonathan."

"You were dancing for Bobby James." He actually seems hurt by the memory. "You said you wanted him."

"I said *take me home*, Jonathan. *Take me home.*"

"I wanted to try and fix it. For the both of us"

"*You were my friend.*" My voice is going shrill. "*Why didn't you help me? I called for you. I needed you to help me.*"

"You said you wanted him."

"*I was fourteen!*"

"What could I do?"

"*You could have done anything!*"

223

"What?"

I sit down hard on the edge of the coffee table and cover my face with my hand. I can't look at him. I'm not afraid of him. I never was. I was afraid of this. I was afraid I'd find my only witness believed his own bullshit story.

That girl, in the back seat of the Nova, on the grass, she really is alone. From the start, she was always alone.

"You won't even tell me you're sorry, will you?"

"I loved you. I can't be sorry for that."

"*Fuck, Jonathan.*"

"I won't be sorry for what I felt for you."

"You know. I liked you, Jonathan. I liked you a lot. I probably liked you more than I liked Bobby James."

There's silence. This is what he's always wanted to hear.

"I could have been your girlfriend."

I want to hurt him, but I'm not making this shit up. If Jonathan Garver was the person who Bobby left me with when he wanted to sneak off with other girls, whose hand I took on Bobby James' joyride that night at the lake, then I mean it. But he's not. He never was.

So, I tell him, "But I'm glad you showed me what a pathetic fuck you are. 'Cause I really didn't need to go down that road."

"Nicki ..."

"You fucked me, Jonathan. You fucked me when you got the chance, when I had no other choice but to get fucked by you. And if I didn't learn who you were then, I might have let you in, and you would never have stopped fucking me."

"That's not true at all."

"Fuck the truth. That's what would have happened."

"Come here." He reaches a hand to me. Just like the hand I reached to him while Bobby James joyrided with us in the back of his Nova.

"Fuck you, Jonathan."

"Be next to me again."

"*Fuck* you."

He drops his hand.

"Why aren't you ashamed?"

"I never would have let anything happen to you that you didn't let happen."

"*You did*. Jonathan! *You did*."

"You said you wanted Bobby."

"I was just stupid. I was stupid and drunk and I needed someone who should have known better to *help me when I screamed*."

"You said."

God, this is a ping-pong game. I smack blame at him, he smacks blameless back.

I stand. "I don't have time for this shit, Jonathan. I'm never going to forgive you. But you're going to help me tonight."

"What?"

"I'll fucking tell you. You're going to help me fuck Bobby James right back."

"What am I supposed to do?"

I tell him. He listens, eyes wide, silent till I finish. Stays silent. He closes his eyes. Shakes his head.

"You're a piece of shit, Jonathan. You are a fucking piece of shit."

"I'll help you, Nicki." I turn and look at Todd. He's still on his knees on the floor. His hands are still behind his back. He looks me straight in the eye. "I'll help you."

"What can you do?" Quinn says.

"I can rally some people. Quick. On the spot."

"Who?" I want to know. He tells us. Sounds like it might work.

I step over to him. "You fuck us, I'll fuck you back, hard."

"Nicki, I want to help. I'm not afraid of you. I want to help."

I turn him by the shoulder and use the razor to cut the duct tape. Quinn looks doubtful as Todd stands to his feet and peels his bonds off his wrists. But Todd doesn't make a break for it. He looks at his uncle. "You owe her." Jonathan cuts his eyes away.

"Jonathan," I say.

"What." His voice is small.

"Look at me."

He raises his eyes.

I have Quinn hand me the roll of duct tape. I show it to Jonathan. "Do I have to make sure you're not going to call Bobby James?"

"I won't call him."

I look at Quinn. He shakes his head in warning. I turn back to Jonathan.

"Don't you let me down this time."

Jonathan shakes his head.

Quinn's not happy. But I see truth in Jonathan's eyes. It may be a short-lived truth, another ping-pong game he plays against himself and a wall, but it'll last until I get what I want. After that, it won't matter what stories he tells himself. Or anybody else who wants to believe him.

I turn back to Quinn and Todd. "All right." I tuck my razor back into my pocket. "Let's show Bobby James something."

"Let's show everyone," Quinn adds.

On the way to City Hall, Quinn takes the wheel of the Tacoma so Todd can sit in the passenger seat and make the phone calls he needs to. As we turn into the parking lot, he snaps his phone shut. "It's all set up."

"When are they going to start?" I ask from the backseat.

"They're moving out right now."

I smile.

Quinn eases the truck up and down the blacktop, palming the steering wheel. I search the line of cars along the driver's side. Todd searches the passenger side.

Quinn asks, "What if it's not here?"

"Then we console ourselves with a big group hug, drive back to your car, and get the fuck out of Dodge."

Todd says, "I'd bet a Franklin it's here. He loves that thing. It's his Sunday-going-to-meeting ride."

I tap on the glass. "See that?"

Quinn squints out the side window. "Shit. That it?"

"Oh, yeah."

Todd leans across the seat to take a look, too. "Yeah. That's it, alright."

I take out the Swiss. "It's ours."

Todd laughs. Quinn brakes the Tacoma. "Then bust ass," he says.

"Bobby James," I whisper. He can't hear me now, but he will. "You're *my* Valentine tonight, sweetie." I jump out of the Tacoma.

Bobby James Sounder's Chevy Nova's metal blue paint job is black in the dark. The sight of that color, and the lines of the chassis, bring a sick ache to my stomach and split me down the middle so that I'm standing with one leg in the-here-and-now and the other leg—a gawky fourteen-year-old leg—in a time by the lake when the summer night air hugged me like a protecting skin and made a promise that I'd never come to know the enormously broken heart of the world.

I barely want to touch the door. But I force myself to reach out and fit the palm of my hand flush against the cold, dead metal. And this time Quinn is with me. This time I have my razor. And this time nobody can hurt me. I take out the Swiss Army knife and get to work.

Doesn't take long before I get the door open and slide into the footwell to get the steering wheel panel loose.

"Got it?" Quinn's hovering outside. I can hear the tension in his voice.

I drop the panel. "Here," I reach the Swiss out to him. "While I'm getting this started, take off the license plates. Lose one and switch the back plate with the front plate from some other car. Peel off the registration tag and stick it to the upper right corner."

He sets off to do that. Before long, I'm getting the engine to turn over. When its rumble is even and unbroken, I slip outside, back onto the blacktop. Todd is leaning his back against his Tacoma's driver's side door. His eyes are roaming the parking lot. He's trying to look casual, and he's not doing a bad job of it, but if I was walking down the sidewalk, oblivious to everything, and I caught sight of him, I'm sure I'd start to think something was up. Makes me just want to get the hell out of Dodge, right now.

"Where's Quinn?" I ask Todd.

He tilts his head to the rear of the Nova. I walk around. Quinn's on his haunches, screwing in a side of the stolen plate.

"All done?" I ask Quinn.

Quinn nods, palms the Swiss closed, stands. "All done," he tells me.

"Well-oiled machine, that's what we are."

"If we weren't already us, I'd wish we were."

"Let's get the fuck out of here."

We do.

In Bobby James Sounder's Chevy Nova, Quinn at the wheel, we trail the Tacoma back to Todd's house. The whole way I'm fighting vertigo. The car seems smaller than I remember, but I feel like I could fall forward into that familiar dashboard in front of me, and when I pull myself back, the interior of the car will be as big as I remember it, and Bobby James will be sitting next to me at the wheel, instead of Quinn. And Bobby will drive me up into the mountains, into the trees, and I won't know anymore how to fight him, and I'll never return.

"You okay?" Quinn asks.

I tell him I am. He takes his eyes off the road to give me a quick appraisement. I pretend not to notice and keep my eyes on our progress.

We make the turn onto Todd's street. Ahead of us, Todd turns his Tacoma into his driveway.

Quinn brings the Nova to a stop at the curb opposite, right behind his own car.

We make quick work of emptying our stuff from his

trunk into the Nova's. I wonder how long it'll all keep us going. I wonder how long the money will last. Then I throw the worry out of my head. Can't matter now.

I snug the last box inside, the one holding Quinn's laptop, against the sides of the others, and slam the Nova's trunk shut after it. When I turn to the street, Todd is crossing the blacktop toward us. Quinn, his back to me, is already stepping to meet him. I can tell by the way he's squaring his shoulders and putting himself between the two of us that he still doesn't trust Todd.

Todd can tell too. He brings himself to a halt just past the yellow line in the middle of the street, jams his hands in his pockets. To me he says, "You out?"

"Yeah." I step up beside Quinn.

"All right."

"Todd. Thank you."

"We good, Nicki? You and me?"

"We're good."

"Take care, then." He glances at Quinn. "The both of you."

Quinn's not impressed. But we're done now. "All right," he says, and turns away toward the Nova.

Todd frees a hand and raises it in farewell. I nod in return, then round my way to the passenger side door.

On the road, I roll down the window and throw Ellis's phone out. Quinn stabs a button on the console with his index finger. A voice blares from the speakers. The both of us jump. "*Jee*-zus!" Quinn shouts, immediately punching the search button to get away from it. On a stretch of static, he stops to adjust the volume.

The radio must have been tuned to the local station. It was broadcasting the debates at City Hall. I'm sure Quinn didn't recognize the voice that came screaming over space and time, but I did. It was deeper than I remembered, but that hard self-confidence, that easy charm, was all the same. The words had something to do with the boardwalk by the lake, its financial importance to the community. Its tone was all business and politics. I did not hear the words *Hey, sweetie!* I did not hear the words *Fuck you, you little cocktease!* But I could never mistake that voice anywhere, no matter what it was saying.

I twist around in the seat, reach my hand over the backrest, and trace my hand over the back seat. Her ghost is there. But she's with me now. At least she's with me.

"*Fuck you, Bobby*," I whisper, so Quinn can't hear me, then sit forward again. Out the front windshield, a sign slips from the darkness into the headlight beam. I blink. "Look!" I point at a sign on the side of the road. "There's one!"

Back at Jonathan's house, before we headed out on our mission, Todd had told us he had some younger cousins who were a bunch of punk rock, malcontent juvenile delinquents. I liked the sound of them. He said they and their friends loved nothing more than to vandalize the social order. For twenty bucks each and a bag of weed, he was pretty sure he could convince them to head out into town and deface every Bobby James Sounder election sign they could find. We talked about what should be written. I think what we came up with was pretty good. *Put it in the simplest terms*, Todd had suggested first as a guideline. *Make it so no one can argue. If they still don't understand it, it's because they don't want to. Those people aren't worth it, anyway.* He'd thrown his uncle a look, but Jonathan had kept his eyes on his lap.

And there it is, in red spray-paint, scrawled across Bobby's name:

> *Nicki Valentine was 14 in 1999.*
> *Bobby James Sounder was 30.*
> *"Darling Nikki"*

An anarchy "A" fills the inside of the zero of the number thirty.

Quinn puts his arm around my shoulder and draws me close. I start to cry. I don't know why, but it feels good, weird as that sounds. It wears me out though. I'm tired. God, I'm so tired.

"Are you going to be okay to drive?" I ask Quinn.

"I'm good to go, Sparks." He kisses me on the cheek.

My eyelids are heavy. "How far're we going?"

"I think we ought to clear the state line before we stop."

"We're going to have to ditch this car, I think."

"We'll see."

"'It doesn't exactly leave a light footprint."

"No."

"We'll have to destroy it. Bobby James can't have it back."

"Well, it's ours now, and we'll ride until it fails us." He says it like he's sure it never will.

I curl onto my side and rest my head on Quinn's lap. He finally finds a station with music and no static. It must be a country station. But it's okay for now, because Patsy's singing. I want to make it through the final part before I fall asleep. Me and Quinn danced to this one time. It's a song about being made to feel crazy for your sorrows, crazy for taking your best shots, and crazy for your final devotion. Patsy sure knew what it's like.

It's almost over now. The final notes are on the way. If you could, before you go, listen to them with me.